ALL THE COLOURS OF DARKNESS

All The Colours of Darkness

LLOYD BIGGLE Jr

NEW ENGLISH LIBRARY
TIMES MIRROR

To Dave Locke . . .
the serendipitous . . .

First published in Great Britain by Dobson Books Ltd in 1964
© Lloyd Biggle Jr 1963

*

FIRST NEL PAPERBACK EDITION OCTOBER 1975

*

NEL Books are published by
New English Library Limited from Barnard's Inn, Holborn, London, E.C.1.
Made and printed in Great Britain by Hunt Barnard Printing Ltd., Aylesbury, Bucks.

45002472 5

1

A sagging floor board caught Ted Arnold's foot. He stumbled and released the door, which slammed with a hollow, echoing clap. Fifty feet away, in the pale wash of light from a dangling bulb, young Jack Marrow leaped to his feet and threw up his arms. When Arnold reached him he was huddled behind the low plywood wall that protected the instrument board.

'Ready to crack,' Arnold thought. 'Too bad.'

Marrow got to his feet and extended one trembling hand to steady himself.

'Everything set?' Arnold asked.

Marrow licked his lips, and glanced behind him nervously.

'Ten minutes,' Arnold said.

He glanced at the setup, found a dial out of position, and moved over to correct it. 'Newark,' he said.

Marrow swallowed, said, 'Oh, I didn't – '

'It's all right now,' Arnold said. 'You won't be needed. If you'd rather wait in the office, go ahead.'

Marrow swallowed again. 'I think – '

He broke off, and headed for the office. Arnold watched him go. The door slammed again, and then there was silence, except for the footsteps that moved tirelessly back and forth behind the rough partition that walled off the office. Pace, *creak,* pace, pace, *creak*. Pause. Pace, pace, *creak, creak,* pace. Arnold listened and counted. There were seventeen creaky floor boards in that office. He knew them all, knew precisely every shade of difference in timbre.

At the distant end of the old warehouse was another shallow oasis of light. In between was drafty emptiness, surrounded by sagging floor and begrimed walls, bare ceiling rafters, and, at one point, a jagged patch of starry sky where the roof gaped. Arnold started the long walk to the other end.

Walt Perrin saw him coming, and waited for him with a grin on his face. Arnold grinned back at him, happy in the thought that there was no chance of Perrin's cracking. He moved around to check the instrument setup. No errors there, either.

Perrin was poking the toe of his shoe at a floor board. The board responded to pressure by bending sharply into subterranean blackness. 'All the time I've been walking around here,' Perrin said, 'I never touched this particular board. Then a minute ago I stepped on it and nearly broke my neck. This dump should be condemned.'

'It has been,' Arnold said.

'Yeah? It'd be quite a joke to have the sheriff show up with an eviction notice just as we're getting started.'

'No danger,' Arnold said. 'The landlord is fighting it. After tonight it won't matter one way or the other. Either we'll be back in decent quarters, or we'll be out of business. Would you mind handling the X-7-R? You'll have plenty of time to get back here.'

'What's the matter with Marrow?'

'Nerves.'

'Tough. Can't blame him. Combing glass out of your hair gets tiresome. Sure, I'll handle it.'

Arnold looked at his watch. 'Four minutes,' he said. 'Better get up there.'

He walked back with Perrin, left him at the X-7-R, and returned to the office.

The Universal Transmitting Company's engineering office looked like the corner of a dilapidated warehouse that it was. The unpainted plywood of the partitions contrasted oddly with the blackened opposite walls, and the plywood was already dusty and smeared with handprints. There was one dirty, unscreened window high up in the wall. From a ceiling rafter hung a single unshaded light bulb. The furnishings were a battered table, a filing cabinet, and a few folding chairs. On the table were three telephones and a fluorescent desk lamp. The small electric fan on the filing cabinet rattled noisily.

Marrow had placed a chair in the protective shadow of the filing cabinet. The other man in the room continued to pace the floor.

Arnold went to the table, lowered himself cautiously onto a folding chair – at least two of those in the room had been known to collapse upon slight provocation – and reached for a telephone.

The pacing stopped. 'Ted?'

Arnold turned.

'Anything yet?'

'A little over a minute,' Arnold said, looking at his watch.

The pacing started again.

Arnold fumbled for a handkerchief, and as he mopped the perspiration from his bald head the pacing stopped a second time. 'A minute, you say?'

Arnold nodded, and picked up the telephone. He dialed a number and waited, scowling impatiently at his watch. Finally someone answered. Arnold heard heavy breathing before he got the irritated growl of response.

'You guys camping out somewhere?' he demanded. 'I want someone on that phone. All the time. Everything ready?'

'Sure. Meyers is ready to step through, if he hasn't already.'

'Twenty seconds, yet,' Arnold said. 'Keep someone on the phone.'

He hung up. 'Newark is ready, anyway,' he said, his eyes on his watch. 'Meyers will be stepping through – just – about – now.'

The white telephone buzzed. Arnold snatched at it.

'Meyers is through,' Perrin said.

'All right, Perrin. Anything – '

The explosion rocked the building. Debris crashed against the plywood partition. Dust rolled over the top and settled slowly. The fan toppled from the filing cabinet, narrowly missing Marrow, thudded onto the floor, and continued to rattle. Marrow sat with his face buried in his hands and ignored it. Arnold caught his desk lamp just as it was going over. He took a deep breath, got too much dust, and sneezed violently.

'Anyone hurt?' he asked the telephone. There was no answer. He shouted, 'Hey, there, anyone hurt?'

'Everything under control, skipper,' Perrin said. 'Just scratch one X-7-R.'

Another telephone rang. 'Carry on,' Arnold said, reaching for it. 'Hello. Arnold.'

'Baltimore station. Our X-7-R just blew.'

'Anyone hurt?'

'Couple of minor cuts.'

'All right. Try to keep to schedule.'

Arnold hung up and leaned back carefully, still dubious about the folding chair. The floor-pacer had slumped onto a chair in the far corner. He sat looking at the floor.

'We'll know pretty soon, now,' Arnold said.

7

The face jerked upwards and stared at him, haggard, almost spectral-looking. Arnold felt a flash of sympathy for Thomas J. Watkins III. As chief engineer of the Universal Transmitting Company, Arnold had nothing more at stake than his pride and his job. His pride had been deflated so often it was immune to punctures, and his job could be replaced in no more time than it would take him to make a phone call.

But Watkins had invested every penny of his own money in Universal Trans, not to mention sizable amounts that were not his own money. He was on the verge of ruin, and he knew it. He looked decades older than his sixty-four years, A younger man would have been able to bounce back, Arnold thought, but let an elderly financier lose his money and he was out of work permanently.

'We're finished, aren't we?' Watkins asked.

'Just getting started,' Arnold told him. 'That was an X-7-R that blew. The old model. The one in Baltimore blew, and Philadelphia – this should be Philadelphia.'

He answered the telephone, listened briefly, and got the Philadelphia engineer's watch synchronized with his.

'That makes it unanimous,' he said as he hung up. 'Those were our controls. Three X-7-Rs. Now we try the X-8-Rs'

'Then – there's still a chance?'

Arnold said gravely, 'I'd say we have a fifty-fifty chance.'

Watkins smiled. 'I've gambled on worst odds than that, and won,' he said wistfully. 'But right now – this thing – '

Arnold silenced him with a wave of his hand. He was on the white telephone, and getting no answer. He reached the door in one leap, and flung it open.

Perrin called to him, 'Sorry. Meyers and I are patching each other up.'

'I thought you said – '

'Just a few cuts. Meyers got a nasty one on the cheek, but he'll be all right. Maybe he could use some stitches later. We'll keep on schedule.'

Arnold walked down to look at Meyers. The scrappy little engineer was grinning as Perrin applied adhesive tape.

'If it's as bad as that,' Arnold said, 'we'll use someone else.'

'Nuts,' Meyers said. 'I've been dodging flying glass for weeks. You think I'm going to quit now? One trip without being blown out of the place when I get there – that's all I ask.'

'I hope you'll get what you ask.' Arnold said. He looked at his watch. 'I have two forty-seven – right – now.'

'Check,' Perrin said. 'Three minutes. We'll be ready.'

Arnold returned to the office. Marrow seemed to have got a grin on himself. He had moved his chair over by the table, and Arnold considered finding something for him to do and decided there wasn't anything that needed doing. Watkins had resumed his floor pacing. Arnold sat down, got the Newark station on one telephone and Perrin on another, and waited, wondering if he had been ridiculously optimistic in rating their chances at fifty-fifty.

'Meyers is ready,' Perrin announced.

'All right, Newark,' Arnold said. 'Get ready.'

Newark informed him that it had been ready for five minutes, and where the hell was Meyers?

'Look at your watch,' Arnold snapped. 'Now, Perrin.'

'He's through,' Perrin said.

'He's through,' Newark echoed.

Arnold clapped the Newark phone to his ear, and waited. He laid down the white telephone, and it was seconds before he realized that Perrin was noisily demanding what had happened.

'Nothing happened,' Arnold told him.

'Nothing?'

'Nothing,' Newark said. 'Shall we send him back?'

'Right. Reverse it, Perrin. He's coming back.'

Silence followed. Then, from Perrin: 'He's back. Everything is all right.'

'Right. Keep it moving. Reverse it, Newark.'

'We have,' Newark said. 'He's through again.'

'Keep it moving.'

Arnold hung up both telephones. Philadelphia called, and then Baltimore. Arnold listened, and told them to keep it moving. He leaned back to look at Watkins. Suddenly he felt very tired. It had taken three years, and he had won – perhaps – and it all seemed anticlimactic.

'I guess that does it,' he said. 'The X-8-R. We're in.'

'It works?' Watkins demanded.

Arnold nodded.

'Then we can go ahead. Then – ' Watkins leaped to his feet. 'Then we can start operating,' he said excitedly. 'We'll get some money coming in, and we'll be all right.'

'At the last minute of the last hour,' Arnold murmured. 'How'd you like to take a quick trip to Newark?'

'Now?' Watkins said, eyes sparkling. 'Do you mean it?'

Arnold led him down to the far end of the warehouse, where a grinning Perrin was presiding at the instrument board. Meyers, in the middle of perhaps his tenth round trip between Newark and Manhattan, darted forward to grab Arnold's hand.

'We did it, Skipper!' he shouted.

Arnold pointed at a metal frame. 'Just walk through there,' he told Watkins.

Without the slightest hesitation Watkins stepped forward and disappeared. Meyers leaped after him.

Perrin scowled. 'Meyers will be breaking his neck, the way he jumped through. Know what that idiot wants to do? Perform a high dive over a concrete floor, pass through a transmitter, and come out over a swimming pool in Miami.'

'Sounds like a good stunt,' Arnold said. 'We may need ideas like that, for publicity.'

Perrin glanced at his board, and threw a switch. Nothing happened for so long that Arnold became uneasy, and then Meyers reappeared.

'The Old Man wouldn't believe he was in Newark,' Meyers said. 'He had to go look out a window.'

Arnold sniffed his breath. 'You're tight!'

'Well – the Newark boys have a little celebration going. They give me a couple of shots every time I touch down there. How long do we keep this up?'

Watkins bounced out in front of them. His face was flushed, his white hair ruffled. He was waving a bottle of champagne.

'Isn't it against the law to bring that stuff across a state line?' Perrin asked impishly.

Watkins roared. 'I didn't see any state line. I'm going to get the directors down here. Every one of them. We'll throw a real party.'

'You may not find them in a party mood,' Arnold said. 'It's three in the morning.'

'They'll be in the mood for this one. I want you to join me. All of your boys, too. They can transmit over here.' He waved a hand at the distant end of the warehouse. 'Plenty of room here for a big party.'

'Sorry,' Arnold said. 'You'll have to count us out. And I'd rather you didn't hold your party here.'

Watkins looked at him, wide-eyed. 'What's wrong?'

'Nothing's wrong. We still have work to do. I have to keep this test going, and I have to think about rebuilding a couple of hundred transmitters. Meyers? Where's – oh. Make this the last run. Newark can tune on Miami, and we'll take San Francisco.'

'Right!' Meyers said, and took a running leap into the transmitter.

2

Leaning back comfortably in the booth, one foot up on the seat, Jan Darzek watched Ted Arnold devour a hamburger. He thought, as he had many times before, that Arnold looked more nearly like a janitor than a brilliant engineer. He was short, fat, and bald. He appeared older than his forty-five years. He also looked slightly stupid.

All of which proved nothing except that looks could be extremely misleading, and no one knew that better than private detective Jan Darzek.

'I had an odd dream last night,' Darzek said. 'I was on the Moon, looking down at Earth.'

'You couldn't,' Arnold said.

'Couldn't what?'

'Look down at Earth. If you were on the Moon. The Earth would be like a large moon in the sky. You'd have to look up at it.'

'Oh. I hadn't thought about that. It proves my subconscious isn't scientifically inclined, I suppose. I looked down.'

'And?'

'And what?'

'What did you do?' Arnold asked. 'Just look?'

'That's all.'

Arnold sighed around a bite of hamburger. 'Seems like a long way to go, just to enjoy the view.' He sighed again, and carefully patted his perspiration-streaked bald head with a handkerchief. 'Air conditioning feels good.'

'It's an infernally hot night,' Darzek said. 'Will you finish that sandwich so you can tell me why you're making a cloak-and-dagger thriller out of this? It hurts my feelings to have my friends going out of their way to add to my daily quota of mystery.' His tone was angry, but merriment sparkled in his blue eyes, and the stern line of his lips did not quite suppress the smile that flickered there.

'What mystery?' Arnold asked.

'Why did Walker insist on our meeting in this – ' he glanced quickly over his shoulder for a lurking waitress ' – dump? Why did you come slinking in out of the night like a fugitive from justice?'

Arnold looked sadly at the bulging white of his shirt front, and adjusted the revolting blotch of purple that was his necktie. 'Men with my build never slink,' he said.

'You slunk. I've tailed too many men myself not to know all the classic symptoms a man displays when he thinks he's being followed. It's a wonder you haven't got a stiff neck, the way you walked up looking over your shoulder. You slunk into the doorway, and spent a full minute watching the passers-by on both sides of the street. Then you had to drag me away from a fairly comfortable chair to a plywood plank so we could have more privacy. And that in spite of the fact that we have this whole crummy joint to ourselves. Even the waitress doesn't hang around. She's carrying on a love affair with the cook.'

'Is she?' Arnold said, looking at the kitchen door with interest. 'Meeting here wasn't Walker's idea. It was mine. I've noticed that the place is usually deserted this time of night.'

Darzek leaned forward, and spoke softly. 'When does Universal Trans open for business?'

Arnold winced and half turned to look behind him. He whispered hoarsely, 'How did you know *that*?'

'Elementary,' Darzek said, still keeping his voice low. 'At the time this stock club of ours liquidated its holdings and invested its all in Universal Trans stock – at your recommendation, you might remember – I scraped together my life savings and brought a hundred shares for myself. Also at your recommendation. I may have mentioned it before.'

'You mentioned it at the time,' Arnold said, 'and you've mentioned it at least three times a week since the stock started to go down.'

Darzek chuckled. 'Have I? I'd forgotten. Anyway, a month ago the market value of Universal Trans stock was maybe a cent a share with no buyers, and a mysterious individual telephoned and offered five hundred for my hundred shares. Said he represented a nationwide syndicate of realtors who were trying to get control of Universal Trans to make something out of the various terminal sites the company has bought or leased around the country. I strung him along, and he's telephoned three times since then. The last offer was two thousand

– just what the stock cost me. Add the fact that Walker has called this meeting. He's probably had an offer for the club's stock. Add the fact that I happened to be walking along Eighth Avenue today, and I saw men at work in the Universal Trans terminal. They weren't tearing the place down, so I kept on adding and came up with an answer. Universal Trans is opening for business.'

Arnold nodded slowly. 'When did this character first offer to buy your stock?'

'A month ago.'

Arnold nodded again. 'Universal Trans is opening next Monday. But a month ago no one knew that. I didn't know it myself, and if I didn't know it no one did. A month ago I wouldn't have given you five hundred cents for your hundred shares.'

'Someone knew,' Darzek said. 'Otherwise, why the pitch?'

'Beats me. We finally got the bottleneck opened up just five days ago, and right up to that moment it looked as if Universal Trans was finished.'

Darzek lit a cigarette, and blew a thoughtful smoke ring. 'Queer,' he said.

'Universal Trans has had queerer things than that happen. What with the stockholders' suits – I think the last count was thirty-one – and the patent disputes, and the congressional investigations, and the Interstate Commerce Commision inquiries, and the Armed Forces threatening to take over the whole works, it's a wonder we still have a company. Then there are the government restrictions – all kinds of governments and all kinds of restrictions. And sabotage. Nothing I've been able to prove, but *I'm* satisfied that it's sabotage. But the worst problems of all were the technical failures. Just when we thought things were ready to roll, bugs would develop. I hate to think how many times that happened. And all along the way I've had the impression that some outsiders know as much about what's going on as I do. Maybe more. I've been followed on and off for the past two years, and it's beginning to make me nervous.'

'Wonder what's keeping Walker?' Darzek said.

'He's on an assignment. He'll be along.'

Darzek leaned back, stretched his long legs out under the table, and studied the flickering neon sign in the restaurant window. He was mentally trying to make something out of the words, DENOITIDNOC RIA, when the door jerked open and

14

Ron Walker hurried in. He came back to their booth without breaking his stride, tossed his hat onto a nearby table, and slid in beside Darzek.

'What's new?' Darzek asked.

Walker shrugged. 'Nothing much. 'Tis rumored the mayor will clamp on water restrictions if it doesn't rain. The weather bureau says this summer of 1986 will be the hottest in forty-eight years. Or maybe it was eighty-four years. Three congressional committees are due in town next week – one of them, incidentally, to investigate Universal Trans again. In Detroit, or maybe it was Chicago, some judge has ruled that a husband's failure to equip his home with an air conditioner does not constitute proper grounds for divorce. Looks like it's going to be a dull summer.'

'Obviously that was the wrong question to ask a reporter,' Arnold said. 'He smells smoky.'

'Warehouse fire,' Walker said. 'Empty warehouse. Dull. Even the firemen were bored. Where's the waitress? I'm hungry.'

Arnold picked up his empty coffee cup and hurled it at the kitchen door. It shattered noisily, and the waitress made a panicky entrance a moment later.

'Put on the bill,' Arnold said.

They waited silently while she brought more coffee and fixed a plate of cold sandwiches for Walker.

'You were right about the cook,' Arnold said to Darzek when she had hurried back to the kitchen. 'She was mussed.'

Walker waved a sandwich. 'Darzek is always right. Time probably hangs heavy on the girl's hands. Look – we haven't had an official meeting since – when was it? Couple of years, anyway. Universal Trans stock has been so low we've been practically bankrupt for that long. How would you like to recoup and make a fair profit?'

'How much profit?' Darzek asked.

'I can get thirteen thousand for our six hundred shares. That's a thousand more than we paid. I don't know what this idiot expects to do with the stock, but I thought you two should know about the offer.'

'Syndicate of realtors?' Darzek asked.

'Why, yes. He said – ' Walker turned slowly, and stared at Darzek. 'How did you know?'

'I own a hundred shares of Universal Trans myself. They approached me a month ago.'

'Evidently they have money to throw away.'

'They're not throwing it away,' Arnold said. 'The stock will be worth double what we paid for it ten minutes after Universal Trans opens for business on Monday.'

Walker leaped to his feet, upsetting his coffee cup. 'Is that offical?' he demanded.

'Official and confidential,' Arnold told him. 'Sit down and start mopping.'

Walker went to work on the spilled coffee with a handful of paper napkins. 'Fine bunch of friends I have,' he grumbled. 'Last month Darzek sat on a jewel robbery for a week, and not a whisper did I get.'

'I gave you a three-hour start when I cracked the case,' Darzek said. 'And I'll give you odds your editor wouldn't use this story. How many grand openings does this make for Universal Trans? Six?'

'Seven,' Arnold said. 'We probably won't even get snide editorial remarks on this one. The official news release goes out at noon tomorrow, and we expect a lot of papers to ignore it.'

'Or bury it,' Walker said. 'Page thirty-two, foot of the obituary column. 'The Universal Trasmitting Company announced today that it would open for business on Monday.' Period. Taking any full-page ads this time?'

'No. We figure people would ignore them, so we're going to save the money. That's what the Boss said, but personally I think he doesn't have the money to save. Anyway, we'll get all the publicity we need once we start moving passengers, and it'll be free.'

Walker nodded. 'I'll get myself assigned to cover the opening. I doubt that anyone else will want it. Everyone in favor of hanging onto the stock? Right. Meeting is adjourned. And Ted, you darned well better be right.'

'I'll be right – barring accidents. And Monday you'll be darned glad we dumped that airlines stock.'

'I want some more coffee,' Walker said.

Arnold summoned the waitress with a shout, and they sat silently while she refilled their cups.

'There's just one thing that bothers me,' Darzek said, when she had returned to the kitchen. 'Why was someone trying to buy my stock long before anyone at Universal Trans knew about this opening?'

'Speculators,' Walker said. 'Or maybe they have a syndicate of realtors. I've heard of stranger things.'

Arnold shook his head. 'More likely someone wants to get control of the company and kill it. Put it permanently out of business. The airlines interests, or the railroad and trucking interests, or – sure. Real estate. Why not? Can you guess what Universal Trans is going to do to real estate values? When we get operating properly a man will be able to live in California and commute to Wall Street by transmitter easier than he can commute now from Central Park West. The cost will be comparable with what the average commuter pays today for a train ticket. You should hear the Boss on that subject. He claims that Universal Trans is going to revolutionize our way of life more than the automobile did, and – '

He broke off and stared at Walker. 'Did you say *warehouse* fire?'

'Over on the west side,' Walker said.

Arnold got to his feet slowly. He walked slowly to the pay telephone, and when he had made his call he sat down on the nearest chair and gazed thoughtfully at a blank wall.

'I don't like this,' he announced finally. 'That was my warehouse. We were using it for some tests.'

'Will this effect your grand opening?' Darzek said.

Arnold shook his head. 'We didn't have much there, and we moved it out this afternoon.'

'Then there's nothing to worry about. Write it off. It was insured, wasn't it?'

'I suppose so. We were just renting it.'

'Forget it.'

'I don't like it. We've had so many things happen – '

'Probably a coincidence,' Darzek said.

'You're wrong there,' Walker said. 'The fire marshal has it down as arson.'

2

3

Only one New York paper gave the Universal Transmitting Company's opening front-page coverage. Other papers across the county treated the announcement as a filler, usually under the terse heading, AGAIN? There was little editorial comment. Even the newspaper editors were tired of pointing out, with suitable cutting sarcasm, that Universal Trans was merely making propaganda to gain itself a temporary respite from the troubles that plagued it.

The average citizen was throughly fed up with Universal Trans. He was not just unenthusiastic, he was uncurious to the point of indifference. As a result, the hour of the opening found the Universal Trans terminals everywhere deserted except for employees.

The swank, half-finished New York Terminal on Eighth Avenue south of Pennsylvania Station was no exception. Ron Walker entered at eight-one that Monday morning, and looked about with the sinking feeling that he'd been had. Getting the assignment had been a problem, not because anyone else wanted it, but because his boss wanted no time wasted on Universal Trans, then or ever. The only thing that kept Walker from turning around and walking out was the knowledge that he had wasted twenty minutes of his editor's time in arguing about the newsworthiness of Universal Trans, and he damned well had to produce some kind of story.

Walker stopped at the information desk and was directed to the mezzanine, where he found a row of ticket windows backed up by ticket agents. He asked for a ticket to Philadelphia. He was sold a ticket to Philadelphia, presented with an artistically printed pamphlet on the joys of transmitting, issued a free fifty-thousand-dollar insurance policy, and directed to a passenger gate.

There he surrendered his ticket, walked through a turnstile and down a short passageway that angled off from it, and seconds later found himself incoherently shouting out his story from a phone booth in Philadelphia. Almost before his startled editor had hung up Walker was back in New York with a follow-up story, and minutes after a messenger reached him with a generous sum for traveling expenses he was on the phone from London. After that performance not even the most hardened skeptic could deny that Universal Trans was in fact open for business.

But the heat-fogged lethargy of the man in the street was not easily penetrated on that sultry July day. By ten o'clock there was only a scattering of pedestrians standing with noses pressed against the towering plate-glass windows of the Manhattan Terminal. A nattily dressed young man waved at them from a platform, stepped through a transmitter, and emerged on another platform eighty feet away, still waving. He moved six feet sideways, stepped through a second transmitting setup, and returned to his starting place.

The average New Yorker watched for three minutes, failed to figure out the gag, and went his way grumbling. Then at ten o'clock a Universal Trans employee with a genius for promotion plucked a shapely brunette from her seat behind a ticket window, sent out for a bathing suit, and set the young man to chasing her from platform to platform. Within minutes the most colossal traffic jam in the entire history of Manhattan was under way.

It required only one final touch of genius to plunge Eighth Avenue into complete chaos. At eleven-thirty the terminal manager supervised the draping of an enormous sign across the front windows. COME IN AND TRY IT YOURSELF – FREE OF CHARGE!

Forthwith the crowd surged into the terminal. The early arrivals may have been more interested in chasing the brunette than in transmitting, but transmit they did, and the brunette was quickly retired as an impediment to traffic. Police fought to keep order in the lobby, and bawled lustily for reinforcements. Cars were abandoned in the street when their drivers, tired of waiting for traffic to clear, fought their way into the terminal to see what the fuss was about. Lines spread around the huge room in fantastic coils as one New Yorker after another cautiously mounted to the platform, stepped through to the opposite platform, returned, and was forcibly moved towards an exit.

No reliable count was made of the number of people who

transmitted that day. Universal Trans claimed a hundred thousand, which was absurd, but one reporter watched for an hour with a stop watch, and stated that a minimum of twenty and a maximum of forty people passed through the lobby transmitters every minute. In midafternoon a change of procedure limited the travelers to a one-way trip across the lobby, thus doubling the number that could be accommodated.

Lines still jammed the lobby at midnight, and business was brisk at the ticket windows. Travelers coming down from Pennsylvania Station to watch the show found their way into the ticket lines, and as a result arrived at their destination hours or days before they were expected. The airlines were receiving an avalanche of cancellations. Wall Street was digging itself out from a panic of late selling that plunged transportation stocks to unheard-of lows. Universal Trans stock had probably soared to a spectacular level, but no one knew for sure because there were no sales. The harassed Universal Trans stockholders were gloatingly hanging onto it.

To any point in the world where Universal Trans chose to set up a terminal, the traveling time by transmitter was zero; or, to be precise, it was the time a passenger required to stroll through an entrance gate, down a short passageway, and out of an exit gate. Boards of directors of many corporations were in session that Monday night, bleakly contemplating that fact and weighing its significance. The more farsighted of them found its meaning ominous, and set about balancing inventories, closing factories, ordering retoolings, and bellowing frantically at research divisions for new products.

The age of the automobile, the air age, were finished. Demolished. Brushed aside to crumble into ignoble oblivion.

And for the first time in three years the directors of the Universal Transmitting Company went to bed early and slept well.

4

Jan Darzek's only full--time employee was a former model named Jean Morris. She was a splendid ornament to his office, which she ran with ruthless competence, and on certain outside assignments her efficiency was deadly. Few people, male or female, could contemplate her superb figure and exquisite features and guess that behind her long lashes both of her large brown eyes were private.

She entered Darzek's employment because she fell in love with him. She quickly learned that Jan Darzek was no mortal man, but an institution of weirdly developed talents, all directed at securing elusive bits of information and assembling them into comprehensive reports to clients. By that time she had transferred her love to the detective business and begun the intense cultivation of her own talents. They made a spectacularly successful team.

On the day of the Universal Trans opening, Darzek returned from lunch and found her puzzling over a telephone call. 'From Berlin,' she said. 'Supposedly from Ron Walker.'

'You don't say.'

'It was a collect call.'

'It would be,' Darzek said with a grin. 'If he calls back, don't accept it.'

'I thought it was a gag. Or was that Ron's twin brother that was here when I came in this morning?'

'Ron hasn't got a twin brother, and it was a gag. This morning he was in New York. Now he's in Berlin. In the meantime he's been in London, Paris, and Rome. He's traveling on a newspaper assignment. I met one of his buddies at lunch, and heard all about it.'

'Oh,' she said. 'That transmitting business.'

'Right. Ron is doing a world tour by transmitter, sending back local color stuff on how the foreign populations are taking it. Naturally he'd like to give me a long personal report, with me paying the phone bill. If he calls again, tell the operator I just left for Siberia by transmitter.'

Twenty minutes later Darzek had a visitor, a businessman who had failed to control his exuberance on a trip to Paris the previous spring. There were complications.

'Paris?' Darzek said with a smile. 'Last week I'd have told you I couldn't spare the time. This week – I'll take care of it tomorrow.'

The businessman delivered himself of a deep sigh of relief. 'Good. I'll leave the whole thing in your hands. When you get back – will you be back by Friday?'

'I'll go over tomorrow afternoon,' Darzek said. 'I'll see the young lady, and come right back. It shouldn't take more than a couple of hours.'

The businessman's brows arched in surprise, then relaxed. 'Ah. Universal Trans. I'd forgotten.'

'You'll never forget it again,' Darzek said.

By Tuesday morning the police had decided to capitulate. Three blocks of Eighth Avenue were blocked off. The perspiring populace jammed the street from sidewalk to sidewalk. Universal Trans developed a sudden and thoroughly justified apprehension that the crowd might interfere with business, and opened a side entrance for paying passengers. When Jan Darzek arrived on the scene Tuesday afternoon it took him forty-five minutes to push his way from Pennsylvania Station to the Universal Trans terminal, and he was restrained from giving up only by the fact that the swelling crowd behind him looked more formidable than the crowd in front.

Finally he reached the terminal, slipped into the side entrance with a feeling of intense relief, and was whisked by escalator to the mezzanine. He paused there for a few minutes to look down on the mob in the lobby below.

Confusion raged about one of the demonstration transmitters. An elderly lady had thrust her umbrella through ahead of her, and then balked at following it. She hauled frantically on the umbrella, two feet of which protruded at the far platform. The umbrella did not yield. The combined eloquence of six guards finally persuaded the lady to push her umbrella the rest of the way through and follow it.

Darzek watched her waddle away, a frown clouding his good-looking face. The temperature was ninety-five, there was no rain in sight, and – why an umbrella? Protection against the sun?

'Down, boy,' he told himself. 'Who do you think you are? A detective?'

A moment later a high school girl changed her mind after curiously thrusting one arm into the transmitter. She hung helplessly, her forearm extending from the distant receiver. Her screams rang out shrilly above the din that filled the terminal. A guard finally shoved her through, and she scampered down the steps and darted furtively away. In the fracas the guard also stuck one arm through, and had to move onto the far platform. The crowd hooted.

'Strictly one-way operation,' Darzek thought. 'But one way at a time should be adequate for most travelers.'

The crowd seemed more amused than alarmed at the two mishaps. The lines kept moving, but Darzek noted that people approached the transmitter warily, tensed themselves as if for a plunge into a cold shower, and lurched through with eyes closed and hands held defensively in front of them.

Darzek tucked his briefcase under his arm and moved over to one of the lines at the ticket window. Directly ahead of him a shapely blonde turned, surveyed Darzek's sturdy six-foot frame and curly blond hair with analytical detachment, turned away. Darzek decided to ignore her.

In the next line a jovial, plump businessman was talking excitedly with a gaunt, unhappy-looking companion. 'Tried it downstairs. Nothing to it. You don't feel a thing. Like the ads said, it's just like stepping from one room to another. Darnedest thing I ever saw. One step and there you are, clear across the room.'

The other chomped nervously on a cigar. 'Across the room isn't the same thing as here to Chicago.'

'Just the same. You can go clear to Singapore – if they have a terminal there – and it won't take any longer than it does to go across the lobby. No more airplane flights for me. They're safe, of course, but now and then a plane does crack up, and this is absolutely safe. That's why they give you the insurance. They're not going to give you fifty thousand dollars' worth of free insurance if they aren't certain that nothing can happen.'

'Humph!' the cigar chewer said. 'They don't do that because it's safe. They do it because this is a new thing, and some people will naturally be afraid of it, and they want everyone to *think* it's safe. Just tell me what would happen if that thing blew a fuse with half of you here and half of you in Chicago.'

'Say – never thought of that! Let's ask when we get to the window.'

Everyone seemed in need of reassurance, and the line moved slowly. The two businessmen reached their window, talked at some length with a patiently grinning ticket agent, and finally bought their tickets. Ahead of Darzek the blond woman was just reaching the window.

She swung a monstrosity of a handbag from her shoulder, opened it, and paused to study herself in a mirror while the ticket agent tapped a pencil irritably. Finally she snapped the bag shut, and regarded the ticket agent with the same analytical detachment she had turned upon Darzek. 'I want to go to Honolulu,' she said.

'Certainly. Do you have some identification?'

'Identification.' It was difficult to tell whether she had asked a question or answered one.

'I need some kind of identification in order to make out your insurance certificate. With your ticket you receive fifty thousand dollars' worth of insurance, effective from the time you enter the transmitting gate here in New York until you leave the receiving gate at Honolulu. Do you have some identification? Driver's license, Internal Revenue ID – '

'Do the passengers wear life jackets?' the woman asked.

The ticket agent caught his breath. 'No. No life jackets.'

'But are you sure it's safe? There's a lot of water between here and Honolulu, and I'd hate to fall in. I can't even swim.'

The ticket agent drew on a thin reserve of patience. 'It's perfectly safe. Nothing can happen to you. Did you try the transmitter in the lobby?'

'Oh, gracious, no! I couldn't get through that crowd.'

'You can watch from here. It's like walking from one room to another. You walk through a door here, and out of a door at Honolulu, or wherever you're going. That's all there is to it.'

'It's Honolulu,' she said. 'I told you I want to go to Honolulu. Don't send me to China or somewhere.'

'You'd like to buy a ticket to Honolulu?'

'That's what I keep telling you!'

'Your indentification, please.'

'You're sure it's safe?'

'Miss, if you have any doubts at all, why don't you go watch the lobby transmitters for a while?'

With evident reluctance she surrendered a driver's license.

24

'I do hope I don't fall in the ocean. Salt water does terrible things to my hair.'

'This is your present address?'

'That's right. I just don't like the idea of going over all that water without an airplane, or boat, or something under me.'

The ticket agent wrote busily. Darzek turned his attention to the other windows. All of the agents looked harassed, and a couple of them were starting to snarl.

The blonde was rummaging in her handbag for her money. Since the operation took place directly under Darzek's nose, he thoughtfully studied the handbag. It was a boxlike contraption of glistening black leather, artfully embossed with a complex network of designs that seemed reminiscent of ancient Mayan art. He couldn't remember ever having seen anything quite like it. He wondered if it were Mexican.

She pushed her money through the window, and received in return her change, a ticket, an insurance certificate, and the Universal Trans pamphlet.

'This book,' the ticket agent said, 'contains all you'll need to know about transmitting. Report at Gate Ten, please.'

The woman carelessly stuffed everything into her handbag. 'You're sure – I mean, all that water – '

'Lady,' the ticket agent burst out, 'you won't even have a chance to wash your feet.'

The woman wheeled haughtily, to the accompaniment of guffaws from the line behind Darzek. Darzek stepped forward.

'Yes?' the ticket agent said warily.

Darzek slid his driver's license through the window. 'This is my present address. Paris, please.'

The ticket agent wrote, accepted his money, made change. 'Here you are. This book – '

'I know,' Darzek said. 'I'll read it after I get there.'

The ticket agent solemnly raised his grille and leaned out to grab Darzek's hand. 'Report at Gate Nine, please,' he said.

There were facilities for perhaps fifty transmitting gates on the mezzanine, with only a dozen in operation. Work was already going forward on the next section. Darzek saw Ted Arnold bustling about, waving his arms in eleven directions and sending men hurrying this way and that. Darzek moved among the waiting passengers with a feeling of exhilaration that only a long-frustrated Universal Trans stockholder could have understood. He found Gate Nine, and got in line.

Pretty young hostesses in smart costumes hurried about,

answering questions, administering bright doses of courage at the slightest sign of faintheartedness. Darzek saw the blonde from the ticket line trying the patience of one of the hostesses. But the hostess was quickly crowded aside by male passengers, who met the crisis eagerly and enthusiastically, congregating around the blonde and reading whole paragraphs of the company's pamphlet to her.

Darzek turned away with a grimace of disgust. There was such a thing as carrying even a good act too far, and the blonde's had been less than tolerable to start with.

A hostess smiled up at him. 'All set?'

Darzek nodded. 'They seem to be moving slowly.'

'That's because there are so few transmitters in operation. We rarely have two passengers in succession for the same destination, and the setting has to be changed every time. This is the European gate, with passengers for London, Paris, Berlin, Oslo, Madrid, Rome, and Athens. When each of those places has its own gate, the whole line will move right on through.'

She hurried off to bolster the courage of a plump woman who had reached the gate and showed signs of wavering. Darzek looked after her thoughtfully. Offhand he could think of at least two ways to solve that particular problem: they could sort out all the passengers for one place, and run them through; or they could schedule a time for each destination. He reminded himself that the company had only one day's experience, and doubtless it would experiment until it found a satisfactory arrangement. And of course more transmitters would help.

Another hostess moved along the line with a speech about the extensive safety checks Universal Trans was applying, and a reminder to walk carefully when transmitting. Only that morning, she said, a man had sprained his ankle when he ran through the transmitter. She was followed by a third hostess who attributed the slow-moving lines to the fact that the passengers were too cautious, and asked everyone to please move through the transmitter quickly. The line edged forward.

The passenger gates seemed to be operating smoothly. Each gate was supervised by an attendant who sat in an elevated control booth. On a signal from the attendant the passenger surrendered his ticket, passed through a turnstile, and turned at a sharp angle into a narrow passageway. He quickly disappeared from the sight of those anxiously waiting in line, but Darzek noted that the gate attendant had an unobstructed view

26

of the slanting passageway, and could watch the passenger until he stepped into the transmitter. The passageways were separated by tall partitions, which kept the passengers from wandering through the wrong transmitters.

Darzek had almost reached his gate when he heard a commotion in the next line. The blonde had been passed through Gate Ten, and then she decided she needed further instructions. The gate attendant and three hostesses pleaded with her as she stood her ground and tapped one expensively shod foot. From long training Darzek had already committed her features to memory. Now he began to study her critically. The mole on her left cheek – she should have that removed. Her long lashes were probably false. She wore more make-up than she needed, and her nervous mannerisms – the foot tapping, the way she repeatedly brushed her long hair back with her left hand, the way her right hand fidgeted with the clasp on her handbag – led Darzek to believe that a psychiatrist could have a very interesting interview with her. She was too obviously the helpless, the dumb blonde. It was an affectation, and she didn't need it. Her face was really quite lovely, her figure lithe and well proportioned, and her white summer suit had a style and simplicity that can only an expensive tailor could have imparted to it. Her appearance was striking enough to attract attention anywhere. Affectations were abominable in a woman who looked like that.

The high-pitched brittleness of her voice turned faces in her direction from the far end of the mezzanine. 'Are you sure? I mean, all that water – '

Finally she turned and stepped out of sight into the passageway. There was a momentary lull while the gate attendant alternating anxious glances between his instrument board and the transmitter, and then the blonde was back.

'What do I do?' she asked. 'Just keep on walking? There isn't anything there but a wall at the end.'

The gate attendant threw up his hands. 'Look, lady. You walk straight down there, and you'll walk through the transmitter and come out in Honolulu. Do you want to make the trip or don't you?'

'I don't want to walk all the way.'

Darzek was staring at the blonde. 'What the devil!' he muttered.

A hand touched his arm. 'Paris, sir?' the hostess said. Darzek surrendered his ticket.

'Walk straight ahead, sir.'

Darzek turned for another look at the blonde.

'We're waiting for you, sir.'

He shrugged. It was, after all, none of his business. He passed through the turnstile and strode down the passageway towards the blank wall at the end. Suddenly, instead of the wall, he saw an exit gate and a smiling attendant waiting for him. He was directed to a fast-moving customs line for passengers with light luggage, and a minute later he strolled out of Universal Trans's Paris Terminal onto the Champ-Élysées.

At the New York Terminal the blonde continued to argue. Waiting passengers set up a volley of blended derision and encouragement. The gate attendant put in a call for his superviser, and that worthy individual took in the situation at a glance and invited the balky passenger back to a ticket window for a refund. Suddenly the blonde turned, walked down the passageway, and disappeared. The gate attendant sighed with relief and watched his instrument board.

Five minutes later he called his supervisor again. 'I don't get any acceptance light from Honolulu,' he said.

'Damn! How long has it been?'

'Over five minutes.'

The supervisor stroked his face thoughtfully. 'Maybe your light is burned out. I'll get someone down here from maintenance.'

'Sure. What about – ' He gestured at the waiting passengers.

'We'll have to shift them to the other lines. Get some hostesses over here.'

They distributed the Gate Ten passengers among the other gates, which took time and did not generate any customer good will. A technician arrived, checked the Gate Ten board, and pronounced it in proper working order. The supervisor swore violently, and hurried off to the staff transmitter for a fast trip to Honolulu.

Three minutes later he was back again, his face a noticeable shade whiter. 'The dame never showed at Honolulu,' he said. 'Her handbag came through, but she didn't. They're still waiting there. She must have ducked out.'

'She did not,' the gate attendant said stoutly. 'She stepped through the transmitter. I was watching her.'

'Then where did she go?'

'How should I know?'

The supervisor was perspiring profusely. 'I'd better get Arnold down here,' he said.

Ted Arnold interviewed the gate attendant, made a round trip to Honolulu, and summoned his staff for a hurried conference. He scattered his men in all directions, to Honolulu, to every Universal Trans terminal in operation, and nervously tabulated the results. Three hours later the chief engineer had to face up to the staggering truth.

On its second day of operation, Universal Trans had lost a passenger.

5

It was not the best speech in the long career of Thomas J. Watkins III, but it was his most important. 'The mission of the Universal Transmitting Company,' he said, 'has been everywhere misunderstood. I have read dozens of surveys. I have heard lectures and debates and discussions and interviews. The gist of this uncontrolled flow of words has been the erroneous assumption that Universal Trans stood poised for the ultimate conquest of linear space.

'These self-appointed experts could not be more mistaken. Man has long since conquered space on this planet. Given the necessary amount of money and time, man has, for years, been able to go anywhere on the surface of the Earth and stay as long as he liked. Universal Trans has changed only the temporal qualification.

'The relationship between time and distance has plagued man since the Pleistocene, and the great transportational developments of the past century and a half have not altered that relationship; they have merely alleviated it. Now the matter transmitter has effaced it completely. Let me repeat: the matter transmitter represents man's ultimate victory over *time*. You, wherever you are, are no more distant from me – in time – than these gentlemen sitting around the table with me. The next room is now no further away – in time – than the next hemisphere.

'Since this fact has not been even partially understood, no one has evaluated its significance, not even the officers of Universal Trans. We have been far too busy with the practical problem of making our transmitters work. But we do know that we are today in the second day of a new era. The transmitter will have a greater immediate impact upon civilization than any other invention in history. By comparison, the notable career of the automobile will appear as no more than a ripple upon the pages of time. And further –'

Watkins leaned forward and touched a button. The television screen darkened. 'Enough of that,' he said.

'But very nicely put,' said the man at his right.

This was Charles Grossman, whose position as treasurer of Universal Trans had been reduced to a purely nominal one until the previous day. He had just read a report on the receipts for the first day's business, and he was in a jovial mood. 'What I especially liked,' he went on, 'was the way you left the implication that one still needs money to travel, even if Universal Trans has eliminated the time requirement. How long do you suppose we'll get away with charging airlines rates?'

'Too long,' Watkins said. 'At present we need all the money we can get, to clear up our debts and expand our operations. But the time will come when lower rates will give us enough additional business to make them profitable. That's when the railroads and the bus companies will start screaming. Right now we're only competing with the airlines. Where were we when that program came on? Oh – the Police Commissioner. He wanted us to call off the lobby demonstration so he could restore order. We were happy to oblige. We needed the transmitters, and that crowd as scaring away paying passengers.'

Grossman chuckled. 'We certainly don't want that to happen.'

'Next item,' Watkins said. 'We have telegrams from everywhere and everybody. Anyone want to read them?'

He glanced around the table. There were only six men present, including himself. It had been planned as a full board meeting, but some directors were not available on short notice, and others hadn't wanted to brave the crowd on Eighth Avenue.

'I have three secretaries sorting them out,' Watkins said. 'Some of them should be answered, I suppose – the President, members of Congress, heads of foreign governments, and so on. I'll see that it's taken care of. Well, gentlemen, that completes the agenda, unless any of you have business that we should consider. 'Yes, Miller?'

Carl Miller, a small, dark, intense-looking man, asked matter-of-factly, 'What's being done about the freight business?'

Watkins concealed his amusement. Miller was a late-comer to the Board, by virtue of a large block of stock he had purchased during the Universal Transmitting Company's darkest days, as well as his control of an impressive number of proxies.

31

He'd had faith in the company, and he'd made himself useful, but he was something of a fanatic on the subject of freight. Watkins preferred to develop the passenger service first. The company would show a greater profit on passenger operations, and there were fewer related problems. Passengers accepted the responsibility for transporting themselves to and from the terminals, and they didn't have to be stored until called for.

'Right now we haven't fully solved the problem of passenger luggage,' Watkins said. 'But we aren't forgetting the freight potential. Arnold has a special transmitter on the drawing boards, designed to handle freight. My feeling is that the freight operation should be kept entirely separate from our passenger operations. I'm certain that in the long run we can set up freight terminals more easily than we can expand and adapt our passenger terminals to handle freight. We also have inquiries from the postal authorities and from several large corporations about the possibility of leasing transmitters from us. The whole matter should be thoroughly explored. Would you like to head a committee to look into it, Miller?'

Miller nodded. 'I agree that it wouldn't be wise to jump into it without extensive planning. On the other hand – '

The door opened. Watkins turned with a smile, and waved. 'Come in, Ted. We were just – what's the matter?'

Grossman took one look at Arnold's face, and threw up his hands desparingly. 'Here it is. I thought things were going too well.'

Arnold wearily pulled up a chair and sat down to tell them about the missing passenger.

' How is that possible?' Watkins asked.

'It isn't possible,' Arnol said.

'But it happened.'

'It seems to have happened.'

'Where could a passenger go?' Miller demanded. 'Into the ninth dimension, or something?'

'Put it another way,' said Vaughan, a vice president. 'How many dimensions are there between transmitter stations? If you engineers really understood how the thing works – '

Arnold interrupted angrily. 'We know how the transmitter works. Let's get that straight right now. We don't know *why* it works, but we have the *how* completely under control. If we didn't, we wouldn't be moving passengers today. There is no "between" when you transmit. You are either at your point of departure or at your destination. If something happens before you leave, you don't go. If something happens after you arrive, you're already there. Look.' He snatched a blank piece of paper from Grossman, and drew large squares in two diagonal corners. 'These are your two transmitter stations.' He brought the corners together, so that the squares were adjacent. 'This is what the transmitter does. As long as it is operating properly, the two stations are locked together. If it doesn't operate properly – ' he smoothed out the paper ' – the passenger doesn't go anywhere.'

'But one has gone – somewhere,' Watkins said.

'One *seems* to have gone somewhere. We have not lost a passenger. We have *apparently* lost a passenger.'

'The passenger would no doubt find that distinction very consoling,' Vaughan said dryly.

'Good Lord!' Grossman exclaimed. 'Another lawsuit!'

Watkins turned to a man at the far end of the table. 'Harlow, what are the legal implications of this?'

'There aren't any,' Harlow said promptly. 'The legal aspects are already taken care of. The company's liability is clearly stated upon each ticket, and is covered by the free insurance given to the passenger. The liability is the insurance company's headache. You don't need a lawyer for this. You need a scientist – or the police.'

'If we'd started out with freight,' Miller said, 'we wouldn't have had problems like this.'

'What police?' Grossman wanted to know. 'New York or Honolulu? Or any of three thousand places in between?'

'The FBI?' Harlow suggested.

Watkins shook his head. 'No. No police. Not if we can help it. We can't afford bad publicity just when we're getting started.

'The publicity will be a lot worse if we don't handle this properly,' Miller said.

Grossman banged on the table. 'Look here. What if the insurance company should decide to cancel our policy? We convinced them there wouldn't be any claims, and here we are only in the second day, and – bang! If we had to stop giving free insurance because we couldn't get anyone to underwrite it, that *would* kill us.'

'We should have started with freight,' Miller said.

'How about a private detective?' Arnold asked. 'I know a good one.'

Watkins looked around the table. 'What do you think? If

3

there's no scientific explanation for this, a detective certainly wouldn't do any harm.'

Four heads nodded. Miller said, 'I still think we should call in the police.'

'Not yet,' Watkins said. 'Get your detective, Ted.'

Arnold telephoned Darzek's office, alerted the Paris Terminal of Universal Trans, and was waiting for Darzek when he stepped through to New York. 'Come along,' he said. 'I have a job for you.'

'Leggo!' Darzek protested. 'I don't want a job. I've had a long evening with a very untractable young lady, I'm tired, and I'm late for an appointment.'

'Evening?'

'In Paris it's evening. Night, now.'

'Oh,' Arnold said. 'You can use the phone in my office to cancel your appointment, and then I'll take you upstairs.'

Black would have been an appropriate color for the room, Darzek thought. The faces were glum except for Arnold's, which was angry. Watkins seemed calmly rational, but his pallor was deathlike.

Arnold spoke, and then Watkins. Darzek listened and watched the faces around the table. Grossman, the plump treasurer, was working at being heroic in the face of adversity. Miller, after one outburst on the virtues of the freight business, sulked in silence. Harlow, the company's legal advisor, had lost interest and was looking at Monday's market reports. The two vice presidents, Vaughan and Cohen, were not listening so much as waiting for an opening to deliver their own gloomy pronouncements.

Arnold was speaking again. 'Everything was clear on both ends. She walked through the transmitter here in New York. Plunk, her handbag came sailing through in Honolulu. We haven't found a trace of her since.

'Anything in the handbag?' Darzek asked.

A billfold with identification and fourteen bucks, plus the usual feminine clutter.'

'I'd like to see it.'

'I'll get it,' Arnold said.

The handbag was produced, and placed on the table. Darzek took one glance at it and started to laugh. The others stared at him, shock and indignation blended in their expressions – exactly, Darzek thought, as if he'd just told an obscene joke in church.

'Now I'll tell you what happened,' Darzek said. 'You've been had. First this woman stirred up enough fuss to get herself noticed by a lot of people. She did that so you couldn't claim afterwards that she'd never been here. Then she walked up to the transmitter, chucked her handbag through, and went back to the gate for another round of arguments. After that she ran out on you. Ducked over into another line, maybe, and left you with a monstrous mystery on your hands.'

The room was silent. Harlow had laid aside his newspaper, and Miller leaned forward and gazed at Darzek, open-mouthed.

'It may be that we were making the mystery overly complicated,' Watkins said finally, 'but you're making it too simple. You're assuming – '

'I'm assuming nothing. I was there. I stood behind that woman when I bought my ticket, and I had a good opportunity for a close-up of this handbag. It's unusual, and it interested me. I was waiting in line at Gate Nine while she was waiting at Gate Ten, and I was watching when her turn came. I saw her start down the passageway towards the transmitter. She had this handbag, not over her shoulder, but in her hand. I saw her come back without it. Obviously she shifted it around in front of her, so your gate attendant couldn't see what she was doing, and tossed it through. I wanted to wait and see what the hell was going on, but my turn came, so I dropped it. I don't know how she managed the disappearing act, but I'm certain it was managed.'

Murmurs of approval came from around the table. 'How do you like that?'

'Lucky thing for us – '

'Bright fellow, to spot that.'

Watkins rapped for order. 'You're an extremely observant young man, Mr Darzek.'

'I earn my living by being observant.'

'That's all right as far as it goes,' Arnold said. 'Smith says – Smith was the attendant at Gate Ten – Smith says, and I quote.' He took a piece of paper from his pocket, unfolded it, and read. ' "I had my eyes on her every minute. She wasn't an easy dame to take your eyes off. She started up there as if she was going on through, and then she turned around and came back, and said, 'Are you sure everything is all right? I mean, it's a long way to Honolulu, and I'd hate to fall in the ocean.

Salt water isn't good for my hair.' And lots of crap like that. I said, 'Lady, if you don't want to make the trip, just step aside. There's people waiting.' Finally I called Mr Douglas, and he asked her if she wanted her money back, and all of a sudden she turned and walked on through as if nothing had happened, but Honolulu didn't give me an acceptance light. I waited, and then called Mr Douglas again." So we're all right up to where Darzek left for Paris. She walked up to the transmitter and got rid of the handbag. Why, incidentally?'

'To magnify the mystery,' Darzek said.

'Of course. If she'd disappeared without a trace, we might not have known we had a mystery. A handbag without a woman attached screams of foul play. She got rid of the handbag, and then she turned around and came back. Darzek left at that moment, but it wouldn't have helped us if he'd stayed to watch. Only the gate attendant could see the transmitter, and Smith swears he saw her step through. And she couldn't have gone anywhere but into the transmitter. She couldn't leave the passageway without coming back through the gate.'

'What about Honolulu?' Darzek asked. 'Could she have got through there without being seen?'

Arnold shook his head. 'I've checked. Believe me, I've checked. I've been onto everyone who was anywhere near that Honolulu receiver. The only way she could have got through there without being seen was to turn invisible. For the time being I'm ruling out that possibility.'

'What do you want me to do?' Darzek asked Watkins.

'Find her.'

Darzek shook his head emphatically. 'Now *you* are over-simplifying things. By this time she could be anywhere. I run a small agency, and the world is a rather large place.'

'Hire as many men as you need.'

'She probably was disguised,' Darzek said. 'I suspect that her long blond hair was a wig, and also that she wasn't accustomed to high heels. I'm certain I'd recognize her if I saw her again, disguised or not, but I've had practice. I'd have a tough time describing her so someone else could recognize her with her disguise off, or with another disguise on. What if she were to change to a red wig, unpad her figure, put on low heels, turn the mole on her cheek into a fancy birthmark, and do another disappearing act – say from your Los Angeles Terminal? Then you'd have two missing passengers, and there's nothing to prevent her from keeping up that indefinitely. I'd suggest that you forget about the blonde, and concentrate on figuring out how she did it.'

'Good Lord!' Grossman moaned. 'This is worse than I thought.'

'There maybe another way to look at this,' Darzek said. 'If you'd be interested – '

'Certainly,' Watkins said. 'What is it?'

'It seems to me that this problem has two angles. One is the mechanics of the disappearance – how the woman worked it, and where she went. If she actually stepped into that transmitter and didn't come out where she was supposed to, that's Arnold's problem. I wouldn't know where to start on it.'

'I wouldn't either,' Arnold said. 'But I agree. It's my problem.'

'The other angle is that someone is obviously trying to embarrass Universal Trans. I'll give you odds that the woman didn't think this trick up all by herself. The question of who is doing it, and why, is a proper one for my type of investigation, and if you want me to take it on I will.'

'It seems a logical approach to the problem,' Watkins said. 'I think we should accept.'

There were frowns around the table, but no objections.

'All right, Mr Darzek,' Watkins said. 'We'll give you every assistance within our power, and naturally we all wish you a speedy success.'

'Do you have some kind of procedure in mind?' Miller asked.

'I have a number of moves in mind.'

'What kind of moves?'

'If you don't mind,' Darzek said, 'I think the fewer people who know about them the better.'

Miller flushed. 'This is ridiculous!'

'Good Lord!' Grossman said. 'If the company officers can't be trusted – '

The door opened. Perrin, one of the engineering staff, stumbled into the room, breathing heavily. He did not speak. He did not have to speak.

'Another one?' Arnold asked.

Perrin nodded. 'Some old dame left on a Chicago hookup.. All that got to Chicago was her umbrella.'

'Umbrella?' Darzek said quickly.

6

Several of the directors were quickly enmeshed in a violent argument, and Darzek sat back calmly and began to study and classify them. Too many times in the past he'd had greater difficulties with the client than with the client's problem, and the longer he listened the less he liked the idea of working for Universal Trans.

Watkins was the philosopher, the man of vision, who was at the same time intensively competent and practical. Watkins was unique. The rotund treasurer, Grossman, swung from bland optimism to dire pessimism, and instantly translated either into monetary terms.

Harlow, the attorney, had already dispensed with the legalities of the situation to his own complete satisfaction, and was unable to understand what all the fuss was about. Miller harped on his freight theme with such single-minded intensity that Darzek suspected unplumbed depths to his character – or no depths at all. Cohen and Vaughan, the two vice presidents, each sought bitterly and transparently to expose the other as a dunce, and both were successful.

Darzek pried the argument apart sufficiently to insert a question. 'How many directors are there?'

'Twelve,' Watkins told him.

Darzek got to his feet. 'I thank you for your consideration, gentlemen, but I've changed my mind. I don't want the job.'

He pushed his chair back, and started for the door.

Arnold, who had lost himself in a perspiring, stricken meditation, snapped to attention. 'What's the matter Jan?'

Darzek turned. 'Gentlemen, I am a Universal Trans stockholder. After listening to you for fifteen minutes, I can understand only too well why the company has had problems. It is said that Nero fiddled while Rome burned. This board would talk while the building was being pulled out from under it. All you have to do is sit here and argue until some police authority gets wind of what has happened, and you'll have no further responsibility for either the investigation or the company.'

Watkins rapped the table sharply, and silenced the ensuing uproar. 'Mr Darzek is right. This talk is getting us nowhere. I'll deal with the matter myself, and see that you are kept informed.

'Just a moment,' Cohen said. 'We didn't even find out what the guy's fee would be.'

'The meeting is adjourned,' Watkins said icily. 'I'm sure I don't have to remind you to make no statements on this matter, public or private.' He hurried after Darzek, and drew him aside. 'Just what is the difficulty?'

'I don't work well with a crowd looking over my shoulder,' Darzek said.

'There won't be. You'll co-operate with Ted to do whatever extent seems feasible, and answer only to me. Is that satisfactory?'

'Perfectly satisfactory – provided I don't have to attend any more board meetings.'

Arnold caught his eye, motioned to him and Perrin, and ambled out. He led them on a reckless dash along a corridor and down two flights of stairs, and pulled up at the door of his own office panting and fumbling with a bunch of keys.

'If I could spare a few transmitters,' he said, 'I'd put one in here and spot the others around this building. For my personal use. I've supervised the development of a revolutionary means of transportation, and I still spend half my time going up and down stairs or waiting for elevators.'

'It's good for the waistline,' Darzek said, following him into the room. 'The stairs, I mean, not the elevators. For heaven's sake – no swimming pool?'

The office was enormous, and virtually empty. A desk stood in one corner, flanked by empty bookcases. There was a swivel chair at the desk, and a battered sofa misaligned in the center of the room, as though the movers had dropped it and fled. Sundry electronic equipment was piled along the walls.

'Swimming pool?' Arnold said. 'Oh, you mean the room. The corporate status system is to blame. My office has to be larger than any of the other engineering offices, but it can't be quite as large as the office of a vice president. I don't do much here except try to think.'

'Watkins must have an entire floor to himself.'

'Just a little cubbyhole. He's beyond status. Well, Perrin, the question of the moment is how to keep it from happening again.'

Perrin gestured disgustedly. 'We might assign a hostess to each gate, and have her lead the passengers through by the hand.'

'I foresee certain difficulties. It would require at least ten times as many hostesses as we have now, and the passengers might resent it.'

'Also,' Darzek put in, 'the hostesses might resent it.'

'That's irrelevant even if it's true. But we'd have to hire special supervisors to route the hostesses to where they'd be needed, and getting them back there after every trip would drive the traffic managers nuts. But I'll think about it. You might as well go back to work. If there are any more disappearances – '

'What?' Perrin demanded.

'Nothing. Just come back here and help me pick a window to jump out of.'

Perrin left, and Arnold sat down at his desk and slipped out of his shoes. 'Can't remember when I've had to spend so much time on my feet,' he said. He tilted back, deliberately placed his feet on the desk, and gazed hypnotically at one toe that wiggled through a hole in his sock.

Darzek removed his coat and stretched out on the sofa, watching him. He had seen Arnold imperturbable in the face of numerous crises, but clearly this turn of events had shaken him. Absently he snapped on his lighter, and singed his nose before he realized that he had no cigarette in his mouth. Then, when he had fumblingly opened a new pack and pried one loose, he forgot to light it. He continued to stare at his toe.

'There's got to be a simple explanation for this,' he announced finally. 'But supposing there isn't? Supposing we *have* sent these people into some nth dimension? It's impossible, but their not arriving at their destinations is impossible, too. So many impossible things have happened with our transmitters, but always before this I could work out some kind of explanation. This time – '

'I'm not a scientist,' Darzek said. 'I won't believe in an nth dimension until I've seen it.'

'If a whisper of this gets out, we're ruined. And I can't see any possible way to prevent that.'

'Can the directors be trusted to keep their mouths shut?'

'Perhaps. But those women must have relatives or friends expecting them or waiting to hear that they've arrived safely. By morning the reporters will have it, the police will have it, there'll be headlines in every newspaper in the country, if not the world, and we'll have had it.'

'That would be unfortunate,' Darzek said. 'I have a feeling that the quickest way to solve this would be to catch them trying again. Obviously if you have to close down we may never catch them.'

Arnold lowered his feet with a thump, and swiveled towards Darzek. 'Did you have to insult the directors that way?'

'I thought it might shock some sense into them. I'm sure Watkins is all you've said he is, but how did he get saddled with a bunch of nincompoops like that? I wouldn't trust Grossman to manage my loose change for me. Harlow exists in a legal vacuum. The two vice presidents are nothing but ciphers with vocal cords. Miller I can't quite make out.'

'He owns a small trucking business,' Arnold said. 'Fancies he's an expert on freight. Maybe he is. When we get around to coping with the freight problem he might be useful – if we're able to stay in business that long. We started out with a first-rate Board, but as our troubles multiplied we gradually lost it. Wise men, as well as rats, desert a sinking ship.'

'Anyway, I've learned from bitter experience not to trust anyone I don't have to trust. As far as I'm concerned, the less the directors know about what I'm doing, the better.'

'What's the dark secret about the umbrella?' Arnold asked.

'Nothing much. I saw an old dame with an umbrella in the lobby lineup early this afternoon. She created a disturbance, and I wondered at the time why she was lugging an umbrella around on a day like this one.'

'What sort of disturbance?'

Darzek told him. 'Not that it helps us any,' he added.

'Might. She could have been attempting a crude form of sabotage, trying to frighten away the paying customers. But don't forget that this disappearing act is on an entirely different level. There must be clever planning behind it, and perhaps organization, and maybe even a better engineering staff than mine.'

'Or maybe just enough money to bribe the right Universal Trans employees.'

Arnold stared. 'The devil! You'll have to work on that angle. I wouldn't know where to start.'

'You might start by buying yourself some cameras.'

Arnold reached for his telephone. 'What sort of cameras?'

'You're the engineer. Something that would photograph each passenger as he approached the transmitter – preferably without his knowing about it.'

'Motion-picture cameras?'

'Not necessarily.'

'Why not? They'd record any suspicious actions that could be concealed from the gate attendant. Such as pitching hand-bags and umbrellas through the transmitter.'

'Suit yourself,' Darzek said. 'All I want is a good shot of the passenger's face. Then if one disappears we'll know what he looked like. If you're worried about concealed actions, why don't you put a mirror at the end of the passageway?'

'Ah! A mirror with a camera behind it. Good idea. The gate attendant would have a front and rear view of the passenger, and the passenger would have something more interesting than a blank wall to walk towards. While he admired himself, a photocell could trip the camera. But it would cost a fortune in cameras.'

'To start with, just enough for the New York Terminal.'

'Why just New York?'

'So far it's the only terminal that's losing passengers.'

Arnold shook his head admiringly. 'Either you're sheer genius, or I'm too shook up to think. I'll get someone started on it. Anything else?'

'I find myself suddenly very curious about your past diffi-culties. You mentioned the other night that you'd been tailed frequently, and that things had happened that looked like sabotage to you. Of course everyone knows you've had a long series of technical failures. I'm wondering what the sabotage was, and if some of those technical failures could have had outside encouragement. I probably won't understand half of it, but go ahead and talk.'

Arnold elevated his feet again and talked for half an hour, while Darzek listened meditatively. 'Well, you asked for it,' Arnold said. 'Want any more?'

'No. I don't understand a tenth of it. What much of it adds up to is that you'd have a problem, and you'd keep trying things until something solved it. But often as not you wouldn't know precisely what it was that caused the problem, and you wouldn't entirely understand how you managed to correct it.'

'Something like that. We're delving into unexplored scientific territory, and it'll be years before our knowledge will be anything like definite. This sort of thing happens whenever man takes on the unknown.'

'You're welcome to it. I'll have to think about this. It's hard for me to read sabotage into your technical failures, and even the more obvious things – the fires, the stuff that fell and smashed when no one was looking – those things could have been accidents.'

'Sabotage with finesse. Or else we're the most accident-prone corporation that ever – '

The telephone rang. Arnold answered, listened briefly, and said, 'Now? I'll be right up.'

'Another one?' Darzek asked.

'No. It was Watkins. He's in the Public Relations Office, and they want to have a press release ready when the storm breaks about the missing passengers. Got any ideas about that?'

'No, but I suggest that you corner the gate attendants and all the other employees who know about this, and tape their mouths.'

'I already have,' Arnold said grimly.

Darzek waited for Arnold to tie his shoes, and they left the office together. At the stairway they separated. 'Where will you be?' Arnold asked.

'I'm going to spend some time browsing around the terminal, and then I'll go back to my office and hire some people. If I find anything to think about, I might even do some thinking.'

'I'll send down a pass so you can see whatever you want to see.'

'I hope Universal Trans took in enough money today to pay me an advance on expenses.'

'If I told you how much the New York Terminal took in today, you wouldn't believe it.'

Darzek took an elevator to the mezzanine. The lobby below was deserted, now that the free demonstration had been canceled, but the mezzanine was more crowded than it had been that afternoon. Darzek threaded his way through to the information desk. 'Open all night?' he asked.

The young lady smiled sweetly. 'People traveling conventionally arrive in New York at all hours. We have to be available if they want to transmit from here. We're the only U.S.-European connection, you know.'

43

'I didn't,' Darzek said. 'You mean anyone traveling to Europe by transmitter has to come to New York first?'

She nodded.

'Well I suppose it's no special inconvenience to walk from one transmitter to another here in the New York Terminal.'

'It requires fewer transmitters that way. Transmitters are our biggest problem right now.'

Darzek smiled back at her, thinking that what she didn't know about the company's biggest problem wouldn't hurt her. 'Very interesting,' he said. 'Thank you.'

Perrin found him a moment later, and handed him a pass bearing the potent signature of Thomas J. Watkins III. 'Do you have time to give me a guided tour?' Darzek asked.

'Sure. What do you want to see?'

'I'd like a leisurely look at the layout of these passenger gates.'

'They're all alike. Come back this way, and you can look at some that aren't in use.'

Perrin led him into a closed-off section of the mezzanine, and opened a passenger gate. Darzek walked slowly to the end of the passageway, and traced his steps. The partitions were six feet high and met the wall solidly. A metal frame with an overhead crosspiece as the only clue to the location of the transmitter.

'Only a pole vaulter could have got out of there without going through the transmitter,' Perrin said.

'Are the receiving gates the same?'

'Exactly the same. Even the instrumentation is the same. Throw a switch, and the transmitter becomes a receiver.'

'Interesting. I'm beginning to see why Arnold is so upset about this.'

'Upset? Listen – it's a wonder it hasn't made a screaming idiot out of him. This is no job for a detective. It wants either a magician or a priest, and if I was the Board I'd hire both. Want to see anything else?'

'Nothing now, thank you.'

Darzek spent another twenty minutes poking about the terminal, getting the enormous place firmly in mind. Then he seated himself near the ticket windows and watched the unending throng of passengers. Ted Arnold found him there, and sat down beside him.

'Anything new?' Darzek asked quickly.

Arnold shook his head. 'Nothing. And I do mean nothing. I haven't the foggiest notion of how to proceed.'

'That describes my state of mind exactly. I might as well go back to my office.'

'I'll telephone you if anything happens. I'll be here until midnight, in case you want me.'

'Right. If I'm not at my office, I'll be home, or on my way there.'

'We'll have the mirrors and cameras ready by morning. I got that much taken care of. We'll also have all the North American operations moved downstairs by morning, which won't make your problem any simpler.'

'Or any harder,' Darzek said. 'See you later.'

Outside he found a long line of passengers waiting at the taxi stand. 'So I might as well travel "conventionally" ' he told himself, and set off on foot.

As soon as he turned off Eighth Avenue he knew that he was being followed – doubly followed, for there was a car and at least one foot operative. He slowed his pace to think the situation over.

Someone rated a capital E in efficiency. If he, or they, were half as effective in other things, Darzek was inclined to believe that Arnold had enjoyed more sabotage than he realized.

Someone also had contacts. Darzek ticked off on his fingers the individuals who knew that Universal Trans had hired Jan Darzek: the six directors, Ted Arnold, and the engineer Perrin.

And someone had blundered badly. Darzek strolled along leisurely, feeling inordinately pleased with himself as he examined the ways in which he might turn this development to his advantage. The foot-snooper matched his stride and kept a half-block behind him – too far back for Darzek to get a look at his face. The car passed him at intervals, its driver carefully looking the other way.

A block from his office Darzek met a patrolman who was an old aquaintance. He stopped to talk with him. The foot-snooper also stopped, and made a production of tying a shoe-lace.

'I've got a tail, Mike,' Darzek said. 'See if you recognize him.'

'Will do,' the patrolman said cheerfully.

'I'll be in my office.'

He turned the corner, and walked quickly. There were no

45

pedestrians about, and the only moving vehicle was the car tailing him. It approached slowly. Darzek glanced back again as he reached the entrance of the building where his office was located, just in time to see the foot snooper hurry around the corner.

That turn of his head proved to be a tactical error. He never saw what hit him.

He regained consciousness looking up into the patrolman's large, ruddy face. With an intense effort he managed to superimpose a grin on his headache. Mike grinned back, a bit anxiously.

'I don't think they busted anything,' he said. 'I guess you got a rap on the head, but I couldn't find any lump. How do you feel.'

'Very odd. Woozy.'

Darzek tried to get up. His legs buckled under him, and his hands and feet tingled strangely. He stayed on his knees, shaking his head, until Mike got an arm around him and hauled him to his feet.

'Better get a doctor,' the patrolman said. 'You may have a concussion.'

'You saved me from being carted off – didn't you?'

Mike nodded. 'They were dragging you to the car when I came around the corner. I blew my whistle, and they dropped you and cut out of here. I didn't even get the dratted license number.'

'I have the license number,' Darzek said. 'That is, I had it. My memory is woozy, too. But – yes, I have it.'

'God. They must have wanted you alive. If they didn't, they had plenty of time to smash your head. You made any enemies lately?'

'Several, but this doesn't make sense at all. Did you get a look at my tail?'

'Never saw the guy before. This is my fault, really. There was a guy standing here in the entrance when I came by. Never saw him before, either. He looked respectable, and we spoke to each other. I thought he was waiting for a cab, or something. Didn't connect him with your being tailed until I was a block up the street. I could have saved you a rap on the head.'

'Think nothing of it, m'lad. By scaring them off you probably saved me from something worse.'

Darzek shook off the patrolman's arm, and leaned against the side of the building. The strange tingling persisted, but his

46

head seemed to be clearing up. He took a cautious step.

'Better get to a doctor,' Mike said again.

'I'll be all right. I have to make a phone call, and then I'll go home. My next-door neighbour is a doctor. He's patched me up so often that I pay him a retainer. Grab a cab for me, will you?'

'Sure. That license number?'

'I'd rather you didn't report this, Mike. I'll see that number is checked out.'

'If you say so. They've ditched the car anyway, by now, or changed the plates. You make your call, and I'll have a cab waiting for you.'

Darzek unsteadily made his way up a flight of stairs to his office, and telephoned the Universal Trans terminal. It took the switchboard operator five minutes to locate Arnold.

'It's me,' Darzek said. 'I've changed my mind. I'm going to work at home. How reliable is your man Perrin?'

"Absolutely reliable.'

'In that case I didn't make the insult to your directors strong enough. One of them is selling you out.'

Arnold said slowly, 'How certain are you?'

'Certain enough to give you a written guarantee.'

7

Universal Trans assigned Darzek to a small office off the mezzanine, and late Wednesday afternoon he was there studying the six photographic enlargements that were spread out on his desk.

Jean Morris had disgustedly retreated to a chair across the room. 'It's hopeless,' she said. 'I've never seen anything like it. They're artists.'

'Or actors?' Darzek suggested.

'Artists. No mere actor could manage such transformations.'

'What do you think, Ed?'

Ed Rucks, an elderly retired cabdriver with youthful enthusiasm for investigative work and a superb eye for a disguise, said mournfully, 'No wonder we can't spot 'em in advance. It's just unbelievable. When you put 'em side by side that way you begin to see resemblances, but otherwise you'd swear they were total strangers.'

'So you know one thing for certain – we aren't up against a bunch of amateurs. Take a set of prints, both of you, and get lost and study them. If the time schedule holds, you have at least an hour before the next disappearance.'

'There's one thing that bothers me,' Rucks said. 'One more thing, I mean. If we are lucky enough to spot one of these dames, what do we do? Scream for help?'

'I'm waiting for instructions on that myself. Just scream for me. I won't be far away.'

'Will do.'

Darzek settled back to study the photos. He had already attempted to sketch faces that could accommodate the various disguises, but this was only an act of desperation to occupy his time between disappearances. He could not recall a job that had plunged him so quickly into total frustration. The wigs were perfect, of course, which was to be expected. But how did they achieve those subtle transformations of nose and chin? And the startling alterations in facial contours? Could this face with sunken cheeks really belong to the same woman whose face had a pleasing plumpness in another disguise? The sheer impossibiity of the thing staggered him.

And yet – it had to be the same person.

Ted Arnold burst in on him, panting violently. He kicked his shoes off, sending them flying against the far wall, and dropped into the chair by the desk. There he loosened his tie and mopped his bald head with a handkerchief, and until he'd got control of his breathing he could utter nothing more than a wheezy remark about how his feet hurt.

'Cheer up,' Darzek said. 'Better your feet than your head.'

'Oh,' Arnold said, instantly sympathetic. 'How's your head?'

'Perfect. I told you – the doctor couldn't find a thing wrong with me.'

'I thought maybe you'd had a relapse. Well, the Boss agrees with you. We're to work together, and you report to me. Anything I think he should know I'll pass along verbally.'

'Good. The way things were shaping up I thought I'd be doing nothing but write reports.'

'Those dunces on the Board – but you can't blame them for being concerned. Anyway, you tell me, I tell Watkins – holding back anything we agree to hold back – and then he tells the directors as much as he thinks they should know. It doesn't look as if the directors will be getting much information, which I gather is the way you want it.'

'Did you tell Watkins he's nourishing a viper?' Darzek asked.

'No. He'd try to smoke him out himself, probably messing up any plan you have in mind. Now that this is settled, how about a report?'

'Yes, Sire. There were two missing women yesterday; there are six today. The six today are revealed, by way of some excellent photography, to be two women, in three disguises each. One of the two – call her Miss X – is my mysterious blonde of yesterday in three new disguises. The other, whom I am calling Madam Z, is undoubtedly yesterday's dumpy old dame with the umbrella. We have accomplished one thing, probably with the assistance of the mirrors. There has been no further sleight of hand with handbags and umbrellas.'

'Neat. I don't suppose you've analyzed their motives.'

'I have not. I have checked out the eight identifications

they used in buying their tickets. All eight are phoney. We may safely conclude that they aren't doing this for the fun of it, and even that they intend to embarrass Universal Trans in some way, though it does seem odd that they haven't made their move yet. By this time we should have had relatives frantically beating on our doors in search of their missing loved ones, or a hysterical woman sobbing to reporters about how she tried to transmit to Minneapolis and ended up in a sewer in Brooklyn. Instead, we have nothing. It defies the imagination.'

'You've made a good point with those photographs,' Arnold said. 'As a standard procedure, as quickly as it can be arranged, we're going to photograph all passengers, both arriving and departing. Then if someone claims we shipped him to a sewer in Brooklyn, we can produce a photographic record of his smiling face arriving in Albuquerque or wherever.'

'With the possible exceptions of Miss X and Madam Z.' Arnold raised his hands wearily.

'Any progress in finding out how its done?' Darzek asked.

'None. The more we check into it, the more inexplicable it seems, If you can give us a lead on who's doing it, and some idea as to why, the how won't be too important – I hope. If we can get our hands on them, maybe the ladies X and Z will tell us what we want to know.'

'Which brings up another point,' Darzek said. 'What do I do if I catch them? Ask them to go home and be good girls?'

'I don't know. No one upstairs will commit himself.'

'What did your legal officer say?'

'He hedged. The board isn't worried about the legal position so much as the unfavourable publicity.'

'The false names and addresses they supplied for their insurance certificates leave them open to a charge of insurance fraud. They have also used four different drivers' licenses each as identification, which would undoubtedly interest the police. Isn't that enough basis for their arrests?'

'I'll ask. You'd have to be absolutely certain it was Miss X or Madam Z you were arresting, or we'd have a whale of a lawsuit on our hands.'

'True. But it may be worth a certain element of risk to cut them off before they suceed in whatever they're trying to do. We still have to catch them, of course.'

Arnold waved his arms forlornly. 'I almost wish they'd make their move, and get it over with. That press release has been rewritten a dozen times without satisfying anyone, and the Public Relations Office goes into a tizzy every time the phone rings. It'd be a relief to know just what they're trying to do.'

'Or even why they thought it was necessary to slap me on the head. You might tell Public Relations to work on the fraud angle.'

'If I could just figure out how they're doing it – ' Arnold muttered.

'Well, shall we go watch for them to do it again?'

Arnold nodded, and went after his shoes. 'One thing more,' he said, panting as he stooped down to tie them. 'You said you got a license number last night.'

'I did. I had it checked out.'

'I suppose the car was reported stolen two hours before you got conked.'

'Not at all. It was never reported stolen.'

'Whose was it?'

'I'm not sure I should tell you.'

Arnold straightened up angrily. 'Are you suspecting *me?*'

'Certainly not.'

'Then whose car was it?'

'Confidentially, it's registered in the name of Thomas J. Watkins III. Now shall we go downstairs?'

Among all the world's passenger terminals, those of Universal Trans were unique. In his first glimpse of the interior of the New York Terminal Darzek had sensed that something was wrong, or at least very different. The atmosphere was electrifying, for there was a dramatic feeling of high adventure in watching friends bid farewell to the traveler who would be, seconds later, at a destination hundreds or thousands of miles away. The year 1986 went its hectic, noisy way along Eighth Avenue, but just beyond the Universal Trans revolving door one encountered the remote future. It was not surprising that such an encounter engendered a feeling of strangeness.

But this was not what had disturbed Darzek. Not until Wednesday, when the lower level was opened to passengers and Universal Trans operations achieved a measure of regularity, did Darzek realize that it was the layout of the terminal that was so different.

There was no waiting room!

There were, to be sure, a number of cozy, conventional

groupings of settees placed at strategic locations, both on the main floor and on the mezzanine, but there were no rows of hard seats for use by weary travelers attempting to make themselves comfortable while waiting for the ten-fourteen flight to Chicago or the eleven-twenty-seven train to Miami. There was no waiting room because, now that Universal Trans had stepped up the efficiency of its operations, there was virtually no waiting. The main floor had an enormous curving row of passenger gates for North American travel. European travelers were accommodated at the shorter row of passenger gates on the mezzanine. You bought your ticket, you walked through the appropriate gate, and you were at your destination.

In Darzek's estimation, Thomas J. Watkins III had grossly understated the impact of the Universal Trans revolution. Time en route was, only too often, the least significant portion of the time expended in traveling. ONLY FIVE DAYS TO LONDON, a ship advertisement would state; but you waited two weeks for the sailing date, or perhaps you had to make your reservations four months in advance.

There were no reservations for Universal Trans. There was no time wasted on awkard travel connections, no layovers, no delays caused by nature or human errors, no obeisance to the tyranny of a schedule. When you wanted to go, you bought your ticket and went.

So there was no need for a waiting room.

Few of the people who crowded the terminal were sitting down. Jean Morris had a whole group of settees to herself, and she sat there comfortably relaxed while she furtively scrutinized the faces of those using the main entrance. At the end ticket window Ed Rucks, protected by a sign that read, NEXT WINDOW, PLEASE, was apparently very busy with a stack of records, and just incidentally keeping the side entrance under unwavering observation.

'It looks as if they have things under control,' Arnold said.

'Two people couldn't possibly keep this situation under control. Neither could two dozen. The terminal is too large, there's a tremendous volume of traffic moving through it, and those women are so expert in disguise that it's not even fifty-fifty that we'll recognize them if we see them.'

'All these years I've been thinking you were an optimist,' Arnold grumbled.

'Go count your transistors, or something. I have to figure out what to do with one of those women if I catch her.'

For the next hour he wove his way restlessly back and forth through the flow of passengers. He nabbed a pickpocket for the terminal police, and neatly tripped up a suitcase snatcher, and both times felt disgusted with himself for allowing his attention to wander. Finally he went up to the mezzanine, found a seat overlooking the main floor, and attempted to pick out familiar features in the blur of faces below. He also kept a wary eye on the gate attendants, expecting at any moment to see the familiar signal that had already come six times that day – 'Another one, Mr Darzek' – but there was no signal.

The constant movement, the incessant babble of hundreds of voices, overwhelmed his mental processes. He returned to the tiny office to reshuffle his ideas, and found it equally difficult to concentrate there. The six faces gazed up at him mockingly from the photographs. The telephone that lurked at one corner of his desk intimidated him. If it rang – 'Another one, Mr Darzek!' – he could only rush down to the lobby, knowing that he was already several minutes too late.

He telephoned his office, and listened patiently while Jean Morris's substitute read the reports that had accumulated. 'If anyone else phones in,' he said, 'tell him to call me at home if it's important. Otherwise, keep it until morning.'

He went back to the main floor. Ed Rucks was still performing his expert imitation of the harassed wage slave. Jean Morris tilted an eyebrow in his direction, but did not shift her attention from the entrance. Darzek summoned both of them with a sweep of his hand.

'Knock it off,' he said. 'Maybe we'll have better luck tomorrow.'

'Why tomorrow?' Jean asked. 'Doesn't this place run all night?'

'It does, but we don't. Those women have had a busy day. Let's hope they're almost as tired as we are. Do your homework, and report here in the morning.'

'Six o'clock?' Jean asked.

'Six o'clock.'

'Slave driver!'

'Darzek telephoned Ted Arnold before he left. I'm going home to do some thinking,' he announced.

'Better let me have a couple of men take you home.'

'No thank you. If I'm dumb enough to walk into an ambush two nights in a row, I deserve it.'

53

'It's your head. Do you really think Watkins – '

'Of course not. I have just proved conclusively that Watkin's car was nowhere near Manhattan last night.'

'Then how – '

'But his license plates were. Or someone has gone to the trouble of duplicating his license plates. The only thing I'm certain about is that the men who were at that board meeting will bear watching. Two of them left town right after the meeting. I've had tails on the others since I left last night.'

Arnold produced a long whistle. 'Paid for with Universal Trans money. The innocent ones will have a fit when they find out.'

'The guilty one will have a fit too.

'Want me to call you if there's another disappearance?'

'If you do, I'll resign.'

Darzek took a taxi, and had himself driven directly to his appartment. No one followed him. He entered cautiously, automatic in hand, and found the place empty. 'So much for that,' he told himself. He had his dinner sent up, and arranged himself to do some serious thinking.

At six o'clock on Thursday morning Darzek was back at the Universal Trans terminal, having breakfast in the basement cafeteria. Jean Morris, seated opposite him, looked amazingly refreshed, but snarled grumpily when he spoke to her. Ed Rucks looked sleepy and talked like a man tensed for action.

'I've been thinking about this,' he said. 'What we need is something that will force their hands.'

'Got any ideas?'

'How about running some ads that brag about how absolutely safe Universal Trans is, and how many thousands of passenger miles have been racked up without injury or accident? If someone is trying to ruin the company's reputation, he might feel he'd have to challenge that.'

'It's an idea. I'll pass it along, though it wouldn't surprise me if the company has something like that planned anyway.'

'Did anything happen during the night?' Jean asked.

Darzek shook his head.

'Maybe we scared them off,' Ed Rucks said.

'I prefer to think that they didn't quite get the results they expected, and they're cooking up something new. I've been asking myself what one sly manipulation would close Universal Trans down instantly and permanently.'

'Is there one?' Rucks asked.

'There is. If they could arrange to have a few passengers depart in the usual manner and apparently reach their destinations as corpses, that would do the job. I mentioned the possibility to Arnold, and he's up in his office right now taking aspirin.'

'No, he isn't,' Rucks said. 'Here he comes, and he isn't after breakfast.

Arnold swooped down on their table, and helped himself to a chair.

'Starting early, aren't they?' Darzek asked.

Arnold nodded.

'No corpses, I hope.'

'No. Just another disappearance. Two more. Only these are from Brussels.'

'So,' Darzek said, pushing back his chair, 'today we work in Brussels.'

'The Brussels Terminal just opened this morning. Its cameras aren't set up yet, so there aren't any photos. It doesn't have the mirrors yet, either.'

'We'll make out with the photos we have. Come, children. You should get more sleep, Jean.'

'Detective work is no job for a lady,' Jean Morris said.

At the Brussels *Gare de trans universel* they found that the unfortunate *Chef de gare* had allowed himself to be overwhelmed by the catastrophe. By the time Darzek arrived, he had been ordered off to hospital for observation.

Fortunately the assistant manger, a Monsieur Vert, had iron beneath his plump little exterior. He had taken charge heroically, conducted his own investigation, and reasoned his way to the conclusion that – as he expressed it to Darzek later – for such untoward events to occur it was required that someone goof. M. Vert quickly established that only two Universal Trans employees had contact with each missing passenger, and it was obvious even to him that he could not blame the ticket agents for what had happened. When Darzek arrived on the scene he found two panic-stricken gate attendants under house arrest, with M. Vert eagerly awaiting permission to call in the police.

Darzek dismissed the charges, read an edict from Watkins concerning secrecy, and assured M. Vert that the disappearances were only optical illusions. He asked to speak with the gate attendants.

M. Vert bubbed enthusiastically. 'But certainly. I shall interpret for you myself.'

'I'll do my own interpreting,' Darzek said.

The attendants immediately recovered their composure when Darzek informed them that such malfunctions had become commonplace in New York. 'I do not mind being blamed for my mistakes, monsieur,' one of them said, 'but if this machine swallows a person wrongly that is no affair of mine.'

'Universal Trans wouldn't appreciate that figure of speech,' Darzek said. 'Tell me what happened.'

The story was both brief and familiar. An elderly woman had made a routine departure for Berlin, but all that arrived in Berlin had been her umbrella..

'Very interesting,' Darzek said. 'Did you speak with her?'

'No, monsieur.'

'But just before she stepped through the transmitter, she hesitated, didn't she?'

'She stopped and looked about, and then she started back towards me and I told her to go straight ahead. But this happens often. The transmitting is such a new thing, and many a passenger is *très confus*.'

'Very good,' Darzek said, turning to the other attendant. 'And your passenger – did you speak with her?'

'Beaucoup, monsieur. Even for a woman her tongue was overworked.'

'In French?'

'Qui, monsieur.'

'How was her French?'

'Very good, monsieur.'

'As good as mine?'

'Quite as good, monsieur. But different. Yours has a slight provincial accent that I cannot place. Hers was pure Parisian.'

'Interesting. You're positive there was no foreign accent?'

'Monsieur, I have been working with travelers all my life, and I speak five languages myself. I cannot remember the last time I mistook a person's nationality.'

'You just mistook mine,' Darzek said. 'But never mind. Tell me what happened.'

This passenger had been a young woman, of striking appearance. Darzek whistled, and the attendant grinned and nodded. 'And blond,' he went on. 'Very blond. Everyone in the terminal stares at her, and for that reason I find her questions much too embarrassing. She wants to know how the transmitter will get her beyond the mountains – does she go over them or through them – and such things as that. She starts down the passageway, she comes back and asks more questions. Finally she steps through, but all that reaches Rome is her purse.'

'Thank you, gentlemen. You have been most helpful. I suggest that you go back to work now, and say nothing more about this to anyone.'

The two attendants left, trailing profuse thanks. Darzek turned to the impatiently waiting Jean Morris and Ed Rucks. 'This may be a break. It was Miss X and Madam Z from Tuesday. If they're repeating their disguises, we've got them.'

'I distinctly heard reference to a *parapluie,*' Jean said.

'The old dame shoved an umbrella through, just as she did in New York on Tuesday. Let's go to work.'

They quickly circled the terminal, and began picking out observation stations. Darzek was weighing the comparative merits of an unused ticket window and the Information Desk when Jean caught her breath and pawed frantically at his arm. 'I think I see your Miss X, disguise B, waiting in the customs line.'

'So you do,' Darzek said cheerfully. 'Ed, we'll take Miss X. Madam Z should be along shortly, and she's yours if you can spot her.'

Rucks nodded, and moved away. Miss X, this time a subdued brunette, passed through customs, paused for a long look about the terminal, and then walked briskly towards the ticket windows. Jean drifted after her. Darzek routed M. Vert from his office, and tersely explained the situation.

'You wish to have her arrested?' that worthy individual demanded, his mind still on the police.

'Certainly not.'

'Our own security staff could detain her for questioning.'

'Perhaps later. I'm reasonably certain that she'll be back in another disguise, and now I want to watch her carefully and see how she operates.'

'Then – we are to do nothing at all?'

'Just brace yourself for another disappearance.'

Miss X left the ticket window, did another careful survey of the terminal and walked towards the passenger gates. Jean Morris was at the ticket window, encountering difficulties with her U.S. currency. At a word from Darzek, M. Vert intervened. She got her ticket.

'Paris,' she whispered to Darzek, and hurried after Miss X.

Miss X was already stepping through the turnstile at the Paris gate. As she moved into the passageway, Darzek and M. Vert unceremoniously rushed Jean Morris to the head of the line.

The attendant's attention was on the passageway. 'Straight ahead,' he called. Then he glanced at his instrument board, gave a matter-of-fact nod, and said, 'Next.'

'You have an acceptance light?' M. Vert demanded.

'But of course.'

The assistant manager turned bewilderedly to Darzek. 'You must be mistaken. She went to Paris!'

Jean Morris thrust her ticket at the attendant, spun the turnstile, and vanished into the passageway in an unladylike sprint. Darzek started after her, and was stopped by the turnstile. The attendant nodded again, and said, 'Ticket, please.'

'You cannot pass through the turnstile without a ticket.' M. Vert said. 'If you wish, I shall arrange a special connection.'

'Damn! Never mind. Jean will manage without me.'

He seated himself near the main entrance, and Ed Rucks walked over with studied casualness to sit down beside him. 'What happened?' Ed asked.

'She bought a ticket to Paris. She went to Paris.'

'So maybe the next disappearance will be from Paris.'

'In that case, why did she come here? Why not go directly to Paris?'

'Afraid of being followed, maybe. Just because they managed eight disappearances from New York doesn't mean they have to do another eight from Brussels.'

'Yes,' Darzek said thoughtfully. 'Yes and no. This terminal has been alerted by the first two disappearances. If she was afraid she was followed, why not go to Paris *via* Madrid? Why return to the scene of the crime, just to pass through?'

'All right. Why?'

'This could be important. I never thought about it before, but their technique may not be one hundred per cent efficient.'

'You mean she tried to disappear, and it didn't take?'

'I don't know what I mean. There's nothing to do now but wait.'

'And keep looking for Madam Z,' Rucks said, and strolled away.

Twenty minutes later Miss X was back in Brussels, followed

closely by Jean Morris. Darzek, taking no chances on Miss X becoming suspicious of Jean, waved her off and signaled Ed Rucks to take over.

'Go have lunch,' he said to Jean.

'I'm not hungry. I just had breakfast.'

'Then stay out of sight.'

Miss X circled the lobby twice. She picked up a handful of Universal Trans literature, seated herself near the ticket windows, and apparently read it. She left the lobby and walked through an adjoining souvenir shop without purchasing anything. Finally she went to a ticket window and bought another ticket to Paris. She took a few steps toward the Paris gate, changed her mind, and sat down nearby to look through the Universal Trans pamphlets again. The puzzled Rucks made himself as unobtrusive as possible on the other side of the lobby. Darzek and M. Vert stood screened by the Information Desk, and watched.

When finally she moved she caught all of them by surprise. With perfect timing she stepped quickly to the gate at a moment when no passengers were waiting. She was through the turnstile before the startled Rucks was halfway across the lobby.

Acting on impulse, Darzek ran. He ignored the open-mouthed attendant, and cleared the turnstile with a long leap to stumble half-falling into the passageway. Miss X looked back blankly. Her split second hesitation enabled Darzek to regain his balance, and as she stepped through the transmitter he dove after her.

M. Vert was talking animatedly with the gate attendant when Rucks arrived. He explained in English. 'There is no acceptance light.'

Rucks said dazedly, 'Then she didn't get to Paris. She's disappeared.'

'Oui, monsieur. And so has your monsieur Darzek.'

8

Ted Arnold had never felt completely at ease in the presence of a woman. When the woman was beautiful, and when she seemed on the verge of either explosive anger or maudlin tears, the only counter-tactic he could think of was flight. He said lamely, 'I'm very busy right now. Perhaps later – '

Jean Morris asked again, 'But where can he be?'

'Darzek can take care of himself,' Arnold said, and wished he felt as confident as he sounded. Jean and Ed Rucks, seated on his office sofa, looked at him glumly.

'He's a rare type of individual,' Arnold went on. 'He's a man of action, and also an intellectual besides which he's as smart as hell. He thinks on his feet. Was he planning on pulling off something like this?'

'If he was, he never mentioned it,' Ed Rucks said.

'Wherever he is, he's all right. Those women never seemed any worse for disappearing. They always showed up again, plague 'em! You say Darzek thought that trip to Paris was important?'

'He thought it might be. He thought it might mean that they didn't always succeed with whatever they were doing. After what happened with Madam Z, I agree with him.'

'Ah! Tell me about Madam Z.'

'She turned up twenty minutes after Darzek and Miss X disappeared. She came from New York, as I found out later, and she was also wearing disguise B.'

'Did you find out where Miss X came from?'

Rucks shook his head. 'By the time we thought to check on it, it was too late. Anyway, Madam Z bought a ticket to London. She went to London. Jean followed her, and followed her back to Brussels, and then I took over. She left the terminal and went for a walk. She browsed through a couple of shops without buying anything, she sat down in a little park and communed with nature for a while, and then she went back to the terminal. She bought another ticket to London. I was right behind her, though not as close as Darzek was to Miss X. I went to London, but she didn't. Ever since then we've been waiting for them to come back to Brussels and try it again. What do we do now?'

'Get a good night's sleep,' Arnold said promptly. 'You've earned it. Tomorrow you can carry on by yourselves until we hear from Darzek.'

'Carry on how?' Jean Morris demanded. 'Jan didn't have a long-range plan. Or if he did, he didn't share it with us.'

'I think he was playing it by ear,' Rucks said.

'Then you play it by ear. Figure out what Darzek would have done next, and do it.'

Both of them scowled. Watching them, Arnold made a discovery that struck him with tumultuous impact. A beautiful woman was – a beautiful woman. She was beautiful when she scowled, and when she was angry, and when she was on the verge of tears. Beauty underwent changes. It had, perhaps, dimensions and facets in infinite measure. But it did not lessen.

Just as an ugly man's ugliness did not lessen, even in his most heroic moments. Arnold patted his ample stomach, and fingered his bald head, and sighed. He probably had more sex appeal than the fire extinguisher outside his door, but not to a noticeable degree. It was the penalty a man paid for doing all of his thinking sitting down. Darzek, on the other hand –

Jean Morris said thoughtfully, 'I'm sure there won't be any more disappearances from Brussels.'

'Then you'll have to wait until we find out where they'll hit next.'

'While we're waiting,' Rucks said, 'we might look at some pictures.'

Arnold arched his brows inquiringly.

'You've been taking photos of all the passengers leaving New York. That's a lot of film. Have you had much of it developed?'

Arnold shook his head. 'Just enough to get prints of the women who disappeared.'

'Get prints of all of it,' Rucks said. 'It'd be interesting to know if the dames had any dry runs here yesterday.'

'You'd better explain that.'

'If a dame disappeared while supposedly transmitting to Chicago, we could check to see if she made a bona fide trip

61

to Chicago a little before that, just as Miss X went to Paris before she disappeared going to Paris, and Madam Z went to London. I'd like to know if they always do a dry run.'

'I would, too,' Arnold said, 'though I don't quite see that it makes much difference.'

'And since Madam Z went to Brussels from New York, we could check to see if Miss X did, too. It may not mean anything, but that's the way Darzek works. He says if you keep collecting information, sooner or later you'll have something that adds up.'

'Good idea. I'll have a room full of prints ready for you in the morning, and you can look at pictures until we get word of another disappearance.'

'If Jan doesn't show up in the meantime,' Jean Morris said.

'Right. He may have the whole thing wrapped up by morning. Do you have any idea how many people he has working on this?'

'None at all. Jan may have put it in a ledger at the office.

'If any of them show up for instructions, just tell them to carry on as before, or if they've finished whatever they were doing use your own judgment. .You two come in at eight, and I'll have the prints in that room Darzek was using.'

After they had left he made a telephone call to start action on the passenger photos, and then for a long time he sat wreathed in cigarette smoke and ideas that never – quite – found a target. Shortly after midnight his door jerked open, and Thomas J. Watkins looked in with a grin.

'Don't you ever sleep?'

'Only during board meetings,' Arnold said. 'What about yourself?'

'I've been riding herd on some auditors.'

'Don't tell me Universal Trans has financial problems!'

Watkins crossed the room and tiredly dropped onto the sofa. 'Call it bookkeeping problems. Which reminds me. I was going to raise your salary. I'll do it first thing in the morning. Have you heard from Darzek?'

'No,' Arnold said. 'And don't ask me where he went. I've been asked that question a hundred and ninety times since he disappeared, mainly by the same two people, and it nauseates me.'

'Universal Trans is deeply indebted to Mr Darzek,' Watkins observed.

'True.'

'To put it bluntly, he has saved our necks. We'd have succumbed to panic that first day if it hadn't been for him, and those photographs were a stroke of genius. That was the most fortunate suggestion of yours – hiring Mr Darzek.'

'Anyone who knew him would have thought of it.'

'But where do you suppose he went?'

Arnold slammed both fists down onto his desk.

'I'd feel personally responsible if anything happened to him,' Watkins added quickly.

'Let me tell you something about Darzek,' Arnold said. 'He carries a gun, in a shoulder holster he designed himself. It's a ridiculous little automatic, and I don't think even an expert could spot it without searching him carefully. And he can hit a pinhead at ten feet and a dime at twenty. Wherever he went, I feel sorry for the people he found there. I've seen Darzek really angry just once, and that was enough to make very good Christians out of a roomful of atheists. Did you notice that there weren't any disappearances this afternoon?'

'That's right. There weren't.'

'I'm betting there won't be any tomorrow.'

'In any case, there's nothing we can do – is there?'

Arnold shook his head. 'There is one problem. Darzek hired a staff for this job, and if he should be – detained – we should advance some money to his office for the payroll, and perhaps we should see that one of his men takes charge temporarily.'

'Certainly. Handle it as you think best, and let me know how much money is needed. Anything else?'

'Not now, no. If I could just figure out how they work those disappearances – '

Early Friday morning Ron Walker came to see Arnold. He leaned far over his desk, looked Arnold steadily in the eyes, and whispered, 'May I ask a question?'

Arnold grunted noncommittally.

Whereupon Walker shouted, 'What the hell is happening with Universal Trans?'

'Plenty,' Arnold said peacefully. 'New terminals opening up, business increasing, records broken almost every hour. There's even a chance that the Russians will relent and let us open a terminal in Moscow. Go down to Public Relations, and they'll fill you in.'

'Damn Public Relations. Where's Darzek?'

'I haven't the vaguest idea.'

'When did you see him last?'

'Yesterday morning.'

Walker pointed a finger. 'I happen to know that he's working for Universal Trans.'

'I never even knew it was a secret.'

'But you don't know where he is.'

'You know Darzek better than that. How long would he stay on a job if his employer made him check in every ten minutes?'

Walker backed off disgustedly, and plopped onto the sofa. 'We had an anonymous letter this morning.'

'About Universal Trans?'

Walker nodded.

'Let me guess. Some woman claimed she tried to transmit to Los Angeles, and ended up in a sewer in Brooklyn.'

'You're warm,' Walker said.

'Let's see it.'

'The boss has it locked in his safe. If true, it's worth its weight in platinum leaf, or something. If it's not true – but either way its dynamite. Did you know that a whole series of Universal Trans passengers walked trustingly into your transmitters and vanished from the ken of mortal man?'

Arnold leaned back and gave what he hoped was a creditable imitation of a laugh. 'I can go you a lot better than that. Go down to Public Relations, and tell them I said you were to see the Crank File. One guy thinks we're changing our passengers into pigeons. He's noticed a dramatic increase in New York's pigeon population since Universal Trans opened.'

'This is no crank letter. At least, it isn't the usual kind of crank letter. It names names, and cites meetings of the board of directors, and even quotes what was said. It claims Darzek was hired by Universal Trans to attempt to locate the missing passengers.'

'It names the missing passengers'?

'No. It names directors, and quotes them.'

'And what is your boss going to do with it?'

'Obviously nothing at all unless he can turn up enough solid evidence to withstand a libel suit. Care to make a statement?'

'I'd be delighted. Of the millions of people who have transmitted since Monday – Public Relations can give you the exact number – there is not even one who is unaccounted for. You may quote me. To your boss, that is.'

'That's fine, as far as it goes. Why did you hire Darzek?'

'Yours isn't the only anonymous letter that's turned up. We'd like to know who's writing them.'

'I see. It sounds so plausible that it's highly suspect. When you see Darzek – '

'What?'

'Never mind. He wouldn't give me a story anyway.'

'I sincerely hope not,' Arnold said.

Watkins had called a special meeting of the board of directors at eleven that Friday morning. Carl Miller had insisted on it, to consider the report of his freight committee. At eleven-fifteen Arnold labored up the stairs with an armful of freight transmitter blueprints, only to find that the meeting was canceled.

'Mr Miller couldn't come,' said Miss Shue, Watkins's private secretary for more years than either of them cared to recall. 'The others on the Freight Committee don't know anything about anything. The Old Man has called another meeting for this afternoon. Four o'clock.' The tough, self-reliant and brutally competent Miss Shue was at least as old as Watkins, but she always referred to him as the Old Man, to the horror of the other secretaries in the executive offices. She would have been equally horrified to know that they referred to her as Old Shue Leather.

'Does he want me this afternoon?' Arnold asked.

'He didn't say. He's been in conference since nine. Some jerk from the District Attorney's office.'

'Ouch! What have we done?'

'I haven't the faintest. Miss Shue regarded him with interest. 'I didn't know you had a bogy, though I suppose you're as much entitled to one as anyone else. Mr Armbruster blanches that way when anyone mentions the Interstate Commerce Commission. Mr Riley is terrified of Internal Revenue, only that doesn't count because everyone is terrified of Internal Revenue. Mr Horner – '

'Did I blanch? I didn't intend to.'

'Of course not. No one ever intends to. Why are you afraid of the District Attorney?'

'It all dates back to that afternoon I murdered my mother,' Arnold said, and walked out, leaving her gaping after him. He threaded his way through the battery of clicking typewriters in the outer office, drawing hardly a side glance from the typists. If Darzek had walked through that office, he told himself glumly, every typewriter in the place would have come to a dead stop.

Darzek. 'Where the devil is Darzek?' he muttered.

Back in his own office, he made a telephone call before he tilted back meditatively and placed his shoeless feet on his desk. It was nearly noon in New York, and late afternoon in Europe, and Universal Trans had yet to record its first Friday disappearance.

Arnold looked in at Darzek's office before he went upstairs at four o'clock. Jean Morris and Ed Rucks were blearily examining photographs. Photographs were piled high on the desk. Photographs had spilled onto the floor, in all directions. Cartons of photographs were stacked about the room – opened and unopened. They did not hear Arnold come in, and he backed out discreetly without disturbing them.

Again he climbed the stairs with an armful of blueprints, and Miss Shue directed him to a conference room. 'The Old Man is still busy with that D.A. fellow,' she said. 'They've started without him. You didn't really murder your mother, did you?'

'Of course not,' Arnold said. 'My baby sister did it, but I got blamed.'

There were only three men in the conference room – Armbruster, a nondescript vice president who had not been present when Darzek was hired; Cohen, a similarly nondescript vice president who had been and Grossman, the Universal Trans treasurer.

'Board meetings shouldn't be called on such short notice,' Armbruster was grumbling when Arnold walked in. 'Strictly illegal. Anyway, no one comes.'

'They shouldn't be called without a darned good reason,' Cohen said. 'That's why no one came. Everyone is fed up with listening to Miller's harangue about the freight business. I wonder why Watkins doesn't turn him off.'

'There's money to be made in the freight business,' Grossman said cheerfully.

'Let the railroads have it. I say, Arnold, could we run a railroad train through a transmitter?'

'Certainly,' Arnold said, 'if we built a big enough transmitter.'

'That might be the answer. Build railroad transmitting

66

points at strategic places about the country, and charge the railroads for using them. The railroads could handle the freight, and we'd handle the railroads. Make a nice profit without all the fuss and bother of setting up warehouses and storage and delivery and that sort of thing. We'd cut days off the railroads long-distance freight runs. How about it, Arnold? Are you listening?'

Arnold started. 'Excuse me. I was half listening. The other half of me was wondering if a train could run through a transmitter and stay on the tracks. Might be messy if it couldn't.'

'Build one and find out,' Cohen suggested.

'Why don't you take it up with the Boss? I don't make policy here. I just follow orders.'

'I'll take it up with Miller. Where is he, anyway? I thought this was his meeting.'

'He's detained out of town,' Grossman said. 'I just talked with his secretary. She doesn't know when he'll be back.'

'Great. He calls a special meeting, and then he can't make it. What are we hanging around here for?'

'That was Miller's meeting that was canceled this morning,' Grossman said. 'Watkins called this one.'

'If he called it, the least he could do is attend. Those disappearances, I suppose. Anything new, Arnold?'

'What did the Boss tell you about it?'

'He said we have the situation well in hand.'

'We have the situation well in hand.'

Cohen glowered at him. 'Where's that detective fellow?'

'I don't know.'

'I thought he was reporting to you.'

'He is.'

'Then why doesn't he report? I know the company's finally making money, but that's no excuse for throwing the stuff away. Anyway, it wouldn't surprise me if someone on your engineering staff was behind that monkey business No one else knows anything about the transmitter, and you guys know all about it, and it seems dratted queer that the disappearances should be such a mystery to you. We should have hired our own detective, instead of one of your pals. We might have learned something – like what engineer has come up with a neat scheme for blackmailing the company.'

'For your information,' Arnold said hotly, 'if there's a crook inside Universal Trans, he's one of the directors. We do know that much.'

'Nonsense,' Grossman said, hastily gushing large quantities of soothing oil. 'Why would a director – '

He broke off as Watkins slipped quietly into the room and took his place at the head of the table. He looked haggard, and so utterly exhausted that Arnold wondered if he'd had any sleep at all the previous night. Before he spoke he closed his eyes for a moment, and pressed a hand to his head.

'I've been waiting for Harlow,' he said. 'But he can't get away. What's the trouble?'

'Nothing much,' Grossman said. 'Here – let me quiet everyone's nerves with a financial statement.'

'Arnold says one of the directors is behind those passenger disappearances,' Cohen said. 'I say only the engineers would have the necessary know-how.'

Watkins turned to Arnold. 'A *director*, Ted?'

'Darzek's idea,' Arnold said. 'He said he'd certify it. Shouldn't have shot off my mouth, but Cohen ruffled me. I'll give you the details later.'

'I'll look forward to hearing them. I've been out of touch today. How many disappearances?'

'None.'

Watkins looked startled. 'None? Do you suppose Darzek is responsible?'

'Wherever he is, I'm sure he's his usual effective self.'

'And Darzek has fingered – that's the term, isn't it? – one of the directors. I regarded that young man highly from the first, but not highly enough, it seems, because he happens to be right.'

The three directors stared at Watkins, who ignored them completely. 'Did he say who it is, Ted?'

'I don't believe he knows who it is.'

'Strange that he should happen onto the idea at all.'

'It struck him suddenly a couple of nights ago,' Arnold said dryly. 'He's been working at finding out who it is.'

'The next time you see him – ' Watkins paused. 'He won't need to work at it any longer. I know who it is. I'm sorry we couldn't have more of the board here, but it was rather short notice. Charlie, I've had auditors on your books since yesterday.'

Grossman froze in the act of lighting a cigarette. He blew out the match, tossed the unlit cigarette into an ashtray, and smiled palely. 'So that's what you've been up to.'

'They say it'll take weeks to get things unscrambled, but

68

they're certain the shortage will run a hundred thousand, and perhaps much more. We've had a specialist in from the D.A.'s office, and the police are waiting now to take you into custody. The D.A.'s man would like to talk with you. You don't have to, of course.'

'I won't.'

'In a way this is my fault. If I'd devoted more time to managerial problems, where I'm an expert, and less time to technological problems, where I'm not, it wouldn't have happened. But I've known you for thirty years Charlie and you're almost the last person – ' His voice had trailed away.

Grossman had recovered his poise, but he avoided Watkins's eyes. His voice was higher pitched than usual, and tense. 'I thought Universal Trans would flop anyway, and I hated to see all that money go down the drain. You say the police are waiting?'

Watkins nodded.

Grossman got to his feet slowly, and started for the door.

'Just a moment,' Arnold called. 'Where's Darzek?'

'*Darzek?*' How would I know? I haven't seen him since the Board hired him.'

'How did you work the disappearances?'

Grossman looked wonderingly at Arnold. 'Do you really think I had something to do with that?' He laughed. 'I always thought you knew your stuff, Ted, but maybe you're a lousier engineer than I am a treasurer. Either that, or one of us is crazy. He opened the door carefully, stepped outside, and closed it.

The two vice presidents had been stunned into silence. Watkins said thoughtfully, 'Maybe he's trying for a deal. He'll tell us what he knows if we agree not to prosecute. He's holding back something to bargain with.'

'You bargain with him,' Arnold said. 'I'm going back to work.'

As he hurried past Miss Shue's desk, she flagged him down with an afternoon paper. 'I meant to ask you. What do you think about this?'

Arnold gazed unseeingly at the headlines. 'Think about what?'

'You mean you haven't heard? Why, everyone's been talking about it all day. The explosion on the Moon, that's what. The government says we didn't do it, and the Russians have just gotten round to claiming they didn't do it, and everyone is accusing everyone else. It's all very confusing.'

'Both we and the Russians have men up there. Did anyone think to ask *them* about it?'

'Oh, it wasn't anywhere near any of the Moon stations. Look – there's a map on the back page, showing where it happened. A scientist like you ought to be interested in these things.'

Arnold waved the paper away. I'm just a dumb engineer with problems. Don't bother me with your Moon explosions. I wouldn't care if the whole damned thing blew up.'

9

Darzek floated.

He was fully relaxed and ready to end his dive with a neat flip onto his feet, automatic in hand if circumstances required it. He was also prepared to talk his way out of an awkward predicament in the Paris Terminal, if that was where he and Miss X emerged.

But he knew instantly that he was not in the Paris Terminal. And he floated.

He soared completely over Miss X, who stood looking up at him, arms half-raised, face immobilized in an expression that had no parallel even in Darzek's considerable inventory of facial expressions. Momentarily he experienced an exhilarating sensation of flying, but his mind was much too preoccupied to enjoy it. He collided gently with the far wall, rebounded a short distance, and twisted to memorize the room with a glance as he dropped easily to the floor.

Instantly his attention was arrested by a grotesquely tall, grotesquely thin apparition that presided over an enormous instrument board near the transmitter frame. Darzek's dramatic entry had caught it in the act of rising from a tall stool. It remained in a half-crouch, one hand frozen in position at the controls, the other waving aimlessly, as though to banish Darzek from its sight.

Darzek had only a second or two to contemplate its impossible expanse of bald head, its weirdly wide face and peculiar, swathing apparel before a sudden movement by Miss X triggered a lightning snatch for his automatic.

But the figure at the instrument board had held his attention too long. Before his hand could reach the gun, darkness crashed down on him.

He regained consciousness slowly, and found himself totally paralyzed. A painful, tingling sensation throbbed through his entire body. It was at once terrifyingly strange and familiar, like the inexplicable recurrence of a half-forgotten nightmare. He struggled furiously, he cried out for help again and again, and when he finally desisted and lay quietly vanquished and soaked with perspiration, he had neither moved a muscle nor uttered a sound.

He was unable to open his eyes, and his head seemed to gyrate strangely. He wondered whether his hearing was affected. The voices in the room sounded enormously distant and babbled impossible, unending chains of hissing and buzzing consonants.

His mind began posing a series of childish questions, and he found much to his disgust, that he did not know where he was or what had happened. Finally he asked himself, 'Who am I?', immediately responded, 'Jan Darzek,' and felt better.

Footsteps padded softly towards him. A hand touched his forehead, a dryly cold, almost abrasive hand that grated his skin, and then lifted his head and dropped it. The strangely familiar tingling sensation had receded to his limbs, and to his delight he found that he could feebly wiggle his toes.

The hand touched his forehead again before the footsteps padded away. The remote conversation continued. 'She shot me!' Darzek's mind exclaimed suddenly. 'Miss X shot me – with – ' There had been *something* in her hand, but he had not even recognized it as a weapon.

A surge of memory flipped him abruptly into the past. He lay on the sidewalk outside his office building, looking up into the patrolman's worried face. His hands and feet tingled oddly.

'So that's how it was,' he mused. 'Just like that night, only a stiffer dose. No wonder they couldn't find a lump on my head!'

The aftereffects faded rapidly. Soon the pain was no more than a dull, numbing throb, and he had full control of his toes. He could have opened his eyes and looked about, but he was determined to risk no movement that might attract the attention of those in the room. He remembered only too well the terrible weakness he had experienced before, his inability to stand without assistance. He would feign unconsciousness until that weakness had passed, and he could, if he chose, come up fighting.

He inventoried his mental picture of the room he had entered so unexpectedly. It was shaped like an enormous cylinder laid on one flattened side. The curved surface was milky white, and it diffused light. At first Darzek rejected the notion; but he had seen no lights anywhere, and yet the room was brilliantly lighted. The soft white glow of the curving walls and ceiling lighted the room.

The transmitter frame stood at one end, with the instrument board angling out from it. A wide ledge ran the length of the room on both sides – for sleeping purposes, perhaps, for there were long objects like sleeping bags lying on it. A curving, glittering metal surface, as tall as the room, bulged from the flat wall by the instrument board. Except for the one stool he had noticed no furnishings.

And he had floated. He thought long about that, hesitant to face up to the obvious implications. He had floated, and therefore there was no gravity. And yet, when he reached the end of the room he had dropped to the floor, so there was gravity. Or would complex factors such as his momentum and the angle at which he bumped the wall control his movement? He wished he had Ted Arnold's knowledge of physics.

If his own specialization was people, what could he make of that person – that *thing* – at the instrument board? The place defied all logic, and so did its inhabitants.

He continued to listen to the voices, and thought he made out the overtones of an argument. For a time he occupied himself with sorting the voices out, and labeling them, and trying to estimate the number of people in the room. He had positively identified four different voices when someone spoke out from close by, and again a cold hand rasped against his forehead. It was all he could do to keep from recoiling.

'You can get up now,' a voice said in English. 'We know you are awake.'

He continued to feign unconsciousness. The argument resumed, and became voluble. A fifth voice joined in. Hands seized Darzek, pulled him to a sitting position and supported him there. He kept himself relaxed, but in the movement he managed to nudge his shoulder holster. They had not taken his automatic. Or had they unloaded it and replaced it?

He weighed his chances carefully, and dismissed the idea of coming off the floor with automatic in hand. For a second or two he would be vunerable from the rear, and he could not handle five of them unless he chose his position carefully.

He decided on a plan of action, opened his eyes, and went through the motions of struggling to his knees.

The argument spiraled away into silence. There were five

73

of them grouped about him, and as they watched him he feigned dizziness, regained his balance, and calmly stared at each of them in turn. To his amazement, they avoided his eyes.

Miss X was still wearing the disguise he had followed into the transmitter. Madam Z was there, in one of her disguises. There was a strange male, an attractive-looking boy in his late teens or early twenties.

And there were two *things*.

At first Darzek had difficulty reconciling the *things* with the apparition he had seen at the instrument board. That figure had been tall and absurdly thin; these were tall and absurdly wide. Only after he had struggled to his feet did he realize that they were wide when seen from the front; thin when seen from the side. Either view was like looking into a distorting mirror.

He continued to stare at them. They appeared not so much like living beings as a patented fabrication for populating nightmares. Their facial features were hideously concave, the enormous widely separated eyes, the single, gaping nostril, the puckered mouth all weirdly inverted as though to open inward on some misshapen fantasy of a drunken artist. There were no ears; there were no hair, no eyebrows or lashes, not even a suggestion of eyelids. The necks were slender pipes. The flesh, what was visible of it, was a ghostly, flaccid blue. They were swathed in what appeared to be unending, over lapping layers of bandage from feet to throat to hands. The hands –

The very ugliness was hypnotic. He tore his gaze away from them, took a step, looked again. The hands had four nailless fingers, which were delicately, almost transparently webbed.

He took another step, and pretended to stagger. Miss X moved to support him, but he shook her off and walked slowly to the far end of the room, stomping his feet as if to restore circulation, rubbing his hands together, pausing once to rub his legs. They made no move to interfere. When he neared the transmitter frame he turned, and his automatic was in his hand.

'Raise your hands above your heads!' he snapped.

For a long moment they stared uncomprehendingly at the gun. Then the male slowly raised his hands, and Madam Z followed. The others made no move at all. One of the *things* spoke, and Miss X replied.

'Speak English!' Darzek ordered.

'She was only asking if it is a weapon, Miss X said.

'She?' Darzek said blankly.

'You would refer to her as – '

One of Miss X's hands leaped, snatched at something in a fold of her clothing. Darzek cooly shot her in the arm. The report rang out thunderously in that bare room, and left his ears ringing. '*Now* will you raise your hands? he asked.

Miss X spoke a single, matter-of-fact word. 'Barbarian.' She raised her hands, and the two *things* followed her example. If her arm pained her she showed no sign of it. Darzek searched the five faces for some trace of emotion fear, anger, perhaps in disgust. He found none. They continued to look imperturbably in his direction, but even across the full length of the room they would not meet his eyes.

'I don't think so highly of you, either,' Darzek said to Miss X. 'Now I suppose you'll have to be patched up. Is there any first aid equipment in this place?'

One of the *things* suddenly became aware of Miss X's wound. It – she – whirled and examined the arm carefully. Then, with a single leap, she soared to the other end of the room, and at her touch a door rippled open in the bulging metal.

Rippled. Darzek thought of venitian blinds and zippers, but neither comparison was adequate. The solid metal rippled aside, and the *thing* darted through the opening and reappeared a moment later, flipping it shut behind her. Darzek followed the movement warily, and watched closely as she went to work on Miss X's arm. She held it firmly with one hand, and dabbed a liquid with the other. Then she turned calmly, faced Darzek, and raised her hands.

Darzek backed slowly away from them, and hoisted himself onto the stool by the instrument board. From there he could keep the five of them under surveillance and also cover the transmitter. He had thinking to do, and he had to do it quickly.

And what he had just seen was enough to unsettle the thinking of any sane man. He'd hoped to inflict a minor flesh wound, but he had to shoot quickly, and the arm was moving, and the tiny slug had struck it dead center. It flattened on impact, which it shouldn't have done, and ripped a dreadful hole completely through the arm.

But it did not strike a bone, and the wound did not bleed.

And under the casual medical treatment he had just witnessed the wound had already closed, except for a gaping tear in what looked to be an exceptionally thick and tough epidermis.

Darzek found his thinking unequal to the situation. 'All right,' he said finally. 'One of you – talk.'

There was no response.

'You.' He pointed to Miss X. 'Where are we?'

No answer.

'Who are you?'

No answer.

It was obvious to him that he would not be in full control until he had mastered these – whatever they were – psychologically as well as physically. He turned for a quick look at the instrument board. 'I wonder where a shot would do the most damage,' he mused aloud. Ted Arnold would have given his eyeteeth, and perhaps a few molars as well, for a look at that board. The controls were cones, built up of variously colored perforated discs that were mounted upon a common center. Some kind of key, inserted in the perforations, could turn the discs individually or collectively – he thought. Other than that he could make nothing of it.

Miss X took a step forward. 'We are on your Moon. If you damage our instrumentation you will never be able to return to Earth.'

'And just where would that leave you?' Darzek asked with a grin. 'Cut off from your source of liver extract?'

'I do not understand you.

'Aren't you taking something for your anemia? You should. You're the first person I ever shot who didn't bleed.'

He scrutinized each face in turn, and found the blankness of expression infuriating. The threat to their instrument board brought verbal protest, but no flicker of emotional reaction. They did not even appear to be indifferent. Just – blank.

He continued to talk, still feeling his way with them, probing for an opening. 'Do you believe that dreams predict the future?' he asked. 'A short time ago I dreamed I was on the Moon, looking down at Earth. It seemed ridiculous at the time, but here we are. How would I go about looking down at Earth?'

He did not expect an answer. *Inhuman,* he thought, as he inventoried the faces again. Or nonhuman. 'Where are you

76

from?' he asked. 'Mars? Venus? Or somewhere – ' he waved a hand ' – beyond the Solar System? You called me a barbarian. I may even be absymally stupid, by your standards, but I've had extensive practice in adding up simple facts. Two of you have family trees that are among no known earthly flora. By fact and deduction the same applies to the other three – in spite of your devilish talent for human disguises. Want to talk about it? No?'

—He looked levelly at Miss X, who turned her head away. 'Then I'll talk about it. If the action I took in self-defense was barbarous, I'd very much like to know how you classify your own acts. You've damaged thousands of dollars' worth of property belonging to the Universal Transmitting Company; you've interfered with the technological development of a civilization that certainly has done you no harm; you've severely and permanently injured Universal Trans technicians; you've – '

He got the reaction he had hoped for, but he savored it not at all. Though they burst into agitated talk, he had no way of telling whether they were angry, remorseful, or amused. Their faces were as devoid of expression as before.

The young male spoke in English. 'None of those men were seriously injured.'

'Two technicians got splinters of glass in their eyes,' Darzek said. 'One of them may lose his sight. Perhaps you don't consider that a serious injury.'

'We are sorry to hear this. We shall be severely reprimanded.'

'What are you sorry about? The injuries or the reprimand?'

There was no answer.

'Considering the damage you've inflicted on persons and property, I'd like to have a definition of that word "barbarian".'

'The word was perhaps badly chosen,' the male said.

'All of your other words seem to be very carefully chosen, and your pronunciation and grammar are flawless. Where did you learn your English?'

He did not answer.

Darzek was beginning to feel angry with himself. His verbal jousting had accomplished nothing of satisfaction, and he could not hold them at gun point indefinitely. Even if he tied them up he had no way of knowing when reinforcements might step through the transmitter, and eventually he would have to sleep.

Again he turned his attention to the instrument board, and

attempted to manipulate the discs. All of them were locked into place. 'Too bad I didn't bring a few tools,' he said. 'A hammer and a crowbar, for example.'

He slipped from the stool and moved to have a look at the other side of the board. The thing was at least a foot thick, fashioned of some nonmetallic substance, with corners and edges rounded and no visible seams. Darzek felt the back, thumped on it, ran his hand along the edge. Suddenly the entire back rippled into the base, and he stood gazing at an electronic engineer's dream world. Sheer, transparent, multicolored threads formed a web of incredible complexity.

'Now that's clever,' Darzek drawled. 'An intelligent spider would die of envy.'

He curbed his impulse to poke the automatic into those complicated vitals. Instead he raised his foot, slipped off a shoe, and with one lightning motion he raked the heel through the delicate electronic web. The slender threads broke easily. Splinters flew in all directions. Sparks snapped and crackled, and wisps of smoke floated from the cabinet.

One of the *things* started towards him. Darzek forced a retreat with a wave of the automatic, and swung the shoe a second time, with equally satifactory results.

The *thing* babbled incomprehensibly.

'Speak English!' Darzek ordered.

'She can't speak English,' Miss X said. 'She says it will take – take hours to repair the damage.'

'That wouldn't surprise me in the least,' Darzek said, surveying the ravaged interior with satisfaction. 'I'd say it'll almost have to be rebuilt from scratch. Odd that there aren't any wires leading into it. I suppose the controls work by radio, and it uses broadcast power, and that sort of thing. What is the power supply? Solar batteries?'

'Could we put our hands down?' the young male asked. 'This it very tiring.'

'Sorry. Until I've finished here, you'll just have to stay tired. In the meantime you might remember that I'm allergic to sudden movements, and I shoot accurately with either hand. Could these knobs on the bottom have anything to do with the power input?'

On the wall behind the transmitting frame he found eight matching crystals. He nudged the wall, rapped on it, kicked it, leaned against it.

'There must be a door here somewhere,' he said.

It rippled open so abruptly that he nearly fell through. He leaped back to regain his balance, and stood gazing into the room beyond. It contained fantastic things – a labyrinth of thick, crisscrossing crystal woven about a darkly looming cylinder that might have been the magic spider herself.

'Ah!' he said triumphantly. 'The power plant?'

He kicked off a long piece of crystal as thick as his arm and tossed it aside. And another. And a third. The last he flung harder than the others, and it bounced twistingly, bounced again, and suddenly there was a flash and a roar, and searing heat. Darzek, knocked across the room by the blast, lay among the aliens, twisted in agony from his burns and totally indifferent to the pulverized fragments of wall that poured down on him.

10

Saturday morning Jean Morris and Ed Rucks came knocking triumphantly at Arnold's office. Perrin, who had been glumly describing the utter failure of an investigation of his own, retired to the sofa, and Rucks eagerly dealt a long row of photographs onto Arnold's desk.

'This is Miss X, leaving New York for Brussels early Thursday morning,' he said. 'Forty-seven minutes later she disappeared while supposedly transmitting from Brussels to Rome. Here she is an hour after that, leaving New York for Brussels in a different disguise. On that trip we spotted her in Brussels. Here's Madam Z, in two disguises, leaving New York for Brussels. On Wednesday –'

'Just a moment,' Arnold said. 'This Miss X disappeared from Brussels, and an hour later she was leaving New York again?'

'Right. Ditto for Madam Z, an hour and twenty minutes later.'

'Why would they come back to New York?'

'To change their disguises,' Rucks said. 'Madam Z doesn't change as fast as Miss X. Wednesday's photos are just as interesting. For the two days we have eight disappearances that were either observed or photographed, and five of those disappearances didn't take on the first attempt. On one of them it didn't even take on the second attempt.'

'Meaning what?' Arnold asked, watching Jean Morris.

'Meaning that Darzek was right. Their technique isn't one hundred per cent efficient. It isn't even fifty per cent efficient.'

'Let me see if I understand this. Five times these woman transmitted normally, came back to New York –'

'To New York or Brussels.'

' – came back to their starting point, bought tickets to the same destination, and disappeared on the second trip?'

'In one case there were two dry runs. She came back twice,

and disappeared on the third trip. That makes six failures for eight successes.'

'Actually, it makes eight successes out of fourteen attempts, which is better than fifty per cent efficiency. But that's only if we assume that the normal trips were attempts to disappear. We can't do that – '

'Who says we can't?' Rucks demanded hotly.

' – except as a working hypothesis, which may or may not be helpful.'

'Do you have any better explanation?'

Arnold shook his head. 'Darzek said it could be important. Right now I don't see how, but I'll think about it. You've done an excellent piece of work, and I hope we'll be able to make something of it. Do you have anything else?'

'Nothing much,' Rucks said. 'I called off the investigation of the directors. You can have the file if you want it, but I can tell you there's nothing in it worth reading. Directors lead awfully dull lives. There isn't even anything about Grossman that would suggest he's been selling you out. Do you want these photos?'

'You keep them. I'd like to have a written report, with the photos and all the pertinent information. When it's ready take it up to Watkins's office and hand it to him personally, to be locked in his safe. Don't make any carbons, and don't keep any notes. Do you have a typewriter down there? Take mine. I never use it anyway.'

'Sure. What do we do when we've finished? Sit around waiting for another disappearance to investigate?'

'No,' Arnold said. 'When you've finished you start looking for Darzek.'

'Are you kidding? If I had any ideas where to start I'd have gone looking for him long ago.'

'I've already discussed this with Watkins. He agrees with me that we'll never find a final solution to this problem until we know what's happened to Darzek. He'll see that you get money or anything else you need. Ask him when you take the report, and then get to work.'

'That's generous of both of you,' Jean Morris said bitterly. 'You aren't especially worried about Jan, but you're going to look for him because you won't know what's been bugging Universal Trans until he's found.'

'What makes you think we're not worried?'

'You seem cheerful enough about it.'

'I do most of my crying in private,' Arnold said. 'Please don't look at me as though I were something you're about to swat. *I* didn't do away with Darzek.'

She smiled. 'No. If it's anyone's fault it's his. Brussels would be the best place to start looking, wouldn't it? Who would have a map of Brussels on short notice?'

'I can think of something more useful,' Ed Rucks said, picking up Arnold's typewriter.

'What's that?'

'A globe. Let's go write our report.'

Jean hurried to open the door for Rucks, flashed another smile, and was gone. Perrin said from the sofa, 'Lovely young lady.'

'Where were we?' Arnold asked.

'How should I know? You can't parade visions of loveliness in front of me and expect me to go on working. I've just been thinking that I've made I don't know how many thousand trips by transmitter, before and after we started operations, and I didn't disappear once. Try applying logic to that, and tell me what you come up with.'

'It's an idea,' Arnold said.

'What's an idea?'

'Apply logic. Forget your scientific theory and your engineering, and reason the thing out. We've been talking about people disappearing, but we know darned well that they didn't disappear. They just didn't go where we expected them to go. First question: Where *did* they go?'

'That's your idea of reasoning the thing out?'

'If we had an ounce of brains between us, we'd have done this the first time it happened. I'll rephrase the question. They went into a transmitter. Where did they come out?'

Perrin stared at him dumbly.

'Where did they jolly well have to come out?' Arnold demanded.

'Out of a receiving transmitter. But look here – '

'One step at a time. We know they didn't come out of one of our receivers. Now where does your logic take you?'

'Right where I was when you started all this reasoning. They had to come out, but they didn't.''

Arnold slapped his desk disgustedly. 'That's the bind we've been in since the beginning. Our minds wouldn't take the next logical step. Look. They went into a transmitter. They had to come out of a receiving transmitter. They didn't come out of one of our receivers. Go on – what's the next step?'

'You mean – they came out of *someone else's* receiver?'

'Right. It sounds incredible, but any other explanation is flatly impossible.'

'But no one else has any transmitters!'

'Go on.'

'I don't get you.'

'Follow that up,' Arnold said, 'and see where your logic takes you. No one else has any transmitters. Therefore, the missing passengers didn't come out of anyone else's transmitters. Therefore – since we know they didn't come out of ours – there were no missing passengers. I prefer it my way. The disappearing passengers had to come out of someone else's receiving transmitter. Therefore someone else must have one.'

'Who?' Perrin demanded.

'Right now I'm less interested in that than in where they got it. It would take a far better engineer than I am to build a transmitter from our patents. The only other explanation – '

'One of the boys sold us out,' Perrin said. 'But I don't believe it.'

'Neither do I. You heard about Grossman, didn't you?'

'Sure. It's in all the papers this morning. Stole a quarter of a million bucks, it said.'

'I'm wondering if he stole anything else, or maybe borrowed a set of plans long enough to photograph them. A lot of well-heeled business interests would love to put us out of business. A set of plans, shrewdly handled, could have been worth another quarter of a million to him.'

'Then you reason that somebody bought the plans, built a transmitter, and rigged all those disappearances, maybe hoping to panic us into stopping our operations. Then Darzek dropped in on them and put their transmitter out of commission.'

'I suppose.'

'That's your next logical step. Why else would the disappearances stop so suddenly? Darzek busted the transmitter, and got his head busted for his trouble.'

Arnold scowled. 'I've always considered Darzek to be indestructible.'

'I hope you're right. I hope he's hanging around to smash their next transmitter, because if he isn't, our disappearances will start up again as soon as they can build another one.'

'I'd like to run an experiment,' Arnold said. 'I want to tune a transmitter to two receivers, and see what happens.'

Perrin stared. '*Two* receivers?'

'It's the next logical step,' Arnold said dryly. 'That has to be how they worked it. They tuned their clandestine receiver to one of our commercial transmitters. The odds would be precisely fifty-fifty that the passenger would come out of their receiver rather than ours. That would account for those dry runs Rucks has been tracking down. Get a couple of the boys to help you, and run a thousand tests. I'm going to ask the Boss to put some extra pressure on Grossman. Maybe we can find out who he sold the plans to.'

The executive offices were deserted that Saturday morning, except for Miss Shue, who was loyally watching over Watkins's door. 'There was a man looking for you,' she told Arnold. 'Did he find you?'

'I don't think so. What sort of man?'

'A newpaperman. A Mr Walker. I think he was trying some maneuver to get to the Old Man by asking for you. I sent him down to your office.'

'Splendid. Perrin will send him back up here, and with any luck at all he'll never find me. Is the Boss available?'

'To you – usually. Go on in.'

Three minutes later Arnold was sole spectator to a rare and entirely unexpected event: Thomas J. Watkins III lost his temper. He seized the dictaphone on his desk and hurled it to the floor. Then he stomped on it twice and kicked it.

Immediately contrite, he sat down again and buried his face in his hands. 'Sorry,' he said. 'I shouldn't have done that. The theft of money I can understand. Theoretically every man has a breaking point where, under certain conditions, he may be tempted to steal, but peddling his firm's trade secrets to a competitor is dishonesty on an entirely different level. Are you positive it was Grossman?'

'All I'm positive about is that it was done. It could have been any of several hundred people. I suspect Grossman because a director had a better opportunity than most, and because as far as I know he's the only crook among them.'

'He still denies knowing anything about Darzek. He offered to take a lie detector test. Supposing I ask the D.A. to give him the test, and slip in a few questions about – this other –'

'I'd be in favor of that,' Arnold said. 'It couldn't do any harm.'

'This test you're going to do. Will it help us?'

'Only to confirm what we already know. But I think I can

84

come up with a gimmick that would prevent this kind of outside interference.'

'I hope you can, Ted, but it won't solve the problem. Not really. The people responsible will still be free to devise some other form of harassment. The problem won't be solved until we find out who is behind this, and take appropriate action to stop them.'

'Grossman might know,' Arnold said.

'I'll certainly see that he's asked,' Watkins said grimly.

Ron Walker was waiting in the outer office, familiarly perched on a corner of Miss Shue's desk. 'Here's my Own Favorite Scientist,' he said, extending a hand. 'Put her there, Own Favorite Scientist.'

Arnold pushed the hand aside. 'If it's a loan you're after, I recommend the Rainy Day Pawn Shop. It's just down the street from Darzek's office.'

'Speaking of Darzek – '

'Which we weren't. What do you want?'

'Authoritative information. An interview. In familiar parlance, a story.'

'I haven't got any.'

'Of course you have.'

'About what?'

Walker smote his brow, and turned imploringly to Miss Shue. 'I spend years cultivating my Own Favorite Scientist. Now comes the one time I can use him, and he pulls the three-monkey gag on me. 'What about?' he asks me. The world is clamoring for information on that Moon explosion, and all the scientists are crawling into their holes and pulling the holes in after them.'

'I don't know anything about the Moon. Go find yourself an astronomer.'

'The astronomers have passed a union agreement not to mention the Moon.'

'Good idea,' Arnold said. 'Now if you reporters would only do the same thing – '

'It's *news*, man! We have a solemn obligation to keep the public informed. Just answer a few simple questions – that's all I ask.'

'If that'll get rid of you, go ahead and ask.'

'What caused the explosion?'

'This is your idea of a simple question? How the devil would I know? I haven't even read a newspaper story, let alone a scientific report.' Arnold wheeled disgustedly, and started for the door.

Walker caught up with him and grabbed his arm. 'Aw, have a heart. Just tell me this – can there be a volcano on the Moon?'

'I don't know. If the Moon wants to have volcanos, that's perfectly all right with me. Why, is that what the explosion was?'

'Well, at first everyone assumed that it was an atomic explosion. But the Russian Government said it wasn't, and then ours said it wasn't, and finally the astronomers agreed. Before they got around to saying what they did think it was, some jerk in Egypt who happened to have an amateur telescope pointed in the right direction claimed it looked like a volcano erupting. The astronomers immediately clammed up. The only official word is that – how did he put it? – "an apparently previously unknown substance" exploded.'

'I can't help you,' Arnold said. 'I don't know any apparently previously unknown substances. Why don't the Moon stations send someone over to have a look?'

'It's too far. Our New Frontier City is the closest, but that's still some seven hundred miles away as the crow flies, with lots of rough country in between, and on the Moon the crow doesn't fly neither does anyone else. They aren't equipped for that much overland traveling, and it might take them months even if they were.'

'Here's a suggestion,' Arnold said. 'Why don't you interview Miss Shue? A lovely young thing like her knows all about the Moon.'

He got through the door in time to dodge Miss Shue's accurately thrown paper weight.

Perrin had the test under way when he got back to his office. 'It's working out roughly fifty-fifty,' he said. 'To be exact, eighty-seven to a hundred and four. A hundred and five,' he corrected, as a bored engineer stepped from a receiver and recorded the result in the appropriate column on a blackboard. 'The interloper ran ahead at first, but now it's slipping back. We're cutting it in on every trail, which is what they must have done. Otherwise they'd have picked up unsuspecting passengers instead of their own people.'

'Good idea,' Arnold said.

'It brings up an interesting question. They must have had an effective means of communication if they were able to cut in just when their own people were stepping through and cut

86

out immediately afterwards. They couldn't have worked it on timing alone, because no one could predict just when a particular passenger would reach the turnstile. Could a small portable radio get through from inside the terminal?'

'I don't see why not. Let's say a very small radio, since no one noticed one.'

'Which means that it couldn't have had much range. If I were looking for Darzek, I'd check the area around the Brussels Terminal.'

'I'll suggest it to Ed Rucks, though I think he has something like that in mind anyway.'

'It should have been done Thursday,' Perrin said. 'By now – '

'I know. By now he could be anywhere.'

11

Darzek's next conscious impression was of a soft tube being gently but firmly inserted into his mouth. For a time he was content to contemplate its unnatural presence resentfully, exploring the oddly serrated surface with his tongue and attempting, once or twice, to jerk his head away from it.

Then it occurred to him that a tube meant food or drink. He sucked on it exploratively, and instantly spat out the gummy fluid that oozed into his mouth. It was tepid, its stinging tartness puckered the mouth and brought tears to his eyes, and its faint odor seemed more appropriate to a motor fuel additive than to a substance intended for human nourishment.

The tube was offered again, and he rejected it with clenched teeth. His waxing consciousness brought a flow of strength, and he attempted to sit up, to open his eyes. In a surge of panic he pawed desperately at his head. His eyes were tightly bound. His head was bandaged, as were his hands, and as far as he was able to determine his entire body was swathed in yards of soft, elastic gauze.

He sank back helplessly. When the tube was offered again he accepted it, and swallowed as much as he was able. He mumbled through his bandages, 'It'll never replace orange juice. Where are we?'

'In the supply capsule,' a voice said.

'Let's see,' Darzek mused. 'There were a couple of *things*, and Miss X and Madam Z, and a young man – that was you. Did all five of you come out of it all right?'

'Oh, yes. We are all right.'

'Supply capsule.' He paused to consider this. 'The metal thing in the corner where it – she – got the first-aid stuff after I shot Miss X?'

'Miss X? I do not quite understand your terms. Yes, that is the supply capsule.'

'The blast got my eyes, I suppose.'

88

'I do not think so. Your eyelids are badly burned, so perhaps you closed your eyes at just the right instant. Your head is burned, and your arms and hands, and part of your body, and we had to cut off what was left of your hair, but you should be fully recovered soon, except perhaps for your hair. We do not know how long it will take for the hair to replace itself. The question has not arisen before, and there is nothing in our files.'

'A long time, I'm afraid,' Darzek said. 'The question hasn't arisen before for me, either.'

'I have often wondered it that unfortunate animality brought accompanying inconveniences.'

'You really should be commended on your English,' Darzek said. 'It's flawless, except for some very subtle inflections that I might not notice if this eye bandage didn't make me concentrate on my hearing. Where did you learn?'

There was no answer.

'You're sure my eyes are all right?' Darzek asked.

'We treated them, just in case, but I do not think they were damaged.'

'What knocked me out?'

'Something struck your head, I believe.'

'Nice of you to look after me, under the circumstances.'

'You should not have done it,' the voice said. Did that rising inflection indicate anger? ' * * * will never forgive you.'

'Who was that?'

He said the word again, an impossible blurring of sounds. 'Our Group Leader and Head Technician,' he added.

'Is that the one who treated Miss X's arm?'

After a long pause, 'Yes.'

'Let's hear the name again.'

Darzek tried to repeat it, and sputtered hopelessly. 'If you don't mind,' he said, 'I'll refer to her as Alice.'

'I don't mind, but she might.'

'Alice is a perfectly respectable name. I had an aunt named Alice. By the way, just what did happen?'

'Our power plant exploded. You should not have done it.' Again there was the rising inflection.

'I'll have to admit it wasn't exactly what I intended,' Darzek said. 'What did I do?'

'I do not precisely understand that myself. It should not have happened. There are many safety devices, but the kind of thing you did was never anticipated.'

89

'Something I threw into the works made a short curcuit?' Darzek suggested.

'Perhaps. In your terminology, perhaps something like running the short circuit through a transformer. Instantly it became tremendous.'

'It certainly did. But even if it was a fluke, it was nevertheless a highly effective one. I agree – I shouldn't have done it.'

'Appallingly uncivilized behavior,' the voice said, swooping upwards. 'Destroying the property of others – '

Darzek stuggled to a sitting position. 'Hold on, fellow! Just who has been destroying all that expensive Universal Trans equipment? Was that civilized behavior?'

'There is no parallel between the two actions,' the voice said. 'Of course you could not possibly understand.'

'I don't believe I could. Vandalism is vandalism, regardless of whose property it is and who is doing the destroying. Never mind. I seem to remember that the roof blew off, and if we are on the Moon, as someone said, you must have saved my life by dragging me here – not to mention treating my burns. I thank you for that. I'll thank the others when I have a chance.'

The voice exemplified commendable modesty by remaining silent. Darzek stretched himself, tested the wonderful softness of the bed he was lying on, and stretched out luxuriously. In the process he discovered that the supply capsule had not been designed as a sleeping accommodation. His feet struck something solid, and when he attempted to edge backwards to give himself more room, so did his head. But none of this distracted from the superb comfort of his bed.

'I'd like to buy a mattress like this one,' he said.

'It is only a sleeping pad.'

'I'd still like to buy one. I've never felt anything like it.'

'It would be less comfortable on Earth. You would weigh much more.'

Killjoy! I wonder if the day will come when people take a jaunt to the Moon to get a night's sleep. Where do you come from?'

'I am not at liberty to tell you. though I do not think it would be meaningful to you even if I did.'

'Probably not. I wouldn't recognize your name for the place, and if our astronomers have given it a name it still wouldn't mean anything to me. If it's outside the Solar System, that is. Is it?'

There was a long pause. 'There can be no harm in telling

you that,' the voice said. 'Yes. My home is outside your Solar System. Would you like more to eat?'

'No, thank you. My stomach hasn't quite decided what it's going to do with the stuff I've already had.'

'I suggest that you rest, then.'

Darzek was moved to protest that he had just awakened, but there was no answer. When he had convinced himself that he was alone, he began to investigate his wounds as thoroughly as his bandaged hands would permit. He had no sensation of pain – only a slight tenderness about his face and head. Eventually, for the want of anything else to do, he slept.

There followed a dreary period in which he rested, took nourishment, rested again. He had so completely lost track of time that he could not even hazard a guess as to the day. It had started on Thursday, a Thursday morning, he kept reminding himself. Thursday morning in New York, and almost noon in Brussels. He fell to pondering what time that might have been on the Moon, and thus managed to occupy himself for an hour or so – or perhaps for only a few minutes.

The young male administered to him conscientiously, but Darzek was unable to draw him into conversation again. His statements were so politely noncommittal, and he avoided Darzek's questions so awkwardly, that Darzek had the feeling he was suffering acute pangs of conscience for his meager confidences of their first conversation.

Finally the moment came when his bandages could be removed. All five of them gathered closely around him in the cramped space by his bed. One at a time the strips of gauze were expertly unwound, and the young male delivered a running commentary on the results. He had healed up very nicely. No, there were no scars. He had not been burned *that* badly.

In the background he heard the subdued buzzes and hisses of the ridiculous alien language.

The bandage that blindfolded his eyes was left until last. It fell away, and he looked onto a dazzling whiteness that made him wince and move to shield himself. His eyes quickly became accustomed to the light, and the whiteness resolved itself into the same softly glowing material that had covered the curved walls and ceiling of the room his explosion had demolished. He blinked, blinked repeatedly, and as he focused on the alien faces all five turned away abruptly and avoided his eyes.

His own face must have mirrored his astonishment. One of

91

them said, 'There seemed no point in maintaining the illusion. And we are much more comfortable this way.'

'Perfectly understandable,' Darzek said, thinking he would have a devil of a time telling them apart.

Three had undergone transformation. Now all of them were *things*, looking down at him from hideous, coldly inexpressive *thing* faces.

There was no mistaking his origial *things*. They were more than two feet taller, and much wider. The three who had been maintaining the illusion were now triplet *things* on a much more modest scale.

'Which of you three is – was – the male?' Darzek asked.

'All three of us are males,' was the answer.

'You mean Miss X and Madam Z – ' He stared unbelievingly. 'All three of you are males,' he repeated slowly. 'Well, I suppose you know if anyone does. A lot of females on Earth would be shocked to hear it. That was quite an illusion that you staged.'

'It seemed to work satisfactorily.'

'And the other two are females. It may take me some time to get used to the idea, but I won't knock it. For all I know, it's a more practical arrangement than the one we humans have arrived at. While we're together, I want to thank you for saving my life.'

'We did not save your life,' one of the males said. Darzek wondered if the inflective droop of his voice hinted at some future threat, or if he was merely adhering to a politely formal code of modesty.

'At any rate,' Darzek said, 'one or more of you brought me here, and treated my burns.'

'That did not save your life, unfortunately. When you destroyed our power plant you also destroyed our air reserves. We have no means of replenishing them. We have no way to reach the safety of your planet. We are not even able to communicate with our people.'

'In other words,' Darzek said, 'my enthusiasm for doing a job thoroughly has landed all of us in quite a fix.'

'In a fix, yes. So you will understand that we have not saved your life. We have only prolonged it and spared you some pain. We would gladly save it if we could, but we cannot. There is a small reserve of air in the capsule. Soon that will be gone, and then all of us will die.'

'Very soon,' another male said, and the third echoed him. 'Very soon.'

The five alien faces gazed fixedly, not at Darzek – they continued to avoid his eyes – but past him. He would have given a great deal to know whether those enigmatically inexpressive faces masked violent emotions of anger, or contempt, or repressed homicidal intent; or – a much more horrifying thought – whether their emotions were as blank as their faces.

12

As soon as Darzek regained his sight and his ability to move about, he found himself confronted with two singular problems.

The first was of his own making. He was quickly able to detect minor differences in stature and facial proportions among the aliens, but he found it utterly impossible to pronounce their names. After one prolonged session of spluttering ineffectuality, he determined to rechristen them with appellations more to his liking.

He had already named one female Alice. He proceeded to call the other Gwendolyn. Miss X became Mr X, and then, because the implied formality seemed ridiculous, Xerxes. Madam Z was altered to Zachary in similar, rapid steps. It then seemed only logical to refer to the third male as Y, which Darzek did until he could think of a masculine name beginning with Y; whereupon he changed the Y to Ysaye.

Alice, Gwendolyn, Xerxes, Ysaye, and Zachary. The aliens themselves could have done no better, Darzek thought; except that the 'Alice' seemed a bit too simple, too earthly, for the spectacularly unhuman alien physiognomy.

He consulted Zachary. 'Do you think Alice would mind if I changed her name to Alithia?'

'I shall ask her.' Zachary said.

He mounted the ladder, and Darzek followed him.

The supply capsule was a tall cylinder with its entire internal circumference ingeniously fitted out for storage. There were deep revolving bins, drawers that pivoted outwards, compartments with doors that rippled down or sideways with the precision and speed of a zipper. The capsule was partioned into four segments, each roughly ten feet in height, and a ladder ran from top to bottom and passed through circular openings in the partitions.

Alice and Xerxes had established themselves on the upper

level. Zachary presented Darzek's question, prounouncing the names Alice and Alithia flawlessly. Alice, who did not speak English or any other terrestrial language, repeated them with equal precision. A discussion followed, which Darzek watched with interest.

He had been unable to understand whether his determination to name the aliens had bewildered them or merely left them indifferent. They responded promptly to their names when he used them, but they politely avoided them when speaking of themselves.

'She would like to know why?' Zachary said finally.

'It seems more appropriate to her personality,' Darzek said.

'How can that be? It not a name only a label?'

'Certainly not,' Darzek said. 'Names have meanings, and the euphony is also important.'

'What do these names mean?'

Darzek searched his memory. 'I can't recall,' he admitted.

'But why did you first call her Alice, if that name was not appropriate?'

'It was the first thing I thought of.'

There was a further discussion, and then Zachary announced, 'She says that you may call her anything you choose.'

'Thank you,' Darzek said. 'But on second thought I'll continue to call her Alice. I've heard it's bad luck to change a name.'

He went back down the ladder, chuckling to himself, while above him the implications of his last remark were discussed and debated. He had, he thought, given the aliens something to think about. He had the feeling that they needed it badly.

The second problem concerned his inability to dress himself. His blindfolded impression that his entire body was swathed in bandages proved correct – because alien clothing consisted entirely of bandages. Wide strips of elasticlike cloth were wrapped in turn about the legs, the lower trunk, the upper trunk, and the arms. When done properly, with precisely the right amount of tension, the result was snug warmth and comfort and an exhilarating freedom of movement. Darzek recalled the elastic stockings and bandages used for certain medical purposes, and wondered if this odd apparel might not also have therapeutic qualities.

His burned clothing had been discarded, but all of his possessions were scrupulously collected together in one small bin in his quarters, which were the lowest level of the capsule. He found there everything his pockets had contained, including his passport, penknife, cigarette case and lighter, pen and pencil, pocket secretary, photographs of Miss X and Madam Z in various disguises – and also his shoulder holster and automatic.

'You're giving this back to me?' he exclaimed.

'Why not?' Zachary asked. 'It's your property.'

'I don't suppose there's much use I could make of it now,' Darzek conceded.

'I do not suppose so,' Zachary said, but whether he was being ironic or merely polite Darzek could not decide.

Having named the aliens and learned to dress himself, Darzek was confronted with the severest trial of his life. He had absolutely nothing to do, and yet he would not, he positively refused to, allow himself to be intimidated by the fact of approaching death.

And the aliens were intimidated. They sought politely to ignore Darzek as he cheerfully invaded their quarters when he used the ladder to test his most recent attempt to clothe himself. They became increasingly withdrawn. At first he thought that they were bitterly and understandably resentful of him, since he was wholly responsible for their plight. It took him some time to decide that they were merely terrified.

Alice and Xerxes sat opposite each other in the cramped space at the floor of the upper level, their gazes fixed upon some object or thought remote beyond the light years, and Alice sang. Her melodic line made slithering ascents and droops, the harsh alien language punctuated it with hisses, and in Darzek's few moments of critical tolerance he found it only slightly less musical than a traffic siren.

Gwendolyn, Ysaye, and Zachary crowded themselves into the level below and played a game – a game that Darzek, after a long session of watching from the ladder, dismissed as a particularly tedious variety of chess, with hallucinations. It was a four-dimensional game, played without a game board. The grotesquely fashioned pieces moved at different levels with the aid of various-sized blocks. The moves depended not only upon position but on the total number of moves that had been made. Darzek's first attempt to understand the game was his last.

He found it difficult to account for his conviction that the aliens had been frightened into an immobilizing hysteria. Their expressionless faces furnished no clues. He was quickly convinced that their voices did, for as his ear became attuned to them he found their speech, even in English, filled with amazing subtleties of nuance and inflection. He had, unfortunately, no way of telling what the nuances and inflections meant – though he reminded himself that he would have encountered the same problem with facial expressions. A smile, on the face of a nonhuman, might indicate anger or deadly insult.

His unaccountable awareness of the presence of a pernicious, all-engulfing dread persisted. He began to feel apprehensive himself, not of the approach of death, but of the aliens' reaction to it.

His wrist watch had stopped while he was blindfolded. When he attempted to reset it, all of his inquiries about the time were politely turned aside. Finally he placed the watch in the bin with his other possessions.

'Why worry about the hour,' he asked himself, 'when you don't know what day it is?'

But the hours to worry about were endless. For a time he allowed his mind to be occupied with the lengthy and involved contemplation of trivialities. He bounced on his sleeping pad and pondered the nature of the smooth fabric and the soft, resilient substance in contained. He touched none of the storage compartments except the bin containing his own property, feeling that the aliens would interpret unauthorized snooping as further evidence of his depraved barbarism; but there were windowed compartments, with openings covered with an invisible, unbelievably tough film, and when he was alone he peered into them and speculated on their perplexing contents.

He puzzled long over the ladder, which was of metal or a metallic-like substance and quite ordinary except for its unusual width and the depth and spacing of its steps. It seemed a fantastically crude object to be placed so prominently amid the capsule's technological sophistication. He decided, finally, that no better method could be devised for making all parts of the capsule conveniently accessible with a minimum sacrifice of space.

Gwendolyn and Zachary were experts in the weird game they were playing; Ysaye was evidently a novice. He was invariably eliminated in the early stages, and occasionally he would come down and talk to Darzek while Gwendolyn and Zachery withdrew into the complicated dimensions of their game and grimly and silently battled to an incomprehensible conclusion.

In the background, Alice's song went on unceasingly.

'I've been wondering about the air,' Darzek said to Ysaye. 'Is it from your home planet?'

'Yes.'

'That means I'm probably the first human who has ever breathed the air of another world. I don't know whether that's a distinction or not, but I like the stuff.'

'It suffers from being stored for so long,' Ysaye said.

'Really? It seems sweet-tasting and invigorating to me.'

'It has much more oxygen than your air.'

Darzek's feeling of physical well-being was such that inaction became intolerable to him. He first occupied himself with the routine exercises that the cramped space around the ladder permitted. Then, for the want of anything else to do, he began to jump. He could, by loosely using the ladder to guide himself, leap through the opening to the level above. With a feeling of sheer elation he dropped back to the first level and leaped again. He wondered if he could, with practice, jump through the two lower levels and disrupt the game in the third.

Then Ysaye came climbing down to him. '* * * says – '

'Who?'

'* * *.'

'Alice?'

'Yes. * * * says that physical effort makes you consume the air faster.'

'Good idea,' Darzek said. 'Why don't we all exercise, and get it over with in a hurry?'

For once he succeeded in disrupting an alien's composure. Twice Ysaye's mouth opened to speak, but he could find nothing to say.

But Darzek resignedly stopped his exercising.

Ysaye was the lonely one among the aliens, the outsider. Darzek felt increasingly sorry for him, and soon began to regard him with an unaccountable liking. Their conversations became more frequent and longer.

'There is one thing that puzzles me,' Ysaye said.

'What's that?' Darzek asked, quickly analyzing the tone of voice for some indication of puzzlement.

'When so many of its passengers did not reach their destinations, why did not your Universal Trans stop using its transmitters?'

'That's an interesting question,' Darzek said. He was savoring the final inch of a stringently rationed cigarette, and he took his time about answering. 'The fact of the matter was,' he

98

went on, 'that there were no passengers who did not reach their destinations.'

'I do not understand,' Ysaye said.

'I could make it clear very easily, I think, but I'm not sure that I should.'

'But why not?'

'You refuse to answer my questions. Why should I answer yours?'

'What have I refused to answer?'

'Why were you attempting to sabotage Universal Trans?'

Before Ysaye could comment, Gwendolyn summoned him for the start of a new game. When next he appeared he picked up the conversation where they had left off. Obviously he had been thinking over Darzek's remark. 'Do you mean that if we were to tell you what you want to know – about us – you would then tell us whatever we want to know about you?'

'I hadn't thought of it in precisely that way, but it sounds like a fair trade.'

'I must first ask * * *.'

'Who?'

'* * *,' he said, starting up the ladder.

'You mean Alice?'

'Yes.'

The song at the top cut off abruptly, and then after a brief interval started up again. Ysaye clambered slowly down. 'She says no,' he announced.

'A pity. We might have had an enjoyable talk.'

'Since we are going to die anyway, I do not understand why you will not tell me.'

'I was thinking the same thing. How much longer do we have?'

'I do not know,' Ysaye said. 'I think * * * knows, but she will not tell us. She thinks it best that we do not know.'

'Anyway, it seems to me that I'd be taking a substantially greater risk. Sooner or later your people will check up on you. What would prevent you from leaving a written record of anything I say? Your successors would no doubt find a way to turn the information to their advantage. On the other hand, there's no possible way I could get any information to my people – is there?'

'I do not think it would be possible,' Ysaye said.

'Even if we're near one of the Moon stations, I doubt that this capsule is sticking up like a sore thumb.'

'Like a sore thumb,' Ysaye repeated. He pronounced the last word with an inflected droop that Darzek was hopefully interpreting to mean puzzlement. 'It is sunk into rock, and we are far from your Moon stations.'

'Just what I meant. My people probably couldn't find it even if they were looking for it. What possible harm could our conversation do?'

'You do not understand. We must follow our Code. We have sworn to follow it. I should not talk with you even this much. * * * thinks we have already told you too much.'

'Or that I've found out too much?' Darzek suggested. 'As I said before, it's a pity. Time hangs heavily here. I've faced death once or twice, but it was something that happened quickly, and I never had much time to think much about it until afterwards. What does it feel like to suffocate?'

He watched Ysaye closely as he spoke. The strangely concave facial features gave an impression only of an immense, utterly frigid indifference.

The six of them waited, tedious hour after hour, with no expectation except for a time when their breathing would become laborious, when they would crowd to the top of the capsule where the air was freshest, or to the bottom – and Darzek spent some hours speculating as to which it would be – and lie gasping in a futile struggle to shred the dead air of its final traces of oxygen, and finally they would die.

Would they be mercifully unconscious at the end? That was another matter for wearisome speculation.

'It's a little like a clock running down,' Darzek said to Ysaye. 'Every breath, or every tick, takes us closer to the end.' moments, 'Tick . . . tock . . . tick . . . tock.'

Ysaye was not amused.

Alice continued to sing. She sang in all her waking moments, with Xerxes listening to her mutely, whether in admiration or nostalgic desperation Darzek could not say. Gwendolyn and Zachary played their game and cultivated their appetites. In a short time their capacity for food became a thing to regard with awe and trepidation.

'We'll run out of food before we run out of air,' Darzek observed to Ysaye, who was dutifully acting as chef and waiter.

'We have enough food to last for – months,' Ysaye said.

'If we do run out, it won't be my fault,' Darzek said.

He ate no more than enough to sustain himself, and merely

to eat that much was a triumph of will power and self-control. The food came in a multiplicity of colors and – Darzek supposed, though he found it difficult to distinguish them – flavors. It was prepared to any desired temperature and served in deep, triangular bowls, sometimes as a thick soup taken with a tube, but more often compressed into small, moist, fibrous cakes that were eaten with the fingers. Whatever the color, or the temperature, or the consistency, Darzek found it uniformly distasteful.

But it was a near-perfect food. The body absorbed virtually all of it, and the large compartment thoughtfully provided on the lower level for the private disposal of bodily wastes saw very little traffic.

The cooking facilities intrigued Darzek most of all. The prepared food was placed in a thin, completely enclosed container that seemed metallic but was surprisingly light. A few seconds in the cooking slot, and the food was heated to order – piping hot for Darzek, or warm, for Gwendolyn's level, or tepid for Alice. The container remained at room temperature.

'Why waste heat to heat the container?' Ysaye asked, when Darzek commented on this.

'What's the source of heat?' Darzek asked.

'The Sun. The capsule stores the heat and uses it as needed.'

'Good trick. Couldn't you use that heat to send up a few distress signals?'

'No – no –'

'Heat is a source of power, isn't it?' Darzek persisted. 'You certainly have all kinds of supplies here, including electronic stuff – or stuff that serves the purpose of what we call electronic stuff. Your technicians should be able to build a radio that would send out a simple SOS signal.'

'Even if that were possible, we could not.'

Darzek looked at him searchingly. For all his provocative prodding and careful analysis, the mind that lay behind those strange facial features was as much a mystery to him as ever. 'Too bad I'm not a psychiatrist,' he said. 'I believe all five of you are possessed of some kind of death compulsion. I can't understand anyone's wanting to die.'

'We do not want to die.'

'Then put Alice and Gwendolyn to work on that radio. Maybe one of the Moon stations could send help, and if not, we might be able to get help directly from Earth. My government has invested millions in the rescue of plane crash or shipwreck survivors. It ought to be ready to spend billions to rescue someone gone astray on the Moon.'

'No. We could not do that.'

'I thought you didn't want to die.'

'We do not. But * * * has considered all the possibilities, and there is nothing we can do. We cannot permit ourselves to be rescued by your people.'

Darzek stared at him in amazement. 'You mean – you wouldn't let my people rescue you even if they were to try?'

'We cannot. We have a Code. We have sworn to follow it.'

'Tick . . . tock,' Darzek said scornfully.

Ysaye fled up the ladder.

13

Ted Arnold invited Jean Morris and Ed Rucks to have dinner with him. Ostensibly the occasion was to enable them to report progress. Arnold knew that the two had no progress to report, but he reasoned that they might have urgent need for a couple of shoulders to cry on, and he had two that were amply padded and had withstood deluges of tears from frustrated Universal Trans engineers that they were virtually waterproof.

He took them to the small executive's dining room of the Terminal Restaurant. They had the room to themselves, and two bowing waiters to serve them, and soft music in the background, and a corner table with candlelight that did bewitching things with a tint of red that Arnold was noticing for the first time in Jean's hair.

The two of them read the menu almost distastefully. 'I'm not hungry,' Jean announced finally.

'Nonsense,' Arnold said. 'There's no point in being miserable on an empty stomach.'

He ordered for the three of them, and then he leaned back, waved his arms comfortingly, and said, 'Tell all to Papa Arnold.'

'There's nothing to tell,' Ed Rucks said. 'It's hopeless.'

'It's never hopeless. Where there's life, there's hope.'

Jean choked on a mouthful of water.

'The police were very co-operative,' Rucks said. 'They got the point right away – a clandestine transmitter opened up all kinds of possibilities for theft and kidnapping and what have you. They gave it the works.'

'Confidentially, I hope,' Arnold said.

'Oh, yes. They got that point, too. Of course we didn't tell them that anything had happened. Just that we were afraid it might happen. They fine-combed the area around the terminal, and got absolutely nothing. We couldn't expect any more than that of them. Brussels is no village, and it would take them years to cover the city.'

'I'll see that they get an official expression of thanks from the company.'

'Yes. Well, we don't really know that the bootleg transmitter was in Brussels, or if it was, that it was located anywhere near the terminal. And even if it was located near the terminal, the odds are that it was moved before they started to look for it. If that doesn't add up to a hopeless situation, Jean's an ugly old hag, and I'm a dashing young optimist.' He ruffled his gray hair disgustedly.

'Do you have anything in mind for your next step?' Arnold asked.

'After Brussels, the world,' Rucks said. 'I suppose we could try the same thing in New York.'

'If Brussels was difficult, New York would be impossible. There are just too many places to hide a transmitter.'

'A fine consolation you are!' Jean snapped. 'What *shall* we do, then?'

'Keep looking for Darzek.'

'Just like that,' Jean said. 'It's like looking for a needle in a haystack when you haven't any idea where the haystack is.'

'Did that guy Grossman give out with any information?' Rucks asked.

'Nary a thing. His knowledge begins and ends in the book-keeping department – or so he says. The two lie detector tests he took didn't contradict him.'

'I'd like to use a good thumb screw on him,' Jean said.

'Don't,' Arnold told her. 'It wouldn't become you. Nevertheless, children, in these days of great and solemn tragedy I see one tantalizing ray of hope. Built into my ingenious little safety device that prevents this sort of thing from happening again, there is a signal light that screams red if anyone so much as tries to cut in on one of our transmitters. To date not one of those lights has flashed. I regard that as highly significant. The parties responsible for this outrage invested a lot of money, time, and inventiveness in the attempt to wreck Universal Trans, and they wouldn't be giving it up if they could help it. Their transmitter is still *hors de combat* and they haven't been able to build another one.'

Jean Morris sniffed disgustedly. 'I suppose all this time Jan has been sitting in a cellar somewhere, holding a gun on them.'

'He probably has them strung up by the toes, and he's tickling their feet to extract a confession.'

Jean smiled – the first time that evening.

'Now, then,' Arnold said, as the drinks arrived. 'To Darzek, wherever he may be. May he never run out of feathers.'

They drank solemnly.

14

The realization came as a shock to Darzek.

He had succumbed to his surroundings, and the aliens no longer looked grotesque to him. Worse, Alice's weird, unending cacophony had begun to sound musical. He found himself listening absently, even following her voice with pleasant anticipation on one of the several songs she repeated frequently. He wondered what the music was supposed to express – what the words might mean.

Understanding came accompanied by a veritable tidal wave of astonishment: they were love songs.

Alice and Xerxes were in love, or some oblique alien equivalent of love. The relationship was, as far as Darzek could tell entirely nonphysical. Except for the hasty first-aid treatment Alice had supplied to Xerxes's wounded arm, he had never seen them touch one another. They rarely spoke. They did not even look at each other, and yet Darzek was certain that the word "love' took him as close as he would ever come to an understanding of their strangely remote intimacy.

He consulted Ysaye about this, and Ysaye, after grappling long with the subtleties of comparative philology, firmly denied it.

'What else would you call it?' Darzek demanded, and Ysaye had no answer.

'I need to do some thinking,' Darzek said.

'Certainly,' Ysaye said, and politely withdrew to the level above. Darzek seated himself on his sleeping pad, lit one of his rapidly dwindling stock of cigarettes, and ordered his mind to think.

The awareness that Alice's strident caterwauling was actually a tender love message brought home to him for the first time the horror of the thing that he had done. Blindly and impulsively, with no thought for the consquences, he had taken action that doomed five living beings. Since then he had been flitting about the capsule like a lunatic on a holiday, treating the aliens with no more consideration than he would have extended to a few denizens of the zoological gardens with whom he had been locked up by mistake, deliberately contriving actions and comments to shock them into responses that he could analyze and classify. He had not thought of them as highly intelligent beings with their own intensely personal aspirations, and sorrow, and frustrations, and depth of emotional response.

He had not thought of them as – as *human* beings, and they were. They were intensely human. They merely revealed their humanity in ways that were strange to him.

'They don't seem to have the grit to face up to a crisis,' he mused. 'Which isn't by way of condemning them, because I've. known businessmen and college professors and bus drivers to lose their heads under far less pressure. The point, I cooked up this mess were in, and getting us out of it is my responsibility. And just how the devil am I going to manage *that*?'

He wondered if the fantastic supply hoard contained anything that could serve as a distress signal. A flare, perhaps, or a signal rocket, or – he brushed the idea aside with a gesture of disgust. He had set off a sizeable flare when he blew up the power plant, and if *that* brought no response, anything less than an atomic holocaust would go unnoticed.

Further, the aliens did not want to be rescued in that way. As he understood their enigmatic Code, rescue by an expedition from Earth would constitute a failure worse than death. He could not expiate his blundering by wrestling them from their present fate, only to push them into one they regarded as incomparably more dreadful.

And he did not blame them. Code or no Code, he could foresee what would happen if the United States Space Administration, or its Russian equivalent, got its hands on these aliens. They would end their days in a custom-built zoo, giving regular performances for scientists and politicians, with matinees twice weekly for reporters.

'If I save them,' he told himself, 'I'll have to do it on their terms. And just for a starter, I'd better find out what their terms are.'

He went looking for Ysaye, found him squatting meditatively on the level above. 'This Code of yours,' Darzek said. 'Tell me about it.'

'I cannot do that,' Ysaye said.

'Why not?'

'The Code does not allow it.'

Darzek turned away to conceal his frustration. 'Since we have to die together,' he said, 'it's unfortunate that we can't trust each other.'

Ysaye gave a clipped utterance of agreement in his own language.

'How about another game?' Darzek asked.

They decended to the first level, and Darzek went to his bin for his pocket secretary and pencil. In a moment of whimsey he had taught Ysaye the child's game of ticktacktoe. It fascinated and delighted him. He was so utterly naïve at the game that he never won without Darzek's contrivance, but no number of defeats could discourage him. They quickly filled Darzek's memo pad with scribbled diagrams, and now they were going through it a scond time utilizing every modicum of blank space. The alien's ineptness intrigued Darzek quite as much as his enthusiasm.

And Ysaye was the lonely one, the outsider. Darzek reasoned that he must be the weakest of the five, and the one most likely to tell him what he wanted to know. Could he find a means of exploiting that weakness?

'Wrong approach,' Darzek told himself. 'The problem is to find out if he has a weakness that can be exploited.'

He passed the memo pad to Ysaye. 'I must concede that your people have outstanding technology and wonderful medical science,' he said. 'I've seen ample evidence of both. It's your ethics that bother me. You realize, don't you, that they are decidedly second-rate?'

Ysaye paused with an X half finished, and carefully looked passed Darzek at the ladder. As familiar as Darzek had become with the aliens, they still avoided his eyes. 'Ethics?' Ysaye said. 'Second-rate?'

'Second-rate,' Darzek said firmly.

'I do not understand.'

'Take this Code of yours. You say you are sworn to uphold it. You're even ready to die upholding it, if necessary, because that was your oath. And you seem to think that makes you a highly ethical people.'

Ysaye waited with pencil poised.

'Perhaps you're right,' Darzek went on. 'But look at it this way. Am *I* sworn to uphold your Code?'

'Certainly not,' Ysaye said. 'You do not even know the Code.'

'Right. But you are forcing me to die to uphold this Code that I know nothing about. How do you reconcile that with your ethics?'

'You do not understand,' Ysaye said.

'I certainly do not, but I would like to understand. If I have to die to uphold your Code, I think I'm entitled to understand. Don't you?'

Ysaye did not answer.

'Is it just for your Code to condemn me to death when I don't know anything about it? Can you have ethics without justice?'

'I'll ask * * *,' Ysaye said.

Darzek laughed. 'Don't you know what she'll say?'

'Yes – yes – '

'Then why ask her? Ethics – ' Darzek pointed a finger. 'Ethics is not something you look up in a book, or run to ask advice about every time you're challenged. Ethics is something you feel deep within yourself. Feel, and act upon. Does your Code say that you can't do what you know is just?'

'You do not understand.'

'Does your own sense of justice say I should die without understanding?' Darzek persisted.

'You are not able to understand. There is darkness within you.'

'Ah!' Darzek had the feeling that he was on the verge of discovering something important, and he chose his words carefully. 'Darkness. Well – there is darkness within everyone.'

'Yes. Within all of your people.'

'And within you, and your people.'

'But the darkness within you – ' Ysaye spoke as if the words were wrenched from him ' – *the darkness within you is the wrong color.*'

'The – wrong – color,' Darzek mused. The conversation had taken an unexpected twist that he did not like. 'But darkness has no color.'

'It has many colors.'

'Many colors – ' Darzek echoed with a smile.

But he had suddenly grasped the full implications of what Ysaye had said, and he was shaken. It was as though some ultimate, invincible power had used this grotesque alien to pronounce judgement on the human race – had judged it, and found it wanting. And there was no appeal.

'It is your turn,' Ysaye said.

Darzek stirred himself, and carefully drew an O. 'Because my darkness is the wrong color, does this mean that I cannot have justice?'

'You do not understand,' Ysaye said. And drew an X.

Ysaye was the misfit among the aliens. If they were given to classifying things in terms of round holes, he was the square peg. Darzek considered him the youngest of the five, but this did not seem sufficient cause to set him apart from the others so drastically.

Darzek's sympathy and liking for him increased in exact measure as his taunts grew bitter and malicious. He sensed that this remark cut the young alien deeply, and he loathed himself for what he was doing.

But now he was determined to know – to know everything.

His 'tick . . . tock' chant was overheard by Zachary, who asked Ysaye for an explanation and then told Gwendolyn. Gwendolyn hurried to relay the information to Alice and Xerxes, and thereafter a single 'tick' from Darzek disrupted the game above and brought Alice's singing to a choking halt.

In the grim psychological battle he was waging, Darzek could count on only one superior weapon. The aliens feared death. He did not, and to sit quietly waiting for it seemed ludicrous. As the unspoken tension fed on the aliens' fright and became a bloated, terrifying force that filled the capsule, his own sense of responsibility staggered him. Fear had immobilized the aliens. They were no longer capable of acting to save themselves.

And Darzek was immobilized by ignorance.

He tried a new tack. 'You went about it the wrong way, you know,' he said to Ysaye.

'I do not understand,' Ysaye said.

'I'm talking about the attempt to put Universal Trans out of business. It seems surprising – you people being the right color, and all that – that you did such a miserably inept job.'

'I have some misgivings about a Code that allows you to go about smashing property that doesn't belong to you. But never mind for the moment I'm just wondering how you happened to botch the job so badly.'

'What should we have done?'

'We've been over that before. I'll trade information, but I won't donate it.'

'We do not smash property if we can help it,' Ysaye said. 'There was no other way.'

'No other way to do what?'

Ysaye did not answer.

'No other way to smash property except by smashing property?'

Again no answer.

'Look,' Darzek said. 'You claim to be a highly civilized, highly ethical people. Surely such a people would not indulge in wanton destruction merely for the fun of it. You must have some overriding purpose or objective.'

Ysaye got to his feet slowly. 'I feel very tired. I must sleep.'

He disappeared up the ladder. The other aliens also seemed to be sleeping. Alice had been silent for an unusually long time, and there were no muttered disputations – or perhaps exaltations, since Darzek had failed utterly to interpret them – from the game. Darzek went to his personal bin, and after some deliberation took one of his two remaining cigarettes and lit it. He stretched out on his sleeping pad.

He was in need of sleep himself. Even after he had come to appreciate it somewhat, Alice's singing kept him awake, and she slept seldom. He felt intensely sorry for her. As the Group Leader she must be suffering a ravaging remorse for the disaster that had fallen upon them. Her wide face was narrower than Gwendolyn's, more perfectly proportioned. Her voice was noticeably less harsh than those of the other aliens, or at least he had come to think so. He wondered if she were considered dazzlingly lovely by her own people. He could – almost – envision her as a thing of beauty, in the way that an abstract painting could be, at the same time, a ludicrous distortion and a work of art.

He finished his cigarette – finished it down to a minute stub that scorched his fingers – and composed himself for an attempt at sleep. For a time his mind kept him awake with unanswerable questions and irrational speculations, but eventually he dozed off. He was aware of Zachary's presence until he opened his eyes and saw the alien seated on the pad beside him.

Zachary said softly, 'I am sorry to have awakened you, Jan Darzek. But Ysaye – ' He paused. The aliens were still grappling uncertainly with the results of Darzek's impromptu christenings, as if they feared that he was somehow insulting them.

111

' – Ysaye is so much with you when both of you are awake that we have little opportunity to speak with you confidentially.'

'Perfectly all right,' Darzek whispered. He sat up, stretched, and rubbed his eyes.

'We have been listening,' Zachary said, 'and we have discussed the matter. We agree that it is unjust to require your death for principles you do not understand. For – ' he crossed his legs, and gazed steadily at a storage compartment behind Darzek ' – for it is true that we could have summoned assistance from your people. We could have employed them to save our lives, and yours, but we did not. Our Code sternly forbids it.'

'That only confirms what I already knew,' Darzek murmured. 'Since your Code sternly forbids your telling me anything about – your Code, I don't see that it alters the situation.'

'The Code requires that we utilize any or every means of preventing outsiders, such as your people, from becoming aware of our presence or objectives. We have reread the Code, and discussed it, and we are agreed that it refers to outsiders as a group rather than as individuals. In all of our previous experience there is no instance in which this distinction has had relevance. In your case, as you have pointed out, there is no possibility of your giving the information to your group. We have decided that the Code permits us to make an exception.'

'It sounds as if an attorney would have a delightful time with that Code,' Darzek said. 'Just what do you mean by making an exception?'

'We have decided to tell you what you want to know.'

'I see. If you don't mind, I'll smoke my last cigarette.'

'Please do. I regret that we are unable to supply you with more, but we did not anticipate the need for them here.' He added, almost apologetically, 'We have never been able to use them ourselves.'

Darzek lit the cigarette, and inhaled deeply. 'You've been reading those old medical reports, I suppose. But I thought the manufacturers had that cancer thing licked.'

'Oh, we do not avoid them for medical reasons. It is just that they make us ill.'

'Understandable. They made me sick the first time I tried them – though I was only about ten years old at the time. You've thrown me for a loop. I thought that if any of you

112

told me anything it would be Ysaye. He seems – I suppose I'd call him the most idealistic.'

'He is,' Zachary said promptly.

'But I couldn't budge him.'

'Of course not. It is precisely for that reason that he would never tell you anything. And I must request, please, that you do not ask him any more questions. You have disturbed him exceedingly.'

'I meant to disturb him, but I certainly didn't get the results I expected.'

'The young are always the most inflexible in their application of the Code,' Zachary said, 'and Ysaye is not only young, but he is also – is it not the same with your people?'

'I wouldn't say so, no.'

'It does not surprise me to hear it. We have noticed many instances where your people are emotionally inverted. I must also ask that you do not mention our conversation to Ysaye. Perhaps later I shall find a way to make him understand. What would you like to know?'

Darzek blew a smoke ring, and watched it float through the opening above. 'Everything,' he said.

Zachary shifted his position to lean against the ladder, and recrossed his legs. 'No,' he said finally. 'I cannot tell you *everything*. You do not need to know everything, and we have relatively little time. Ysaye will be awakening soon.'

'Tell me what I need to know, then,' Darzek said with a grin.

'Perhaps you would prefer to ask questions.'

'All right. Why the vendetta against Universal Trans?'

'Our action against Universal Trans – and it will resume as soon as a group is sent to replace us – has two important purposes: to protect the inhabitants of the planet you call Earth, and to protect the inhabitants of other planets of which you could not possibly have any conception.'

'Interesting,' Darzek said. He was taking long, slow puffs on his cigarette, on the general assumption that this would make it last longer. It was another scientific problem he would like to have discussed with Ted Arnold. 'You are protecting us, and them, against what?'

'Against each other.'

'Sounds like a noble objective,' Darzek said. 'But putting aside for the moment the question as to whether these various inhabitants and planets want or need such protection, what does Universal Trans have to do with it?'

'Universal Trans has perfected a type of matter transmitter. With this achievement your people are but two steps removed from absolute mastery of space travel.'

'Ah! Mankind is reaching out for the stars, as the poets put it. But I don't think Universal Trans or anyone else is aware of this.'

'They must not become aware of it. For this reason Universal Trans must, and will, fail. Your transmitter must, and will, develop – ' He paused.

'Bugs?' Darzek suggested.

'Bugs. Defects, that will hold back its effective utilization for many, many years. Your people are not ready for space travel, and will not be for generations.'

'Because our darkness is the wrong color?'

'The color,' Zachary said deliberately, 'is horribly wrong. Do you have any more questions?'

'Not more than a few hundred. I'm still grappling with the connection between the transmitter and space travel.'

'It is difficult to discuss even your crude transmitter in simple terms, but nevertheless the device represents what you would call a breakthrough. A decisive first step. Once its principles are mastered – and Universal Trans has mastered them even though its engineers are far from understanding them – it becomes relatively easy to process to step two, which is the transmitter that works without a receiver. The third step is the transmitter that transmits itself, also without a receiver. This is the only practical kind of spaceship. The rockets your people have been developing for so many years are crude toys by comparison.'

'I see. Very neat. All the glowing advantages of Universal Trans travel applied to batting about the Solar System. Mars and back before breakfast, and that sort of thing.'

'Not only the Solar System. Your galaxy – and others.'

'I won't pretend that I understand, but I'm willing to take your word for it. Limitless distances in one instantaneous twitch, and no wonder our rockets look crude to you. What I don't see is what our color has to do with it – of darkness or whatever.'

Zachary spoke with the lofty patience of an adult instructing a child. 'Think! Your darkness is so deeply ingrained that your people are generations away from merely mastering your relations with each other. You exploit the weak. You defy the strong with nuclear weapons. You pervert and distort your own justice, even where justice exists. Your honor is for sale in every market place. You persecute those of your own kind who have different hues of skin – and what minute differences they are, compared with the variegated colors of the inhabitants of other worlds! You even wage war among yourselves over trifling contradictions of words in what you choose to call religion – and what feeble contradictions, when compared with those of the major religions of only this galaxy! You have not even mastered the relationship between your sexes, you who are so fortunate as to have only two. We cannot – we must not – permit your people to leave your Solar System. The galaxy has myriads of worlds with power and technology beyond your comprehension. You are pugnacious, and resourceful, and at the mercy of your own darkness. You would inflict grievous harm upon others, but they would utterly destroy you. *Now* do you have any other questions?'

'Only one more – for the present, anyway. Who are you?'

'You might call me a policeman,' Zachary said. 'I fear that my superiors will consider me – consider all five of us – highly inept policemen. We should have recognized that the Earth situation had developed beyond our control, and asked for assistance. Not that it will really make any difference. We are due for resupply in approximately seven of your months, and then our superiors will learn what has happened. A reinforced group of specially trained officers will be brought in, and it will halt the operations of your Universal Transmitting Company permanently.'

'Thank you,' Darzek said. 'You have given me much to think about.'

'Whenever you have questions. I invite you to ask them. I shall probably feel free to answer most of them.'

He withdrew up the ladder, and Darzek held a cold fragment of a cigarette between his fingers and gazed blankly after him.

He felt torn between two conflicting desires. His loyalty to his fellow men demanded that he bend every effort to put a halt to the activities of these super-smug aliens. On the other hand, he felt morally obligated to save the lives of the five aliens entrapped through his blundering.

But the conflict was at worst an academic one. There was no possible way of him to do either.

15

Circling the ladder slowly, Darzek made one of his periodic checks of the capsule's air. He took long, steady breaths, drinking deeply of it, dragging it past his tongue with gastronomic deliberation; and short, powerful sniffs that sought to gauge its freshness around a cloying host of alien odors.

It always tasted and smelled the same to him.

Ysaye descended the ladder on one of his culinary errands, stepped carefully around Darzek, and expertly mixed up six servings of food. He left Darzek's portion at the foot of his sleeping pad, and went back up the ladder adroitly cradling five triangular bowls between his arms and body. He neither looked at Darzek nor spoke.

Darzek nibbled at the food distastefully, and abandoned his air supply speculation to wonder about Ysaye.

Immediately after the conversation with Zachary, Ysaye began to avoid Darzek. He remained in the upper reaches of the capsule, still the lonely one, estranged now even from his human friend. Darzek could not decide whether the young alien was horrified that Darzek had confided in him, or merely embarrassed because he had not dared to do so himself. Or perhaps some exotic twist of alien mentality was involved.

Or perhaps –

Zachary's mention of humanity's good fortune at having only two sexes had startled Darzek into mental immobility. Could it be possible that the aliens had three, that there were *two male sexes,* and Ysaye was the second – useful, even essential, but fiercely resented?

He hesitated to inquire. As Zachary had said, it was not necessary that he know *everything;* and at every point that he met alien psychology and physiology head on, they baffled him.

He turned his thoughts again to the capsule's air supply. The air circulation system was wonderfully efficient. It filtered the air, removed carbon dioxide and impurities, restored the oxygen content to specification, and returned the air to use. Now that the system had been explained to him, Darzek's hunch was that the air would never grow foul. The capsule would continue to remove the carbon dioxide and restore oxygen as long as the supply of oxygen lasted. Then it would circulate air that contained no oxygen. Darzek did not expect a sudden drop from ample oxygen to none at all, but he felt certain that the end would come with very little warning.

All of this was by way of attempting to figure out how much time he had in which to concoct a miracle. Between the capsule's outer and inner shells was an enormous storage capacity for air and water; but how much air had been stored there, and how quickly they were using it, were matters vague beyond conjecture.

But the essential ingredient in this miracle that Darzek must shape was not time, but distance. He could save the aliens only by moving them to safety. His adversary was the ruthless, uncompromising reality that lurked just beyond the capsule walls: the Moon. Neither man nor alien was a match for it without the sustaining resources of another world.

Zachary descended, emulating Darzek's technique of sliding down the ladder. 'Have you enjoyed your cigarette today?' he asked.

'Not yet,' Darzek said. 'But this would be as good a time as any.'

It had been Zachary's suggestion that they attempt to manufacture cigarettes. He produced a crisp, clothlike material, and in this they rolled such substances as the capsule was able to supply. Some of these burned slowly, raising a veritable fog of choking smoke; others burned with sputtering rapidity of a time fuse. Finally they found a dark, granular substance that proved to be almost smokable – though it gave off a nasty-smelling, purplish smoke and left Darzek's mouth in a state of acutely puckered sensitivity – and Darzek fashioned himself a reserve of a dozen cigarettes.

During one of the least successful experiments Alice and Xerxes came to investigate the source of the smoke. Alice informed Darzek, by way of Zachary's translation, that a burning cigarette needlessly squandered oxygen.

'So does breathing,' Darzek responded cheerfully, and Alice received the translation and retired without further comment.

Darzek yearned again for the presence of Ted Arnold. Arnold would have calculated the precise amount of oxygen burned in each puff of a cigarette, and knowledgeably estimated the number of seconds of life lost thereby. Arnold would have been a man after Alice's own heart.

Darzek lit a synthetic cigarette, and tried not to wince on the first puff.

'If you would care now to teach the game to me, I have brought the materials,' Zachary said.

'Certainly,' Darzek said.

The game that had so intrigued Ysaye had aroused Zachary's interest, so they proceeded to fill with ticktacktoe diagrams several large sheets of the same material that had been used for cigarette papers. Zachary proved quite as inept as Ysaye had been, but Darzek suspected that his mind was on other things.

'You mentioned,' Zachary said finally, 'that you would trade information.'

'Any information you want,' Darzek said, 'provided I have your pledge that you won't record it for your successors.'

'Certainly. They would not accept it if we did. Because we have failed, any message from us would be suspect.'

'But surely they will try to find out what happened – where you went wrong, and that sort of thing.'

'They will know at once that our power plant exploded,' Zachary said. '*That* they will investigate carefully. Such a disaster as this one has never occurred in all of our history, so of course much will be made of it. From your presence they will conclude that we blundered or violated the Code, but no time will be wasted in speculating as to why we blundered or violated the Code.'

'My people would speculate,' Darzek said. 'They would want to know why, so they could avoid a recurrence.'

'Indeed. But perhaps your people are more uniform in thought and action. What I would like to know – only from what you would call curiosity – is why Universal Trans continued to accept passengers when some of its passengers were not reaching their destinations.'

'There's a simple explanation. There were no such passengers.'

Zachary laid down Darzek's pencil. 'We know that the company was informed. The subject was discussed by the directors. You were hired to investigate it. We ourselves wrote letters to newspapers so that everyone would know about it. And yet the company proceeded as if nothing had happened.'

'Nothing had happened,' Darzek said. 'If a bona fide passenger had failed to reach his destination, friends and relatives would have complained, the police would have made inquiries – even one such disappearance might have stopped the company's operations. As soon as our investigation revealed that the missing passengers had used phony identifications, the disappearance were recognized for the fraud that they were. The company's attention was directed entirely at figuring out how the fraud was carried out.'

'But our identifications were flawless!'

'With nothing to back them up. No matter how perfectly forged a driver's license is, it won't stand up to investigation if no one of that name has ever lived at that address, or if there is no such address. Of course the newspapers would ignore your letters unless they had some way of proving the allegations.'

'I understand. Our plan was doomed from the start. It could not possibly have succeeded.'

'Not only that, but sooner or later your phony identifications would have gotten you into trouble. You shouldn't have copied the number of a Universal Trans officer when you forged license plates.'

'It seemed that all of the numbers were taken, and that one was as good as any,' Zachary said. 'Even so, I believe that we should have succeeded had it not been for you. You have more than justified my apprehensions.'

'That night outside my office!' Darzek exclaimed. 'What were you going to do? Salt me away somewhere until you'd finished your job on Universal Trans?'

'Nothing as drastic as that,' Zachary said. 'A few changes in your thinking, a little memory erasing, and you would have declined the Universal Trans position. You would have been home no more than two hours later.'

'*Memory* erasing?'

'It is a common procedure among us, with a number of valuable applications. No doubt the concept is strange to you.'

'Not at all,' Darzek said. 'It didn't occur to me at the time, because I didn't know you were aliens. Aliens *always* erase the memory. We have a substantial literature on that subject.'

'I do not understand. We never had occasion to use it on one of your people before.'

119

'Perhaps it's unfortunate for both of us that you missed your chance then.'

'I agree, but the policeman had blown his whistle and we feared that the situation might become complicated. We decided to wait for a better opportunity, but we found none.'

'At least one of the directors was passing information to you,' Darzek said. 'For a price?'

'Indeed, no. One of the directors is merely a good friend. We own some of the Universal Trans stock, and we have permitted this friend the use of the proxies. It is only natural that we expect him in turn to inform us concerning the company's activities.'

'Which of the directors was it?'

'Mr Miller. Mr Carl Miller. We have given our support to him because his own business makes him interested in freight. It would have greatly simplified our problem if the company had concentrated on freight instead of passengers. We could then have destroyed its equipment without the worry of inflicting injuries.'

'The same way you were blowing up Arnold's transmitters, I suppose.'

'We passed a small explosive through whenever they were used. Then your friend Arnold improved the design, and this no longer could be done. It was very clever of him, since he did not know what was causing his failures.'

'Arnold is a very clever man. I take it you were also behind the alleged syndicate of realtors that was buying up Universal Trans stock. You must have a well-established base of operations in New York, to develop so many valuable contacts.'

'That is correct. Gwendolyn operated our New York — base, as you call it. If she had been there when you caused the explosion, we should have been rescued long before now. Unfortunately all of us had assembled here to discuss the situation and to assist Alice in dealing with you.'

'In erasing my memory?'

'It is an extremely delicate operation. Is your understanding complete, now?'

'I doubt that it'll ever be complete. Why go to such amazing lengths to conceal your activities on Earth?'

'Our system has worked with complete satisfaction in our relationships with more worlds than you could count.'

'But do you always operate to block a world's technological development?'

'Of course not. We do this only when the development might threaten others, exactly as you would feel free to place an adult weapon beyond a child's reach and return it to its normal play with proper toys.'

'Meaning that the human race must grow up, or mature, before it can have the transmitter?'

'Perhaps I over simplified,' Zachary said.

'Then we will never be allowed to have the transmitter because our darkness is the wrong color.'

'My people are vastly longer-lived than yours, Jan Darzek, but even we hesitate to use the word "never".'

'Well, is your activity always destructive, or hindering, as it has been on Earth, or do you sometimes help a planet – say, to scientific discoveries or a better food supply?'

'We frequently intervene to accelerate a planet's development. It depends upon the classification.'

'In other words, on the color of the population's darkness.'

'I suppose this is true, indirectly.'

'And are you just as secretive when you help a planet as when you hinder it?'

'Naturally. That is our Code.'

'What would you say if I told you your Code represents the maniacal conceit of a smugly self-righteous and disgustingly imperious race of misguided zealots?'

'I should regret it exceedingly if your feelings were to force the use of such language upon you.'

Darzek turned away resignedly. 'What's the racket up above?' he asked.

'We are moving essential supplies out of the upper two levels,' Zachary said. 'We're going to seal them off. Alice feels that we will use our last oxygen more efficiently if we concentrate it in a smaller area.'

'I don't suppose she's told anyone how much time we have left.'

'No. I would guess no more than a few of your days, at the most, but of course I have no way of knowing. It cannot be very much longer. Obviously.'

121

16

Jean Morris set down her water glass, and leaned forward. 'Don't look now, but we're being watched.'

'What's that?' Arnold said, glancing in the direction of the bar. 'Oh – him. He's just a reporter who haunts me from time to time.'

'Name of Walker.'

'Right. Does he haunt you, too?'

'He's a friend of Jan's. Right after Jan disappeared he haunted the office trying to see him.'

'When he's not working, he's a very friendly guy. It's really too bad that he's always working. You say Ed went back to Brussels?'

'He's feeling awfully low, but he won't give up. He thinks if there's a lead anywhere it'll be in Brussels.'

'He may be right,' Arnold said. 'Finding it is something else, though.'

'Has your boss kicked about the payroll yet?'

'He hasn't even twitched about it. He won't, either. As long as Ed wants to keep looking, Universal Trans will pick up the tab.'

'Just the same, don't you think it's a hopeless waste of money?'

'It won't be a week until tomorrow. No, I wouldn't say it's hopeless, but I think Darzek is likely to find us before we find him. To state the situation honestly, either Darzek is dead, or else he'll turn up – what's the matter?'

'Your haunting reporter is coming.'

Ron Walker calmly filched a chair from the next table, and joined them. 'This is three nights in a row I've seen you two having dinner together,' he said. 'A fine friend this Ted Arnold is. He sends Darzek out of town, and then while he's gone he steals his girl.'

'His *office* girl,' Jean said icily.

'I keep forgetting,' Walker said. 'Jan doesn't practice monogamy.'

'He doesn't practice anything. He's a machine.'

'Jan the robot. Sorry to hear it. I've often wondered.'

'Are you still pretending to work on a Moon story, so you can charge all this night life to your paper?' Arnold asked.

'If you're angling to be interviewed, you're days too late.'

'Glad to hear it. I don't know any more now than I did when it happened.'

'What's this about?' Jean asked.

'The explosion on the Moon,' Walker said. 'Ted pretends to be a scientist, but when a real scientific problem comes along he runs and hides.'

'You see how he exaggerates,' Arnold said. 'Imagine me running and doing anything. What's new on the Moon?'

'No one is saying anything, but the best guess is we're in another Moon race. The powers that be, or that would like to be, are waiting with bated breath to see if we can get there before the Russians.'

'We're both already there.'

'Not where the explosion happened. Word is that we're frantically getting ready to plant a new base right smack on top of that volcano, or whatever it was, and it is assumed that the Russians have similar ideas. The U.S. Space administration is working around the clock, and gnawing its collective nails for fear it will find a USSR Station II on the spot when it comes down.'

'I thought USSR Station II was on the far side of the Moon.'

'Not confirmed. You know the Russian psychology is different from ours. We like to do a little bragging all the time. They prefer to save things up, so periodicaly they can blow themselves to a big brag. This explosion, if it was one, took place so far from any of the present Moon stations that the quickest way to get there is directly from Earth. Hence the Moon race. Too bad you don't have a few Universal Trans terminals spotted about the Moon, so an honest and enterprising reporter could get information without waiting for handouts from a flock of stupid scientists.'

'I doubt if the traffic would warrant it,' Arnold said with a grin.

'Don't kid yourself. It'd be the greatest sight-seeing attraction in history, not to mention various side benefits any shrewd promoter would be happy to fill you in on. A honeymoon hotel, for example. What a play that would get from newly-weds – HONEYMOON ON THE MOON! To date, Universal Trans hasn't needed any promoting, but the time will come when you'll pay big money for ideas like that one.'

'No doubt,' Arnold said. 'Not my department, though. Still – there'd be some interesting problems.'

'There sure would. Those honeymooners would get a jolt when they returned to normal Earth gravity.'

'I was referring to scientific problems, and don't forget there's a lady present.'

'Isn't gravity a scientific problem?'

'Not your kind of gravity. I suppose such a project would be worth considering. No doubt it would bring in millions of dollars' worth of publicity.'

'You mean a honeymoon on the Moon?' Walker asked. 'I'll offer my congratulations now. How are you going to manage it?'

'Not a honeymoon, dolt. A transmitter.'

Walker jerked erect. 'Now *that* would be a story. Can I quote you?'

'You cannot. I haven't said anything yet. It's – let's see – about two hundred and forty thousand miles from Earth to the Moon, give or take a few thousand miles, and there'd be at least that many miles or red tape to cut. Fortunately Watkins is an expert at unsnarling red tape, and he has all kinds of connections in Washington. If they're planning a new Moon base they'll be sending up tons of supplies, and they should be able to find room for one transmitter. And once we've got the transmitter operating it could be a hundred times as much payload as it displaced in the first hour. Do you have any idea when they're going to shoot?'

Walker shook his head. 'This one they're not talking about.'

'I'd better get moving. Is there a telephone – excuse me.'

He darted away, narrowly missed a tray-laden waiter, collided with a drunk near the bar, and finally escaped into a telephone booth.

'Quite a guy,' Walker said.

'He is that.'

'I'm glad you think so. I thought no woman would ever have the brains to see it. Take warning, though – the gal that marries Ted Arnold marries his slide rule, too. He'll do the household budget on it, and use it to figure out the baby's

124

formula. He may even take it to bed with him, for all I know. Have you two set a date yet?'

'Are you serious, or do you do a gossip column on the side? We've only had dinner together a few times, and –'

Arnold made a reckless dash back to their table and looked down upon them, breathing heavily. 'I'll probably be working all night. Would you take Jean home, Ron?'

'Glad to oblige, old man.'

'I'm awfully sorry, Jean, but an opportunity like this one won't come along every day. We can't expect USSA to wait for us – we'll have to be ready when it's ready.'

'You haven't had your dessert yet,' Jean said.

'Ron will eat it for me. I'll take care of the check on my way out. Good night. I'll telephone you tomorrow.'

'Say good night to your slide rule for us,' Walker called.

Arnold turned. 'Not a word in the paper, Ron.'

'Go soak your transmitter. The things my friends ask me to do –'

Arnold spoke briefly to the cashier, pointed in their direction, and dropped a bill on the counter. He charged into the revolving door and was gone.

Walker raised his hands despairingly. 'Page one stuff, and he says not a word. He won't even tell me the time, unless I promise not to quote him. Ever since Darzek – by the way, where *is* Darzek?'

'I haven't the vaguest idea.'

'Honestly?'

'Honestly.'

'Wherever he is, there's a story there, too. I spent days bugging Arnold about it, and checking places where Jan is seen now and then, and talking to people who know him. Know what? Darzek's whereabouts are so secret that even Darzek doesn't know where he is.'

Perrin interrupted the conversation long enough to unfold a map and plunk it onto the table. 'Just so we know what we're talking about,' he said.

'Where'd you get it?' Arnold asked.

'U.S. Government Printing Office. Price eighty cents.'

'Sounds like a bargain.'

'It is. Here is where the alleged explosion occurred, the crater Abenezra. And here is New Frontier City, at the crater Plinius, where the Mare Serenitatis connects it with the Mare

Tranquillitatis. In order to reach the crater Abenezra they'd have to travel down to the southern reaches of the Sea of Tranquillity, and maybe around through the Sea of Nectar, and they'd still have two or three hundred tough miles to go. Lunaville which is at Kepler, in the Ocean of Storms, is even worse off, and the Russian base at Archimedes is completely out of it.'

'I see what you mean. The highway system on the Moon is somewhat underdeveloped.'

'Except on the *maria*, travel in a straight line is difficult if not impossible – so all the bases are located where the so-called seas permit some range of exploration. At least, I'm sure that's what we had in mind. I don't know about the Russians. How about it, Major?'

'I doubt if the Russians even tell themselves what they have in mind,' Major Gorelick said.

'I take it that no one at USSA knows anything about a USSR Station II on the far side. Is it true that we're going to put one there?'

'We were, until this explosion thing came up. It is now planned for the crater Abenezra, as soon as we can get there. In my opinion it's a lousy place for a base, because once we set up in the crater we may have a problem getting out, and even if we get out we can't go anywhere, but that's where it's going to be. I should tell you now that your proposition has been turned down flatly, and I'm here only to observe and to placate you if possible.'

'You can expect revised orders any minute, now,' Watkins said. 'I just talked with the President. The only condition is that we have to be ready when you are.'

'How much time does that give us?' Arnold asked.

'I'm only an errand boy. I'd guess twenty four hours.'

'Ouch!'

'You're lucky, at that. If it weren't for the fact that we just supplied the bases there wouldn't have been this much delay.'

'You people at USSA move so quickly that you're generations behind the times,' Arnold said irritably. 'The rest of the world has been traveling by transmitter for a week and a half. If the USSA bigwigs would now and then look at a current newspaper, and co-ordinate what brain power they have so as to figure out which way is forward, this inquiry would have come from them instead of from us. As far as I'm concerned, I don't care where the transmitter goes – New Frontier

126

City, Lunaville, or this blah-blah crater. Once we start operating, the place will be supplied from Earth a lot more efficiently than I can get a sandwich from the cafeteria downstairs It can have all the supplies it wants, twenty-four hours a day. We'll even rig up portable receivers for your exploration teams. They'll stay out for months, and receive their supplies direct from Earth. As a matter of fact, they'll work the standard six-hour day, and spend their evenings and week ends with their families on Earth. We're going to revolutionize Moon travel the same way we've revolutionized Earth travel.'

'Cheers,' Major Gorelick said with a grin. 'If there were no pressing circumstances, we'd all go wild with joy. Right now it wouldn't matter if you could furnish the means to transplant New York City to crater Abenezra – if the Russians should get there first with one temporary hut. Why don't you work things out at your leisure, and let us shoot your transmitter up to one of the bases on a regular supply run. The Moon is going to be there for a long time, and so are we, and it can't matter much to you whether you revolutionize Moon travel now, or six months from now.'

'How about it, Ted?' Watkins asked. 'Is there any chance of your being ready in twenty-four hours?'

'There's a chance, yes.'

'Then I say let's make the effort. If this expedition is only being made for purposes of prestige – '

'Whatever happened at crater Abenezra may have considerable scientific importance,' the major murmured.

'Or it may have no importance whatsoever. From what I've read, more than one scientist thinks the explosion was an hallucination.'

'It was an unusually widespread hallucination, and it photographed beautifully.'

'Photographed?' Watkins said. 'I don't recall reading – '

'I should hope not. Look – for centuries there have been reports of curious phenomena on the Moon. Observers have seen mysterious lights, and clouds of gas, and changes of color. As recently as 1958 Russian scientists saw some kind of gaseous emission in the crater Alphonsus. There are two significant differences about the Abenezra report. For one, the explosion, if you will pardon the expression, occurred at a wonderfully opportune moment. The line of sunrise lay across the area, and for excellent reasons understood best by themselves, astronomers frequently study the movement of sunrise

127

across the Moon. Seven reliable amateurs in Europe and Africa were looking at that precise area, and saw the whole show. In a further extension of coincidence, another amateur was making a series of photographs to study the measurements of this adjoining crater. It wasn't until he developed his negatives that he found he had two very good shots of the explosion. The observers saw the flash clearly because it occurred in the crater's shadow and lasted for several seconds; and they saw the accompanying emission of ionized gas because it was blown, or ascended, high into the sunrise. All of which makes for a thoroughly documented hallucination.

'The second difference is that we now have the means of getting there promptly and making an on-the-spot investigation. This is one plum we don't want the Russians to grab off. Fortunately we've been able to sit on those photographs, and if the Russians think the whole thing was an hallucination right up to the moment we land in crater Abenezra that's all right with us.'

'Scientific importance or not,' Watkins said, 'you people wouldn't be in such a panic about this if it weren't for the prestige, and as long as Universal Trans has a valid contribution to make, we might as well share the prestige with you. There'll be enough for both of us, if we can bring it off. Where are you going, Ted?'

'I'm going to soak my head, for even suggesting this. Twenty-four hours! How do we pack a transmitter for shipment to the Moon? There's no point in sending it up there if it'll arrive smashed. When it does arrive, they can't just plug it in and start operating. It'll have to be redesigned to use whatever power source is most effective on the Moon, and God and everyone else may know what that is, but I don't.'

'That's what Major Gorelick is here for. He'll know, or he'll know where to find out.'

'We'll also have to train some Moon men to operate the thing, since USSA certainly won't want to take one of our engineers along.'

'If they can operate it just once,' Watkins said, 'we'll send them an engineer.'

'In the meantime – but never mind. The first thing in the morning I'll send Perrin down to the Cape for liaison. If we're lucky, we might just bring it off. Just barely.'

Five hours later, with the last error found, and the last objection stilled, and the coffeepot empty, Arnold got up from the drawing board.

'Build them,' he said.

And they built them. Every engineer on the far-flung Universal Trans staff, every technician Arnold thought might be of use, labored and perspired along rows of benches set up in an unpartitioned section of the uncompleted Universal Trans terminal. Arnold placed guards at the door, with strict orders: no telephone calls, no messengers, no interruptions of any kind. If there were failures in the Universal Trans passenger network on that day, the traffic managers could route the passengers around them.

They built two dual-function transmitters, one for the Cape and one for the Moon. They were battery-operated, and they incorporated refinements of design that had been neither necessary nor thought of in the commercial models. The maws were short and broad, sized to take shipping containers of a precribed shape, rather than passengers, and though the personnel would have to stoop to pass through, Arnold anticipated no complaints. A couple of steps, stooping, were no inconvenience when compared with the long, cramped rocket ride.

At five-seventeen that evening they conducted their initial test. By six o'clock one Special had been edged through a standard transmitter to the Cape, and they were running tests between the Cape and New York. At the same time a crew of Moon men received an elementary course in operating a transmitter. At eight o'clock, after as meticulous a job of crating as time and materials allowed, Arnold turned one Special over to USSA.

And at 3 a.m. he stood with a group of distinguished guests watching the long tongue of flame speed the rocket skyward.

It was dawn in New York when Arnold, drunk with fatigue, staggered into his apartment. A figure twisted in his bed. Ron Walker sat up, and said brightly, 'Give with the news!'

'You!' Arnold exclaimed bitterly.

'Who else? Your landlady took pity on me, or maybe she thought my sleeping on the doorstep would give the house a bad name.'

'You took Jean home –'

'I escorted her modestly and safely to her own front door, though I didn't for a moment think she needed it. Some of the things she told me about jujitsu –'

'I was supposed to call her today. Yesterday.'

'I told her you'd forget all about it. What's up?'

'A rocket is up,' Arnold said. 'And a transmitter.' He flopped onto the bed, raised up tiredly, and said, 'But don't quote me.'

17

From immediately above Darzek came a sharp cry, instantly drowned in a high-pitched eruption of alien voices. Darzek stirred resentfully, and decided to ignore it. Days, or perhaps even hours, before such an outburst would have triggered him into a clawing ascent of the ladder. But he had been doggedly attempting to extract nonexistent ideas from his barren cranial lodes, and in addition to feeling disgusted with himself he was mentally exhausted.

His only firm conclusion was that these aliens had been tracked down by the wrong man. Ted Arnold might have thought of something – but Arnold wouldn't have smashed the instrument board and blown up the power plant. He would have gleefully analyzed and studied the thing to the exclusion of everything else until the aliens got the drop on him again.

And never, but never, would Arnold have leaped the turn-stile after Miss X. If only the talents of Ted Arnold could get them out of their predicament, Darzek had at least the consolation that only the talents of Jan Darzek could have got them into it.

Zachary came sliding down the ladder, demonstrating a speed and agility that Darzek had never suspected. He opened a compartment at eye level, and Darzek, standing at his side, found himself looking out onto the bleak glare of moonscape.

'What do you know?' he breathed, taking in at one glance the dullish gray, flat plain and the distant line of jagged heights beyond. It was not the scenery that impressed him – both the American and the Russian Moon stations had recorded vastly more spectacular views. 'I didn't even know this thing was here,' he said. 'Is it a window?'

'No,' Zachary said. And added, 'Until now, there was nothing to see.'

'There still isn't much to see,' Darzek said. The view swung slowly along the curving, precipitous rim and lifted to the black sky beyond. Even Darzek's rudimentary knowledge of the Moon was sufficient for him to identify the place as one of the thousands of much publicized craters.

Then he caught his breath again, and grabbed at Zachary's arm. He had seen the rocket.

Its flaming descent was caught in the center of their round screen as if TV camera were following it down. It dropped below the lacerated rim, and an adjustment in magnification took them leaping towards it as it touched down, vanishing in the swelling cloud of vapor.

Darzek gasped his surprise. The dullish, dead plain had leaped to life as the ship landed, splashing outwards and shimmering in swiftly running ripples. 'Water?' he explained incredulously.

'Dust,' Zachary said.

The vapor dissipated almost at once, leaving the ship erect on its wide tripod of spindly, jointed legs, its very symmetry making it appear misshapen against the cragged irregularity of the distant rim.

'It's ours, I think,' Darzek said. 'I mean – it isn't Russian, is it?'

'It is a United States design. Your people are at last investigating the explosion of our power plant. We wondered if anyone had noticed it.'

'I suppose you're right. Of all the thousands of craters the Moon has, it'd be asking too much of coincidence to think they picked this particular one by accident. Do you suppose they'll find us?'

'No. They will not find us.'

'That explosion must have left quite a hole.'

'It left no hole at all. It blew the cap from the safety vent, but Alice replaced that while you were unconscious.'

'I see. I suppose that safety vent is why we survived the explosion. What about this?' He thumped the side of the capsule. 'But someone said it's sunken into a hole. And this isn't a window?'

'It is a viewer. There is one on each level, connected with – I do not know exactly how to explain.'

Darzek thumped the capsule again. 'But they might have instruments for detecting metal. There must be a lot of metal in this thing.'

'Their instruments will not detect this metal,' Zachary said. Darzek looked at him quickly. Had there been a note of laughter in his voice? That was one emotion he'd had little opportunity to classify. Since the moment of Darzek's unwelcome intrusion, the aliens had had very few occasions for laughter.

'So they won't find us,' Darzek said resignedly. 'And of course you're not going to run up an SOS now, any more readily than when you had to send it all the way to Earth.'

'We must adhere to the Code. I realize that this is a bitter blow to you, Jan Darzek, to have to die with help so close at hand. Perhaps I have erred in letting you know about this arrival. If we had our instruments intact, and could alter your memory – but even that would not suffice. We should have to implant some explanation for your presence on the Moon, and there is none. So we cannot permit you to save yourself.'

'Even so, I see this ship as an opportunity.'

'What sort of opportunity?'

'Perhaps we could filch a supply of air.'

'I fear not, Jan Darzek. If the rocket is unmanned it will not contain supplies of air. If it is manned we could not take supplies without risking detection, and the supplies we took would be needed by its crew. We must not condemn others to death in order to futilely extend our own lives. It is manned, I think, because the navigation was very precise. I doubt that your people could have achieved it with instruments alone. Unfortunately this does not alter our circumstances in the least.'

'It alters them considerably,' Darzek said with a grin. 'They'll be setting up some kind of base, and exploring the crater. At least we'll have something to watch while we're dying!'

For a long time the stubby ship rested motionless, dipping the toes of its slender, protruding legs into the purplish shadow that sprawled beneath it. Darzek regarded that shadow curiously. For the first time it occurred to him to wonder just where on the Moon he was.

He asked Zachary.

'We are in the southern part of your Moon, on the side that faces Earth,' the alien said.

'I was wondering about the shadow,' Darzek told him.

'It was now afternoon, here. In another of your weeks the crater will be dark.'

'Then this viewer faces – north?'

'South. On your Moon the sun sets in the east. If we continue

133

to watch, you will see the shadow of the eastern wall move across the crater. Why do you ask?'

'Put it down to what I would call curiosity,' Darzek said. 'And isn't it about time . . . ?'

Abruptly a hatch opened, a flexible ladder unrolled, and a bulky, gleaming figure backed down it, feeling awkwardly for the rungs. A second followed, and a third, and the three slowly circled the ship in a heavy, stiff-legged, dragging strides that splashed and stirred manifold ripples in the dust.

Suddenly one figure leaped high, leaped again and again, like a small child seized by a fit of inexplicable exuberance. Another took long, soaring strides with incongruous grace and ease. The third stood looking on like a disapproving parent.

Darzek chuckled. 'Just a guess,' he told Zachary. 'We have two novices on their first Moon landing, and one old hand who is wishing they'd get it out of their systems so they can get down to work.'

'I was wondering,' Zachary confessed. 'Much that your people do surprise me.'

'Likewise,' Darzek assured him.

Eventually the cargo hatch was opened, and a bundle of silver fabric was carried some distance toward the nearest crater wall, unrolled, and inflated into a long, low, curved-roof hut. The hatch was emptied, its contents sorted out and placed strategically around the hut or carried inside. The cargo hatch was replaced, and the men vanished into the hut – to have, Darzek thought, with a sudden, stinging hunger for a cup of coffee, their first meal in the new Moon base.

'They work very efficiently,' Zachary observed.

'They probably practiced the whole operation back on Earth.'

'But why do they need such enormous quarters? One would think that twice or three times as many men could be accommodated there.'

'I thought the same thing when I first saw your installation,' Darzek said. 'Perhaps there is another ship on the way.'

'Another ship would of course account for it. Our bases are planned for many contingencies, and this one has been here for many of your years.'

'Then at one time there were more of you – policing Earth?'

'That is correct.'

The men did not reappear, and Darzek quickly became bored with watching the inert hut. He retired to his sleeping pad to rest and dream of food. Not until that moment had he been aware of his intense craving for his normal diet. For a cup of coffee, for an egg – fried, scrambled, boiled, or raw – for a steak, for a pie à la mode. He swam in a conjured-up aroma of food, but his mind persisted in returning to the hut, and its piles of supplies. At long last it had something of substance to work on, and if he could get some sleep, and rid himself of this enfeebling exhaustion –

'Grilled chops,' he murmured, and slept.

Abruptly the aroma of food resolved into the sharp, lingering scent of the last synthetic cigarette he had smoked, and Zachary was shaking him awake. The alien was incoherent with excitement. He pointed a trembling hand at the viewer.

Darzek stared. There were *four* silver-suited figures engaged in the assembly of a queer-looking land vehicle. Two more men came from the hut's air lock as he watched, and stood looking on. Others began to pass in and out, stacking crates of supplies around the hut's perimeter.

'So the other ship arrived,' Darzek said.

Zachary spoke in the alien language, and the viewer jerked to a lower magnification and took in a larger slice of the crater. The ship stood as he'd last seen it. One ship.

'All of those men were in that ship?' Darzek asked incredulously.

'Only the three you saw,' Zachary said. 'This – thing – they build did not come from the ship, and they have brought much more material from the hut than they took in.'

'They can't be pulling men and vehicles and supplies out of a hat.'

'Out of a transmitter,' Zachary said. 'I would say that they brought one of your transmitters.'

'A *transmitter*?' The casual remark's significance did not penetrate at once, but when it did Darzek was electrified. 'Then – this stuff is coming directly from Earth!'

'And the men,' Zachary said.

'Wow! Right about now Ted Arnold is turning handsprings, and Universal Trans stock has gone up another hundred a share. If I ever get back to Earth I can retire.'

'It will certainly effect some remarkable economies and efficiencies in your Moon exploration. We have wondered how long it would be before your people thought of it.'

'The possibility never occurred to me,' Darzek said. 'No reason why it should. I never gave much thought to the Moon

135

before I got here, and I can't even claim to have given much thought to it after I arrived.'

Zachary made no comment. He was listening to the voices on the level above. For the first time since the early hours of Darzek's invasion of their base, the aliens were talking loquaciously among themselves. Loquaciously and, apparently, with excitement.

At the new base the greatly augmented force worked with miraculous speed and organization. The Moon vehicle sped away on its inflated rollers to circumnavigate the crater. Groups of men spread out on foot to investigate the crater walls. Supplies continued to arrive. Another hut was inflated, larger than the first one. A radio antenna was erected.

'They're planning on a long stay,' Darzek observed.

'I think it more likely that they do not wholly trust your transmitter.'

'Why do you say that?'

'If the transmitter were to fail, they would have a difficult time supplying so many men. They are building a safe reserve.'

One group of foot explorers approached the capsule – approached so closely that rock tappings rang out clearly. Zachary was apparently unperturbed.

'Aren't you going to haul down your periscope?' Darzek asked.

'Periscope?' Zachary said blankly. 'We have no periscope.'

'Then how does this thing operate?' Darzek asked, indicating the viewer.

'Not with a periscope.'

That was as much as Darzek ever learned about it.

But already he had noticed a subtle change in the aliens' attitude, as if their fear had acquired a new veneer of anxiety. At first he attributed this to a natural concern that one of the search parties might stumble onto their position, for it seemed to him that the explosion must have left traces. After several groups had passed around them, and over them, and even scaled the crater wall above them, he was forced to the conclusion that these aliens were supreme geniuses in the art of camouflage.

It was evident that observers on Earth had pinpointed the location of the explosion, for the exploration teams were concentrating on one short stretch of crater wall. It was equally evident that they were not going to find anything.

Darzek marked up one more mystery to the Moon, and

perhaps a collection of red faces to some alert and highly competent astronomers, and turned his attention to a new mystery of alien psychology.

Why this added tension, this uneasiness that at times seemed almost volatile?

They feared Jan Darzek.

The relaxed friendliness that had grown between him and Zachary was abruptly terminated. His every remark was followed by a flow of alien conversation, as if it were immediately analyzed and its import discussed at length. His movements set off ripples of uneasiness. He was never left alone. Not only did one alien remain on the lower level with him, but there was invariably another watching surreptitiously from the level above. Once, when he went to his bin for a synthetic cigarette, he caught the glitter of the aliens' strange weapon held in readiness.

He wondered that they did not take his automatic. Apparently some quirk in their Code prevented them from depriving him of his property of inhibiting his freedom of movement until the precise moment when property or freedom became a threat. But they were watchful, and they were waiting. They valued their Code more highly than their lives, and they feared, they anticipated, they fully expected that he would attempt to betray them.

Somehow he felt sympathetic towards them rather than resentful. It would not occur to them that all of his scheming was directed at saving *their* lives.

'But it does lead to a very interesting question,' Darzek told himself. 'Just how do they expect me to do it? Sneeze violently when one of these exploring parties is passing by? Run to the window and scream for help? Open the door –'

He dropped meditatively to his sleeping pad, and muttered aloud, 'I think, Mr. Darzek, that it is high time you became a detective again.'

'I beg your pardon?' Zachary said, turning towards him.

'Nothing,' Darzek said, waving him away.

The door. Logic insisted that they would have some kind of exit; and if logic was a dangerous thing to apply to aliens, there was supporting evidence. Alice had repaired the damage done by the explosion. She had replaced a cap, or plug, or whatever, and expertly removed the external traces, if there were any. How did she get outside to do it? Or could she have done it from inside?

137

Darzek conceded himself one door.

The next question was more difficult. How did they expect him to use it? Fling it open and leap out into the arms of the explorers? He would be dead before they were fully aware of his presence. Call out to them and then slam it and wait until they came with an extra Moon suit? Sound did not travel on the surface of the Moon – he must have read that somewhere – and if it did they wouldn't be able to hear him through their suits. Leave the door ajar – it must have an air lock, like the huts – and thus attract attention? Perhaps. Its camouflage would be perfect, but opening it could be expected to destroy the effect somewhat. This proposition seemed naïve to Darzek, but – perhaps.

'Wait!' he muttered.

If Alice went outside to repair the explosion damage, she must have had some kind of Moon suit of her own. Perhaps all of the aliens had such suits. If, with the help of his automatic, he obtained possession of one, what would prevent him from strolling over to observe the activities of the new base at close range?

'That's it!' he told himself.

It was the only explanation that made any sense. But where did they keep the suits, and where the devil was that door? Perhaps both were within an arm's length of him, but he had no way of knowing. He had scrupulously refrained from snooping about the capsule when he had the chance, and now he regretted it.

But at last he had an idea.

He went to his bin, fully conscious of the watchful eyes above him, and nonchalantly picked out his watch. 'What time is it in New York City? he asked Zachary.

'I do not know,' Zachary said. 'Why do you ask?'

'Never mind. I'll manage without it.'

The greatest detective job of his career was just before him.

18

Darzek watched the new base incessantly, taking brief catnaps when he had to, and then leaping back to the viewer with frantic concern for what he might have missed. The flooding shadow of the eastern rim came into sight, creeping relentlessly towards the silver huts. Darzek's eyes returned to it again and again – uneasily, because it marked the silent passage of time.

And he did not know how much time he had.

For the first twenty-four hours the activity about the base was chaotic. For the second it was merely confused, but it was not until midway through the third day that Darzek could discern the emergence of a routine.

A few casual inquiries of Zachary, an innocent-appearing request to see as much of the crater as the viewer could show him, and the pattern was suddenly crystal-clear. Darzek exultantly retired to his sleeping pad to contemplate the significance of what he had learned.

There were undoubtedly worse places on the Moon for a base than this particular crater, but they could not have been much worse. Or so Darzek reasoned. The rim looked formidable, and even if trained men were able to climb or blast their way out it seemed certain that the operation would not be worth the effort. There were few places to go once they got out. The crater was, Zachary assured him, located at the approaches of one of the Moon's most rugged wastelands. It was virtually inaccessible from without, and the without was virtually inaccessible from within. The aliens had located their base in its rim for that very reason. The crater offered nothing that could not be had in hundreds of more conveniently located craters, and the aliens had confidently expected that this one would long remain unmolested.

Suddenly this obscure crater had become important. Fire flashed on the edge of its northern rim. Earth scientists considered the occurrence of sufficient import to justify a special expedition. The other disadvantages remained, however, and in the normal course of events, once the expedition had convinced itself that the explosion, or eruption, or whatever, had left no traces – if indeed there had ever been one – and perfunctorily examined the crater, it would have achieved its purpose. The ship would be off on its return journey to Earth, or to replant the expedition in some more promising location.

But something had occurred that swung events far from their normal course. The expedition's equipment included a transmitter, and it worked. Anyone could visit the Moon in no more time than it took to step through a doorway, and the volume of supplies the expedition could expend each day was limited only by the volume that could be hauled through that same doorway in twenty-four hours.

It was perhaps unfortunate that this unexpected largess could not be directed at New Frontier City of Lunaville, where it could be legitimately absorbed without appointing a committee to think up a use for it; but no matter. Transmitters would be shipped to those bases with their next supplies. In the meantime, here was this out-of-the-way crater, comparatively safe as landscape went on the Moon, unexciting and unimportant since there really hadn't been an explosion, but instantly accessible to anyone or anything that could pass through a transmitter.

What better place could be devised for training novice Moon explorers? They could accustom themselves to the gravity, to the Moon suits, to the vehicles, to the general living conditions, and be served a sampling of problems in Moon exploration in properly diluted form. They could follow a carefully contrived, step-by-step training schedule, two hours of this and one of that, and work up to overnight expeditions to the other side of the crater and mountain climbing on carefully selected slopes of crater wall. The crater would contain them more effectively than a fenced yard ever contained children at play back on Earth. They might find places to hide, but they would have a devilishly difficult time getting lost.

Further they could receive this training without consuming costly, rocket-borne supplies. They could return to their Earth base at the end of the day, or if their training schedule permitted, even for lunch. For the first time in the history of Moon exploration, Earth's twenty-four-hour day had become something more than an abstract reference.

Darzek wondered wryly how the cantankerous lunatics at

New Frontier City and Lunaville would take to the transmitter. Their belovedly hostile Moon environment would grow soft, and plush, before their disbelieving eyes.

Once Darzek had pursued this line of thought to its logical conclusions, he had little difficulty in sorting out the routine of the new base. The novices arrived twice daily, and marched out in formation for two-hour romps in Moon environment. Three men, evidently scientists, arrived each morning, Earth time, spent the day methodically searching the crater wall with instruments, and went home to Earth – at night. There were innumerable sight-seers whose portly importance was masked by their Moon suits. They were taking advantage of the transmitter for a first-hand glimpse of the Moon, and they gawked, walked about cautiously, and then returned to Earth.

And there were three men who acted as caretakers. They remained at the base, superimposing Earth's day and night activities upon Moon's diurnal month. These men interested Darzek intensely. Apparently they had first established themselves in the smaller hut, where the transmitter was located; but they quickly came to resent the volume of traffic that passed through their living quarters, and on the second day they moved into the large storage hut. Darzek silently but fervently thanked them.

The scientists had a small hut of their own, which they set up near their work area. It was perhaps designed for some technical or emergency funtion, but Darzek surmised that its principal use was as a site for midday meals and coffee breaks. The scientists also had their own vehicle, of which there were now four in the crater, and the assistance of any or all the novices when they required it.

The third day came to a peaceful close. The novices left in midafternoon; the scientists, working late by Darzek's calculations, in the evening. The caretakers moved about leisurely, shifting supplies, tidying things up. Finally they retired to their quarters. Darzek continued to watch at intervals until his calculations told him it was midnight.

His plan was ready. There was only one more thing that he needed to know: How much time did he have?

He said to Zachary, 'I think we should have a conference.'

'Certainly. What would you like to confer about?'

'All of us, I mean.'

'If you like.'

They filed down the ladder and stood in a tight arc facing him. Their expressions were blank as always, and yet he felt as certain of their emotions, now, as if they were crisp messages received on radar. The aliens were suspicious, agonizingly suspicious. They expected trickery, and they were alerted to deal with it. And they were afraid.

Darzek stood with his back firmly against the bin holding his personal possessions. 'I have a plan,' he announced, 'but I need to know something. How much time do I have in which to carry it out?'

'Alice feels that we should not know about the time,' Zachary said.'

'Ask her – but never mind. First I must supply a reason for her to change her mind. You have a Code. You are sworn to uphold it. I, also, wish to swear to uphold it, or as much of it as I know. What ceremony would be appropriate?'

The reaction was a breathless, dumbfounded silence. Alice finally asked a question, received an answer, and the five of them stared at the top of Darzek's head.

'We do not understand,' Zachary said. 'Why should you swear to uphold our Code?'

'Why not?' Darzek asked. 'Isn't it a good Code?'

There was no answer.

'I have a plan that may well save all of us – save us as you would wish to be saved. To carry it out we must work with mutual trust and co-operation. Therefore I must accept your Code without qualification, and you must accept me as one of you. I have thought long about this. It is the only way.'

'We, too, have thought long about it – about saving all of us,' Zachary said. 'There is no way that does not involve excessive risk.'

'An argument will settle nothing,' Darzek said impatiently. He raised his right hand. 'I solemnly swear by all that is sacred to your people and to mine that I will uphold and adhere to your Code as it is known to me. Is that satisfactory?'

'Perfectly satisfactory,' Zachary said. 'I cannot see that it alters our situation, but it may seem preferable to you to die in a just cause.'

'My concern is with living in a just cause. You said you had a base in New York City. Tell me this – is there a transmitting device in that base?'

'Certainly.'

'Is it still operating?'

'It operates automatically when –'

'Never mind. Would it operate *now* if you had access to the transmitter out there at the base, and made contact with it?'

'Certainly. Believe me, Jan Darzek, we have considered this. It would require delicate adjustments, perhaps even drastic changes, to make that transmitter operate with ours. These would require much time. We are certain that one of us could not reach that base, and work long on that transmitter, without being detected. We cannot take such a chance.'

'Now look at it my way,' Darzek said. 'I understand these men as you never will, and I understand their routine. I would not be running the same risk as you, simply because I am a man, and could possibly talk my way out of any difficulty that developed. Whichever one of you worked on that transmitter would have me standing by. But I must know how much time we have. Just to be on the safe side I'd like another day, to confirm my observations. Will you ask Alice if our air will last for – oh, make it twenty-six hours.'

The aliens continued to stare at him; or rather, past him. Zachary translated his question, and for a long time Alice said nothing at all. Suddenly she looked at Darzek. Never before had one of them met his gaze directly, and he realized with a start that her colorless, sunken eyes were faintly luminous. Then she spoke – one word.

'No,' Zachary said.

'No? Then it will have to be done tonight. Immediately. They're asleep now, and we should have plenty of time before morning. Certainly the job could be done in two or three hours. Do we have three hours left?'

Zachary translated. Alice did not answer.

'Tell me this,' Darzek said. 'You do have some space suits, don't you? Or Moon suits, whatever they are.'

'We have only one vacuum suit,' Zachary said, 'for emergencies. We did not come here to explore your Moon.'

'I'm sorry to hear that. I'd hoped for two, at least. That means we'll have to steal one from the base.'

'You cannot be serious,' Zachary said. 'Do you expect to find such equipment lying around for the taking?'

'Certainly. With as many visitors as they've had, they would have to keep a number of suits on hand for emergencies. I've

143

seen a spare one on the scientist's vehicle, and there's certain to be a rack of them at the base. Do we have three hours?'

Zachary translated again. Alice looked long at Darzek, and then she spoke.

She said no.

19

Darzek looked blinkingly at the silent aliens. He'd had almost no sleep for three days, and he was fearfully tired. 'How much time *do* we have?' he demanded.

Alice answered at some length, and Zachary translated. 'We are now using our last reserve tank, and the gauge reads empty. The gauge may not be precisely accurate, but it is certain that we have very little time. Once the tank is empty we have only the air on these two levels of the capsule, and we use air much faster than your people, Jan Darzek. We are truly sorry that we cannot use your plan, but as you see, it came much too late.'

'If we start at once, it might be done in one hour. What do we have to lose?'

'Everything,' Zachary said.

'Yes. You're right, of course, but if we manage this thing properly we have nothing to lose. At least let's try the first step, and see if we can get hold of another suit. Where do you keep yours?'

The silence was long and tense. Darzek looked from one blank face to another, and hoped fervently that he would not have to use the automatic. He watched Zachary expectantly, but to his amazement it was Ysaye who moved.

'I shall get the vacuum suit,' the young alien said, and rippled open a tall compartment. He hauled out the suit, and handed it over to Darzek. 'It will not fit you,' he added.

'I'll make it fit,' Darzek said grimly, but as he held the enormous thing up full length he had more than a few misgivings. It was of soft, blackish fabric, and the air tank was a bulging sausage that protruded from the back. It was designed to accommodate the eight-foot stature of an Alice or Gwendolyn.

'I see what you mean,' Darzek said. 'But I'll manage. I'll have to. Is this tank full of air?'

'It is kept ready for emergencies,' Ysaye said.

'If there'll ever be an emergency, this is it. Where's the exit?'

Ysaye turned to the compartment again, rippled open a door at the back, and revealed a long tunnel that slanted down to a dead end. It was brightly lit with the same glowing material that lit the capsule.

'Right,' Darzek said. 'Come along, will you, and help me get this suit on. The rest of you can watch, and if you know any prayers you might even pray a little. I'll be back soon – I hope.'

The others had neither moved nor spoken, but when Darzek stepped towards the tunnel Zachary leaped to block the way and Xerxes snatched his gleaming weapon from his clothing. Darzek sprang aside, and as the weapon's full impact struck Zachary he brought the edge of his hand down on Xerxes's arm with vicious force. The arm seemed to snap, and flopped uselessly. The weapon clattered on the floor. Zachary sprawled motionless in the entrance of the tunnel, and Xerxes stood calmly contemplating his helpless arm.

'You're quite the triggerman, aren't you?' Darzek said to Xerxes. 'But your draw is a bit rusty. You need practice. When business is less pressing, I'll give you lessons.'

He nodded at Ysaye, who pulled Zachary aside. 'The two of them stepped into the tunnel. 'Look after Zachary,' Darzek said, and rippled the door shut behind them. They walked quickly down the slope together.

The tunnel leveled off towards the end. 'Is this the inner door to an air lock?' Darzek asked.

'Yes. Yes, you would call it that.'

'Just so that's what it is. The outside door must look just like the face of the rock. How do I get it open when I come back? Or even find it?'

'Come back?' Ysaye repeated. 'You are coming back?'

'Of course.'

'I understand. You will bring your people here.'

'Certainly not! Didn't you hear what I said about a plan?'

'I did not think you meant it,' Ysaye said simply.

Darzek regarded him with amazement. 'Then – why are you helping me?'

'Because I do not want you to die.'

Their eyes met, and Darzek reached out and took the young alien's cold dry hand. He had never felt such compassion for a living creature. Ysaye's utter isolation, his unplumbed depths of loneliness, were such that in the end he was ready to violate the Code in recompense for those few meager gestures of

146

friendship that Darzek had extended to him. What that decision was costing him Darzek could never know.

'I think,' Darzek said slowly, 'that a friend of yours enjoys a much greater friendship than he realizes.'

Abruptly he turned away. 'The suit,' he said.

It drooped over him in cumbersome folds, and he swam in it. The helmet was so large that he had to tilt his head forward to see through the visor. The joints were adjustable, as was a beltlike arrangement around the body, but between these points the oversized suit ballooned out alarmingly. The inflated legs rubbed together; the suit's hands, even under mild pressure, popped away from his hands and dangled free at the ends of the long arms. Darzek removed the helmet, and watched his bulging belly collapse into sagging wrinkles of fabric.

'I'll manage somehow,' he said. 'How does the outside door work?'

'It pushes out. Then it opens on - on hinges.'

'How do I open it from the outside?'

'There is no way,' Ysaye said. 'It is only for emergencies. It must be propped open.'

'I don't like that,' Darzek said with a scowl. 'But if it must be left open, then I'll prop it. A rock will do, I suppose. You wait here, just in case it closes on me. If I can't get back in, I'll have no choice but to go back to the base and formally introduce myself. 'Do you understand?'

'I – yes, I understand.'

Darzek snapped the helmet into place, and pushed on the circular inner door. It opened easily, closed behind him. Whether it slammed, clicked, or closed noiselessly he could not say, because he now moved in a void of uncanny silence. He could see no door ahead of him, but he pressed on the blank wall. A jagged section moved outwards – moved with stiff resistance, as though strong springs were holding it – and then pivoted. He stepped through, into the bleak shadow that cloaked the eastern end of the crater, and held the door until he could wedge pieces of rock behind it on both sides to prevent its snapping back into place. Then he backed off and spent several minutes studying the barren slope of crater wall. The door matched so perfectly that even with its slight protrusion it was invisible except from close by. He needed a few landmarks, so he would not waste valuable time in looking for it.

Finally satisfied, he turned and looked about him. As he glanced upwards stars leaped into view, stars by the dazzling thousands and tens of thousands, of startling brightness. Balanced on the rim of the crater was a rakish, glowing cresent the Earth, either waning or waxing, and whichever it was Darzek couldn't have cared less.

He moved off, following the crater wall for a hundred yards or so, awkwardly stumbling over rock debris and circling enormous chunks of rock that had been eroded from the rim in whatever mode of decay afflicted Moon craters. Darzek was not interested enough to speculate, his only reaction being to damn the process for cluttering up his route. On level ground the dust seemed impervious to tracks – his footprints filled immediately behind him – but on regular ground the dust could be scraped away, and drifts of smaller rock fragments also recorded his passing. Darzek doubted that anyone could have distinguished his tracks from those of the exploration parties that had tramped along the wall and crisscrossed that section of the crater, but he cautiously followed a wide detour, taking no chances on laying down a trail that would lead directly to the aliens' door.

Finally he struck off across the crater, heading down the long, almost imperceptible slope towards the base.

It was only when he lengthened his stride and attempted to take advantage of the low Moon gravity that he realized he was trapped in a deadly struggle with the aliens' vacuum suit. The contraption possessed a built-in determination to seek its natural shape. His feet slipped easily from the large feet of the suit, and when he took a long stride, a leg from the knee joint to the foot, would pop out to its full length while he was in mid-air, and become entangled with his feet when he came down. On a particularly long leap both legs popped out, and nearly tripped him up. He kept the sleeves in place with a desperate grip on the huge mittens, though his hands quickly became cramped. The rubbing legs worried him. He began to wonder if the bulging torso would permit him to bend over. His body was uncomfortably warm; his limbs distressingly cold. He floundered and perspired forward.

The aliens' viewer had misled him as to the distance. He'd thought the base less than a mile away, but he quickly raised his estimate to three miles. 'But what are a couple of miles on the Moon?' he asked himself exultantly.

148

Then he crossed the shadow line, and the blast of the sun's heat struck him.

For a terrifying instant the heat overwhelmed him. Just as abruptly the suit reacted, and he began to feel almost comfortable. He slowed his pace as he approached the base, but that was only so his awkwardness and inertia would not carry him completely past it. He had already decided that caution would only waste time, and would entrap him as certainly as recklessness. The base had no hiding places – not for a man who was thousands of miles across space from where he had any right to be, and most particularly not for one wearing a misshapen, miscolored, and otherwise designed-to-stand-out-like-a-sore-thumb alien vacuum suit.

There were no windows in either hut, a fact for which Darzek as profoundly grateful. There were, however, single windows in both doors of the air locks, to prevent collisions, or, more likely, to prevent the two doors from being opened simultaneously. Darzek went directly to the transmitter hut, paused only for a moment to peer through the doors, and resolutely entered.

The hut was softly lit by the penetrating sunlight. The transmitter stood at the far end, in an open space reached through a narrow alley formed by cases of supplies. Darzek was chiefly interested in two things, an extra space suit and a spare cylinder or two of oxygen, and he saw neither. He pawed at the crates, squinted at the stenciled labels, and found himself at a frantic dead end. He circled the transmitter, looking at it carefully, and then he left the hut.

The weird silence had so unnerved him that he found himself tiptoeing, though he knew that no sound could reach the sleeping men in the other hut. He turned to the scientists' vehicle, which stood nearby. It had a large air cylinder clamped to it with metal straps – they used it to inflate their hut and to replenish their suits' air supply – but even if Darzek could have coped with the bolts holding it, he would not have dared to take it. It would have been no more conspicious to swipe the whole vehicle.

An extra suit, on the other hand, might not be missed immediately, and could be presumed lost, mislaid, or borrowed. He opened the vehicle's storage compartments, one by one. There was no suit. The scientists' hut was a gleaming speck far off by the crater wall. They could have left their spare suit

149

there, but he would not risk a fruitless trip, and had no time for any kind of trip.

The gauge on the supply capsule's last reserve tank still read zero. If Alice or Gwendolyn had come, instead of Darzek, the work on the transmitter could well have been finished by now. But neither of them would have come – not alone. He had to have a suit.

He went slowly to the second hut, and peeped through the air lock. Crates were stacked high at the rear, perhaps to form a partition. He entered the air lock, and slowly, hesitantly, opened the inner door. If they were awake, the slightest noise would trap him.

The suits hung to the right of the door. A row of them. Darzek helped himself to one, and backed away. His confidence returned in a rush. He closed the doors carefully but deliberately, and even paused outside for a glance at the suit, but he could not inspect it, not there, fighting the cumbersome alien suit. He could only hope that it was in working order, and that the air tank was full.

As he turned away he saw, on the far side of the transmitter hut, a large air cylinder. He loped over to pick it up. With cylinder under one arm, suit under the other, he started back to the supply capsule, making the best stumbling speed that he could manage.

The alien suit had begun to do strange things to him. His human metabolism was bringing about violent reactions from its delicate mechanisms. At first it merely probed at him in a cautious puzzlement; then it asserted itself. It blasted him with heat. Just as abruptly it flushed him with cold. A low humming sound replaced the silence of the helmet. As he began to shiver violently, another blast of heat sent him reeling. He dripped perspiration now, and this seemed to infuriate the suit. The hum crescendoed maddeningly.

He staggered the last few yards alternately shocked by heat and cold. He hauled open the camouflaged entrance, kicked the rocks aside, and dropped the stolen cylinder and suit on the floor of the air lock. Ysaye was waiting inside the inner door. Darzek unsnapped the helmet, and gasped, 'Get me out of this thing!'

Ysaye stripped the suit from him, and Darzek sagged against the wall and brushed perspiration from his forehead. 'First it burned me, and then it froze me,' he complained.

'I hoped you would not wear it long enough for that to

happen,' Ysaye said. 'We do not perspire, you see, and our body temperature is lower.'

'So the suit was trying to stop my perspiration and lower my body temperature. I'm glad it didn't succeed. When that happens, a human is usually dead.'

He picked up the stolen suit and the cylinder, and led the way back up the tunnel to the capsule.

Zachary lay on Darzek's sleeping pad, still unconscious. The others were grouped around the viewer. Xerxes's arm bore a voluminous bandage.

'Anything stirring?' Darzek asked.

'We have not noticed anything,' Xerxes said.

'Good. Who is coming with me? Alice or Gwendolyn?'

'What exactly do you want of us?' Xerxes asked.

'I want one of your technicians to use that transmitter to get back to your New York base. From there she can make contact with us here, and rescue all of us. I don't pretend to understand how she'll do it, but one of you told me it could be done.'

'Yes. It could be done. It would require much time, because she would have to build –'

'Never mind how, or how much time. If it can be done, let's get moving. There are plenty of tools there in the transmitter hut.'

Xerxes's translation brought about another prolonged discussion. Darzek turned his attention to the stolen air cylinder. He twisted the valve – and nothing happened. Ysaye came to assist, and then Alice. 'I fear that it is empty,' Ysaye said finally.

Darzek slumped dejectedly, and pawed at his flourishing growth of beard. 'Of course,' he muttered. 'Dumped outside the hut until they could get around to sending it back for a refill. Just finished it yesterday, I suppose, and – this obviously isn't my day.' He got to his feet again, and reached for the stolen suit. 'Now that I think about it, there was a whole row of cylinders in the other hut. All I was concerned with was getting out of there with the suit. This time I'll take a couple of them.'

'What we do not understand,' Xerxes said, 'is what you propose to do yourself.'

'I propose to mount guard while your technician works on the transmitter. If anyone approaches the hut I intend to way-lay him, and delay, divert, or commit mayhem, if necessary,

151

so your technician won't be interrupted until she finishes whatever it is she has to do, and gets out of there. Then I'll come
back here. With luck, I'll bring a couple of *full* cylinders.'

'You may be captured yourself.'

'That's possible,' Darzek said. 'I'll do my damnedest to
avoid it, but it's possible. And if I am captured, I'll invent a
story about sneaking through the transmitter from Earth
because I had a long-suppressed passion to see the Moon.'

'I doubt if such a thing would be possible.'

'Probably not,' Darzek conceded. 'There'd be a tremendous
flap, and I'd be third-degreed interminably, but not even the
Chinese water treatment would extract the truth from me. And
remember this – even though the high brass back on Earth
would never understand how I managed it, at least it wouldn't
be *unbelievable* – as it would be, for example, if I were caught
wearing your vacuum suit. I'll take off this clothing before I
start, and if I am caught they won't find anything about me
that wasn't made in the U.S.A.'

'We cannot do what you ask,' Xerxes said. 'The risk would
be too great, and the time too little.'

'Look. For the moment I'm not questioning your allegation
that your darkness is the right color, and I can't fault your
courage. It must have taken a lot of courage to bring off the
things you accomplished on Earth. But you certainly lack
spunk. Either you make this effort or you die here like rats in a
hole, for all your lovely color.'

Xerxes did not answer. Darzek brushed him aside, took
the suit from Ysaye, and offered it to Alice. Their eyes met
Then she spoke a single word, and as the others watched
silently she took the suit and put it on. Darzek unwound the
strips of alien clothing and struggled into the stolen suit, with
Ysaye fussing around him anxiously. His tenseness vanished
as he found the control on the air tank and got the helmet
into place.

Ysaye trailed after them faithfully as far as the air lock.
Darzek waved a final salute, the inner door closed, and they
stepped outside. He wedged the rocks into place again, and
they set off on the circuitous route Darzek had used before.

They moved with incredible swiftness. Darzek's suit was
bulky and primitive when compared with the aliens', but at
least it almost fit him. He took enormous, soaring strides, and
had to exert himself to keep pace with the tremendous bounds
Alice made.

When they reached the transmitter hut he pointed at the air lock, and she stooped low to enter. He was about to follow her, to show her the switch on the light that illuminated the instrument board, but she found it immediately. He watched through the windows as she removed her suit and went to work on the transmitter, her enormous, stooped form looking weirdly out of place in the low hut.

He turned speculatively towards the other hut, wondering if he should try for the air cylinders at once, or wait until Alice had finished. He decided to wait. Then, if he muddled the job, he would have only himself to account for.

He moved to the side of the hut, and found a place of relative concealment behind the supply crates stacked there. He was beginning to feel excessively warm, and he mentally directed a deluge of corrosive curses at all vacuum suits, their designers and makers. In his rush to get into the suit he hadn't thought to look for anything as incidental as a thermostat. He clumsily explored some controls without result, and found he'd been fussing with the radio. Eventually it occurred to him to move into the crates' shadow, and he soon felt comfortable again. And as soon as Alice –

'Damn! he exploded, and immediately hoped he hadn't broadcast the word.

He would have no way of knowing when Alice completed her mission. Even now he might be standing guard over an empty hut. His only means of checking on her progress was to move around and look through the air lock, and this exposed him to a sudden exit from behind the other hut.

If he'd had an iota of foresight he would have arranged a signal – she had only to bat the side of the hut when she was ready to return to Earth – but now it was much too late. He knew better than to enter the hut and try to get the idea across to her by sign language. It would waste valuable time, and he would probably fail anyway.

He darted to the air lock for another look. Alice's huge form was still bent over the transmitter. She did not appear to have moved since he had seen her last.

He returned to his hiding place, and continued to search for the suit's thermostat. He watched, and waited. An hour? Two hours? Three?

He wondered what sort of havoc Alice was working with the transmitter. If none of the base personal was enlightened in the ways of the gadgets, an engineeer would have to be sent

153

from Earth by rocket to untangle the mess she would leave. It struck Darzek as a tolerably good joke, and he might have enjoyed it immensely under less pressing circumstances.

His terrible fatigue, and the intense strain of suspenseful waiting, had set his nerves to jangling like a misstrung harp. And in the supply capsule, the gauge on the last reserve tank still stood at zero. He started to his feet for another look at Alice, and sank back again as a silver-suited figure emerged from the other hut.

Frantically he fumbled with the radio controls.

' – ready yet?' a voice rasped.

'We're coming.'

A second figure emerged. And a third. Darzek could only pray fervently that their schedule of yesterday would hold, that they would turn to the right.

They did. They moved off in long leaps, heading towards the far crater wall. It was their after-breakfast constitutional, and if they followed the previous day's timing they would be back in about thirty minutes to open the base – and the transmitter – for the day's operation.

For a few valuable seconds the other hut lay between them and the air lock, and Darzek was able to risk another check on Alice. She was still at work. He took up a position behind the hut and waited, wondering how the radio operated. Did he have to push a switch to talk?

He clucked his tongue sharply.

'What did you say?' was the immediate response.

'I thought that was you.'

'Your teeth are rattling.'

The three figures soon separated, one of them heading for the eastern shadow. Darzek had a momentary twitch of uneasiness about the entrance to the supply capsule, but the man moved only a short distance into the shadow, where he seated himself, perhaps to admire the awesome display of stars. Another turned in the opposite direction, and had soon diminished to a rapidly moving, glittering speck. The third, a short figure with a rolling gait whom Darzek had already identified as the transmitter operator, continued straight ahead. Darzek relaxed, and began once more to search for the thermostat. Now that he'd moved into the sun, his suit was heating up rapidly. He *had* to find the dratted thing, but the gloves transmitted no information to his hands, and he had difficulty examining himself through the visor.

154

He glanced up to check on the positions of the wandering Moon men, and instantly forgot about the heat. The transmitter operator was returning.

'So they got a late start today,' he told himself, 'or maybe the guy wants to get to work early.'

There was no time for another look at Alice. He moved off a hundred yards, and waited. The operator came on at a springing jog, heading directly for the transmitter hut. Finally he saw Darzek, and waved.

'That you, Sam?'

Darzek waved back and spoke, trying to imitate one of the voices he'd heard. 'Come on. Wanna show you something.'

'Can't,' the operator said. 'I gotta sweep out the hut for that goddam VIP.'

'Aw, come on. It won't take long.'

'Where is it?'

'Not far.'

Darzek turned, started off, and the operator followed him. He looked again for the other two men. One was still seated in the shadow, gazing up at the stars. He could not locate the other, which suited him perfectly. He lengthened his stride.

The operator was hurrying to catch up with him. 'I haven't got all day. What is it? Where is it?'

'Up this way,' Darzek said, veering towards the crater wall and increasing his speed. They jogged on for some time without speaking. The heat in Darzek's suit had become intolerable, and he was beginning to feel dizzy. He moved along the base of the wall, zigzagging among the fallen rocks. They had covered a considerable distance, and the two huts were only bright mounds in the plain behind them.

'How far are you going?' the operator demanded.

Darzek looked back. The operator had halted, and was looking towards the huts.

'Just a little way,' Darzek said. It was the literal truth. He knew that he was about to have a heat stroke, that his next step might be his last, and there was nothing he could do about it. He staggered into the shadow of an enormous chunk of rock, and sank to his knees.

The operator was walking away. 'I'm going back, Sam.'

Darzek did not answer. He heard a muttered, 'Now where the hell did he go?' but the operator continued to walk back towards the base. Darzek flopped over as heavily as a hundred and ninety pounds could flop under Moon gravity. This was

155

not what he had planned, but he was unable to so much as lift his throbbing head again. He had done his best, and his best had gained at most an additional thirty minutes for Alice. The rest was up to her.

20

For a long time Darzek lay motionless, too weak and nauseated to stir himself for a glance in the direction of the base. Perhaps he lost consciousness momentarily. He neither knew nor cared. His next coherent awareness was of an outraged voice screaming angrily in his ears. *'Which one of you idiots has been messing with the transmitter?'*

A second voice answered immediately. 'What'd you say, Perrin?'

'I said – get back here, both of you.'

'Coming. What's the matter?'

Darzek muttered exultantly, 'She got through! She got through!'

'What'd you say, Perrin?'

'I said get back here. Sam? *Sam!*'

'Maybe he's out of range of your suit radio. Turn on the relay.'

'Nonsense. I left him over there – '

'He headed out across the crater. I can't even see him now.'

'I tell you he came back. I just left him. Sam!'

'I don't see him.'

'He found something over there. Maybe he's in a cave.'

'There aren't any caves.'

'Well, he said he found something. Sam!'

Darzek lost interest. The suit had cooled off miraculously, and his perspiration-soaked body was soon shudderingly cold. This time he was able to locate the thermostat and adjust the temperature, and he wondered if there was a loose connection that had somehow been corrected when he flopped down.

Sam returned, angrily protesting that he had been nowhere near the base, had found nothing, had not seen Perrin. All three men went into the transmitter hut. Darzek did a quick review of his position, and decided that he didn't like it. Once Perrin became convinced that he hadn't been following Sam,

157

it was only reasonable to assume that he'd be mildly curious to know whom he had followed. The most casual search would lead directly to Darzek.

He weighed his chances carefully, and decided to move. By this time, he thought, the three men would be out of their suits and assessing the damage to the transmitter. The others might even stand around to watch while Perrin went to work on it.

He moved off, keeping close to the curving crater wall and traveling with as much speed as his weakened body and the accumulation of fallen rock permitted. The rock debris was often treacherous underfoot and forced him to follow an exhausting, meandering path, but he did not dare to leave the wall. The rocks also supplied the crater's only hiding places.

He had reached a point almost directly opposite the base when the three men reappeared. Darzek leaped for cover, ducking behind a rock and moving a few more yards at a crouch to the protection of a cluster of large rocks, but the men did not look in his direction. Perrin, gesticulating excitedly, indicated the precise spot where he had last seen the phantom Moon man. He returned to the hut, and the other two trotted off to investigate. Darzek settled down comfortably behind his rocks, and waited.

The two searchers wandered about aimlessly, grumbling and arguing, not entirely convinced that Perrin had seen anything at all. Time passed. One of them abandoned the search. More time passed. A few minutes? An hour?

A squad of novices filed from the transmitter hut. Perrin had completed the repairs.

'So I'm marooned here,' Darzek thought. 'But it could be worse.'

He was perfectly safe. Even if they searched in the direction they would not find him unless they walked up to his cluster of rocks and looked in. If they came after him in numbers he might be able to join the search and pass himself off as one of them. He could not change his position until their midday break, but as long as his air lasted he had nothing to worry about.

Nothing except the zero gauge on the supply capsule's last reserve tank, and the stolen empty air cylinder that he should have returned, and the full cylinders he had promised but now would be unable to deliver. He felt sick with apprehension. Had Alice got through from Earth – in time? Would they, after all their pious pratting about their Code, abandon him on the

Moon, to talk his way out of the situation as best he could?

The base seemed to be following its normal routine. One group of novices prowled the area of the phantom Moon man's disappearance, but the others had advanced as far as lesson five, mountaineering, and were working their way up one of the easier slopes of crater wall. The scientists had packed up their hut and driven off out of sight to stake out a new area of investigation. Darzek explored the available wave lengths on his radio, and listened to a sharp-voiced instructor berate the novices, to some incomprehensible scientific chatter, to the inane remarks of a carefully herded group of VIPs. The midday break arrived without incident. The novices marched in for their return to Earth, and the base appeared deserted.

Darzek cautiously ventured out of his hiding place.

He had not taken a dozen steps when a man came out of the transmitter hut and stood gazing in his direction. 'Be natural!' Darzek told himself. 'You're one of them. Be natural!' The man turned abruptly, and stalked off to the other hut. Darzek ducked for cover, wondering who the man thought he'd seen.

He expected him to reappear shortly, with reinforcements, and when he did not Darzek started out once more. This time he recklessly left the crater wall and headed directly for the supply capsule. In his haste he overshot the camouflaged entrance, and had to spend several frenzied minutes searching for it. He turned for a last look at the base, and then he slipped inside, kicked the rocks away, and let the door snap shut behind him.

He opened the inner door, and stumbled over the prostrate form of an alien.

He ripped his way out of the suit, and knelt down. It was Ysaye, apparently dead. Darzek searched for a pulse with a fumbling, inexpert finger, felt for a heart beat, found nothing. There was no sign of breathing, and the alien's flesh had taken on a faint brownish tint, as though the body were already in an advanced state of decomposition.

Darzek rocked on his heels despairingly. He called out – the door was open at the end of the tunnel – but there was no answer. The air seemed fresh, but he realized that he was breathing with some difficulty.

He searched again for a pulse, a heart beat, wondering if the aliens possessed either. And how could he go about giving

159

artificial respiration to a creature whose lungs were as likely to be located in its ankles as its chest?

He detached the helmet from the space suit, and slipped it over Ysaye's head. Seconds passed without any response. Darzek began to push roughly on the abdomen and chest, to push, crush with his full weight, and release.

Ysaye jerked and stirred, and began to breathe deeply. The brownish tint faded. Soon he was able to sit up.

'So you have returned, Jan Darzek,' he said, his words muffled by the helmet.

'Take it easy,' Darzek said. 'Keep breathing deeply.'

'Alice – '

'I think she got through all right. I couldn't go back to see.'

'We watched. Your plan worked splendidly. Gwendolyn thought you meant to betray us, but I could not agree with her. But I did not think you meant to return.'

'I took an oath,' Darzek said. 'Remember?'

'The others – are they – '

'I haven't even looked for them. I fell over you as I came out of the air lock.'

He ran up the tunnel to the capsule, and looked inside. There the air seemed worse, and the three aliens lay in pathetic, browning heaps. Darzek raced back to Ysaye, snatching the helmet from his head, and dragged helmet and suit up to the capsule.

He bent first over Gwendolyn. The helmet was hopelessly small for her enormous head. He attempted unsuccessfully to fit the bottom opening to her face, and finally he leaped to his bin, snatched his penknife, and sliced the air hose. He cupped it to her face with his hands, and pressed his weight upon her body, pressed again and again.

'It is no use, Jan Darzek.' Ysaye had crawled up the tunnel, and he lay in the doorway, looking in. 'It is no use. Go back to your people. You must not feel obliged to die with us. You have saved Alice – that is enough.'

'Nonsense. You're not going to die.'

Gwendolyn was responding. As she stirred and sat up, staring at him uncomprehendingly, Darzek jerked the hose away and went to work on Xerxes. Before he had arrived that alien Gwendolyn had collapsed again, and Ysaye lay unconscious at the opening of the tunnel.

'Screwy metabolisms,' Darzek muttered, working frantically

on Xerxes. 'I'll have to put them in a circle, and let them take turns.'

In his own weakened condition the effort taxed his strength to the utmost, but he finally got all of them revived and seated so that the hose could be passed from one to the other. Gwendolyn, Xerxes, and Zachary seemed dazed. They acted almost automatically, seizing the hose, gulping at it, handing it along, keeping their eyes always on Darzek. Ysaye was in better shape, perhaps because the air in the tunnel had not given out as soon as the air in the capsule. He passed up several of his turns to argue with Darzek.

'Don't be silly,' Darzek said. 'I can't run off and leave you to die. I couldn't leave now if I wanted to. I cut the suit's air hose.'

'You can repair it. When your oxygen is gone we will die anyway, and you with us. It will not last long, and we are wasting much of it.'

'I suppose we are. Pity there isn't a more efficient way to use it. Still, it may improve the air to the point where you can breathe that again. Quit arguing, and store up as much reserve as you can before it gives out.'

'Do you need some yourself?'

'So far I don't.'

'I forgot. You who live on Earth are accustomed to bad air.'

'We aren't accustomed to air that's this bad, but I'll manage. What's keeping Alice?'

He went to the viewer for a look at the base. The novices had returned, and some of them were searching through the area where Darzek had been seen. If he hadn't been so tired, so utterly exhausted, he would have enjoyed watching. His foot found his discarded strips of clothing, and he dressed himself wearily and went to sit in the tunnel entrance. He leaned back and closed his eyes.

He was awakened by a tug on his leg. 'We wish to say goodbye to you, Jan Darzek,' Ysaye said. 'While we are still able.'

They had cast aside the air hose, and the other three sat looking blankly at Darzek, or perhaps at nothing at all. Already they were breathing laboriously.

'Tank empty?' Dazek said. 'But you're able to breathe without it.'

'Yes, a little,' Ysaye said.

'Good. What *is* keeping Alice?'

'There was not enough time. We knew that when you started.'

'Enough time for what? She's had hours.'

'We had not the necessary apparatus at our Earth station. We had no use for it, until now. Alice must build it, and when it is built she must – adjust it, which is a delicate process requiring much trial and arror.'

'I can imagine,' Darzek said. 'It wouldn't be easy to hit this precise underground spot from the Earth. How much time should it take?'

'We do not know. Alice did not know. She has never before built such apparatus. That is why the others did not consider it – consider your plan – worth the risk.'

'Well, there's nothing we can do but wait,' Darzek said. 'I'm sure she'll work as fast as she can.'

'Our most earnest wish is that she will finish in time to save you. Since you are able to breathe this bad air, and we – '

'You're breathing it,' Darzek said. 'Better save your breath.'

The aliens were soon taking in great, wracking breaths, their bodies heaving convulsively. Darzek could do nothing but affect calm and optimism and watch them, one by one, topple over. No kind of artificial resperation would have helped them without oyygen, and he had no more oxygen.

Ysaye held out the longest, but finally he, too, slumped to the floor, leaving unanswered Darzek's question as to whether it would be best to move all of them into the tunnel. Darzek went to investigate himself, and decided that the air there was not discernibly better. He returned to the capsule and stood looking despairingly at the inert, browning bodies of the aliens. There was still time, perhaps, for him to summon help from the base. He could patch up the suit adequately for him to step outside for a few seconds at a time and signal.

But the aliens would prefer death, and in a calmer moment, when he had not anticipated having to watch them die, he had agreed with them. And he had taken an oath.

But he had not, until this moment, realized how badly he had wanted to save them. With a sob he dropped to one knee beside Ysaye, and took the alien's hand.

A blast of cool, fresh air struck him, and Alice stepped from nowhere to stand beside him.

21

Alice lifted Ysaye as an adult lifts a child, and was gone, leaving only a swirling of dead air to mark her passage.

She returned before Darzek could comprehend the manner of her going, stepping from a shimmering nothingness, from a mere trickery of optics that played delicately near the ladder. Xerxes followed, and then Zachary, and she had uttered no sound, had not even glanced at Darzek.

Not until she attempted to lift Gwendolyn's huge form did she falter. Darzek sprang to her assistance, seizing the legs. Gwendolyn seemed ridiculously light, to him, but her weight plainly distressed Alice, who hauled pantingly at the shoulders as she edged her way backwards. Darzek never saw exactly where it was that he went. One instant he was breathing the lifeless air of the capsule; the next instant, in mid-breath, as it were, the air he sucked in became coolly delicious, and Gwendolyn's weight was staggering.

The laboring Alice had sunk to her knees, but even so she allowed Gwendolyn to drop the last few inches to the floor. Darzek slowly lowered the legs, and straightened up to look about him. The shock of recognition left him blinking. The room appeared to be an exact replica of the wrecked Moon base. It had the same curved and glowing walls and ceiling, the same ledges with sleeping pads, the instrument board, the transmitter frame from which he had just stepped.

In his exhausted state the sudden change to Earth's stronger gravity left him with a frightful sensation of fatigue and weakness, and he needed no further proof to convince himself that he really had returned to Earth.

He seated himself on a ledge, and watched Alice minister to the unconscious aliens. Except for Gwendolyn, they lay on sleeping pads on the opposite ledge, and Alice moved tirelessly from one to another, giving them oxygen through a queerly flat face mask. They revived one by one, and sat up, but continued to gulp greedily at the oxygen when it was offered.

For a long time they spoke in hushed tones among themselves, and seemed to be studiously avoiding as much as a glance in Darzek's direction. It was Ysaye who finally got to his feet and moved falteringly across the room.

'Well Jan Darzek – '

His hand clutched Darzek's arm. His other hand wiped the bubbling saliva from his mouth, wiped it again and again, and Darzek felt an overwhelming, incomprehensible surge of affection for this hideously faced, dry-eyed creature who was thus sobbing out his alien gratitude.

When the others, even Alice and Gwendolyn, began to display the same disconcerting emotional symptoms, the embarrassed Darzek felt constrained to divert their attention to more practical matters. He announced, 'I'm hungry.'

The five of them stared at him.

'I can't remember when I ate last,' he said 'It certainly wasn't today – now that we're back on Earth I suppose I can start thinking of time in terms of days. I don't accuse you of intentionally mistreating me, since you had no advance notice that you were going to have a guest of my gastronomic inclinations, and I don't doubt that the predigested sawdust you've been feeding me contains enough food value to sustain life, but if you have anything on hand that a native of this planet would loosely classify as food, I'd like to see if I still have a stomach.'

Much to his bewilderment, this intensified their distress. Ysaye bubbled apologies . The others engaged in an agitated exchange that resulted in Zachary's darting from the room through one of the camouflaged collapsing doors. He was gone for some time, and he returned, not with the food Darzek expected but attired as the alluring, blond Miss X of the Universal Trans terminal.

'What would you like me to bring you?' he asked.

'I'd like a steak with french-fried potatoes and various other trimmings, lots of coffee, and blueberry pie à la mode. But my stomach has probably shrunk to the size of a golf ball, and it would kill me to see all that food, and smell it, and taste some of it, and not be able to eat it. Let's start out with coffee and a couple of sandwiches. Any kind of sandwiches will do.'

Zachary departed, and the other aliens suddenly rediscovered their own appetites and broke out a set of their triangular utensils. Darzek declined a portion with a shake of his head, wondering if his food was equally distasteful to them. Zachary returned in a surprisingly short time with an enormous tray of a dozen kinds of individually wrapped sandwiches and six cartons of coffee, and Darzek ate slowly, savoring every delectable bite, sampling all the sandwiches and finishing none.

While he ate, he listened to the aliens.

They were laughing.

The unpleasant hisses and buzzes of their language had unaccountably acquired musical overtones. There were quavers, lilting inflections, that he had never heard on the Moon. Every clipped, strident utterance vibrated with hilarity. They laughed at themselves, individually and collectively. They laughed at Darzek, at the tasteless fodder he was chewing with so much relish, at his perplexed reaction to their laughter. No condemned man suddenly granted a pardon ever found life so magnificently delightful.

Darzek reluctantly pushed the sandwiches aside. 'I've mangled all of them beyond repair, but I can't eat any of them,' he said sadly. 'Never mind. Tomorrow is another day. If you have a refrigerator, stow them away and I'll have another crack at them for breakfast.'

'Is there anything wrong with the sandwiches?' Xerxes asked, his voice consumed by laughter. 'Do you wish for something else?'

'The trouble is with my stomach, and only time and a steady diet can correct that. What I would like now is some sleep. In a genuine bed. It seems ages since I had any, and I can't remember my last really restful sleep.'

The laughter tapered off as unaccountably as it had begun. 'We should talk,' Zachary said, 'but there is no reason why you should not sleep first. We have much else that must be done.'

'I will show you the way,' Ysaye said. 'Come.'

He rippled open a doorway, revealing a tunnel that slanted upwards. Another doorway, and Darzek followed him out into a quite ordinary basement. The squat furnace and its insulated hot-air pipes, and the one dimly burning electric bulb, were comforting monuments to a reality Darzek had almost forgotten. The basement windows were covered, but even in the feeble light of the one bulb Darzek could see that the place was conspicuously clean and quite empty.

Ysaye led him up the basement stairs to the first floor, then along a lighted hallway. The windows they passed were heavily curtained; the doors closed – but otherwise Darzek's impression was of an altogther ordinary house.

They climbed to the second floor, and at the end of the hallway Ysaye opened a door and turned on the light. 'This room should be quietest,' he said. 'The bathroom is opposite. Can you find your way down to us again if you need anything?'

Darzek sniffed the air. The bedroom, like the rest of the house, was hot and stuffy, as though it had long been vacant and closed up. 'I don't know,' he said.

'You need only to go as far as the basement and call. I wish you a pleasant rest, Jan Darzek.'

'Thank you,' Darzek said.

The door closed, and Ysaye's light footsteps receded.

Darzek went immediately to the window, raised the shade and opened it. Sounds drifted in from outside – passing autos, children being called in from their play. It was dusk, and he looked out onto a well kept cement courtyard, set amid a quiet neighbourhood of well-kept yards and cheerfully lighted brick houses. The spire of the Chrysler Building loomed conspicuously above the trees. After a moment's reflection he knew almost precisely where he was.

He cautiously opened the bedroom door. The silence within the house was absolute. He tiptoed carefully along the hallway and down the stairs. He tried the front door.

It opened.

Gently he nudged it shut until the lock clicked. He went back to the second floor, and quietly investigated the other rooms there. All of the bedrooms were tastefully furnished. The beds were made up, the rooms ready for occupancy. The polished bureau tops were not even dusty. He hazarded a guess that none of this furniture had ever been used, and wondered if the aliens had a maid, a human maid, who came twice weekly and was delighted with the immaculately tidy habits of her employers.

He returned to his own room, turned off the light, and stripped the swathing cloth from his body. The bed was comfortable, he was more exhausted than he had ever thought possible, and yet for a long time he could not fall asleep.

He had, since he dove into the transmitter in Brussels, observed and been a party to many miracles, but these seemed trivial compared with the miracle he had just witnessed.

The aliens trusted him.

22

A softly closing door awakened Darzek. He lay staring at the ceiling and listening to the reassuring street noises. Two women began a backyard argument somewhere nearby. The house was as restfully silent as it had been the night before.

He turned over lazily, made himself comfortable again, and then lay gazing incredulously at the clothing that had been draped over the rooms two chairs. His clothing. The suit was his, as were the socks and necktie, and it seemed only logical that the shirt, underwear, shoes, and handkerchief had likewise been lifted from his wardrobe. He wondered by what sleight of hand they had entered his appartment, and got the answer when he sat up and saw on the bureau the personal possessions he had abandoned on the Moon, including his keys. The alien garment strips had disappeared.

There was also a tray packed with sandwiches and cartons of coffee.

The coffee was hot; the sandwiches as various as the night before. He managed to eat three, with three cartons of coffee, and then dressed himself slowly and spent some time contemplating the strangely pale, bewhiskered face that stared back at him from the bureau mirror. His burns had healed without scars, but it would be a long time before he could comb his hair properly.

'Might as well get a brush haircut and have done with it,' he told himself resignedly. 'But it'll have to grow some before it's even long enough for that!'

The beard he could do without, and would as soon as he got his hands on a razor. Otherwise, except for his hair, he had come out of his experience in surprisingly good shape.

He knotted his tie, and went downtsairs to join the aliens.

He first searched for the collapsing door in the basement wall, and could not find it. Feeling slightly foolish, he backed off and called. A moment later the door rippled open, and Darzek stepped through.

'Good morning,' he said. 'Or good afternoon. Did I sleep until the next day or the day after that? I feel as if – '

He broke off confusedly. It was a male alien who stood before him, an alien of smaller stature, but it was not Xerxes, nor Ysaye, nor Zachary. Darzek stared blankly. 'Who are you?' he demanded.

The alien did not reply. He led Darzek down the tunnel to the underground room, and with a sleight-of-hand gesture produced another doorway. Darzek stepped through, and it closed behind him.

In this room, a diminutive replica of the other, a female alien was seated on the floor. A desklike contrivance stood in front of her, and across its surface flickers of light darted in incomprehensible patterns. Beside her stood a solidly human chair that looked, in those glowing surroundings, like a crude relic of some long-forgotten primitive civilization. Over the chair a silver space suit was draped.

The moving lights faded, and the alien rose to greet him. 'Mr Darzek,' she said. 'Mr Jan Darzek.' It was not a question.

Darzek began a polite bow, and halted it to accept the hand she extended to him.

'I don't believe we've met before,' he said.

She was enormous, like Alice and Gwendolyn, but she appeared to be infinitely older. Her face was a mass of sagging wrinkles. The delicate blue tint had faded from her skin, but there were disfiguring blotches, like large bruises. The webbing of the fingers, which had been delicately transparent with the younger aliens, had a loathsome appearance of dark, decaying flesh.

As he looked at her she said with a smile – and the smile was in her voice – 'I do not think you find us beautiful, Mr Jan Darzek.'

Darzek said slowly, 'I find you strange. I think only a very rash man would attempt to evaluate the aesthetic attributes of something totally beyond his experience. No doubt your people could use our beauty queens in your chambers of horror, if you have such a thing.'

She gazed at him steadily without answering. Her eyes, like Alice's, were without color and faintly luminous. Then she turned, and removed the space suit from the chair. 'Please sit here,' she said. 'I thought you would be more comfortable if you had one of your chairs to use. Our talk may be a long one.'

Darzek seated himself. She laid the suit aside, and sat down on the floor facing him.

'You have an excellent command of English,' Darzek said. 'So do the others – Xerxes, Ysaye, and Zachary, that is – and they speak other languages like natives. Is it an innate ability?'

'Ability and training. We are chosen for that ability, and we are trained meticulously. Long ago, when Moon bases and matter transmitters were at most subjects of speculative thought among your people, I served my apprenticeship on this planet. Its rustic depravity and senseless wars made it an excellent training ground. Afterwards I returned and wrote its present classification.'

'Then you're the one who plastered the NO TRESPASSING signs around this Solar System.'

'Listen.' She leaned forward, and there was no mistaking her earnestness. 'Your planet has long been used by us for training purposes. Its scientific development has accelerated in the past century, but that was only as we anticipated. The matter transmitter was several centuries in your future. Suddenly, through some freakish accident, its principles were discovered. It could not have happened at a worse time. Our Group here consisted of a newly arrived Group Leader on her first assignment, an apprentice technician, one apprentice observer, and two observers who are permanently assigned here because they have never demonstrated sufficient ability to attain rank. The Group should have requested a consultation, but it thought it could handle the situation. It thought it *was* handling it. It will receive a severe reprimand.'

'In my estimation,' Darzek said, '*you* should receive the reprimand.'

'*I*? Why do you say that?'

'You underestimated the inhabitants of this planet, and sent an inadequate force to deal with them.'

'So you defend the Group,' she said. 'You actually defend it. I did not think it possible, but they were right. You do consider them your friends. Such a thing has never happened before.'

'Are you so incapable of friendship yourself that it surprises you to find it in others?'

She did not answer at once, but whether she was offended or only nonplussed he could not decide. Then she spoke with oracular deliberation. 'The Group will receive a reprimand, not because it failed to handle the situation here, but because it attempted to handle it. It should have taken into consideration the crudeness of your transmitting device, and done nothing.'

'It works,' Darzek said.

'Barely. It is of a wholly unique design, and it is self-limiting. It does not point to further discoveries, it prevents them. It is so clumsy in its operation that Alice – ' Again the smile was in her voice. 'I would very much like to know the sources for those names, but our time is limited. Alice was almost unable to use it. That fact should have been determined at the beginning..'

'Ah! Those three steps to space travel. Then you think our transmitter is so crude that we're stranded on the first step.'

'Your transmitter is so crude that you cannot be said to have taken the first step.'

'Then – you won't smash Universal Trans?'

'What has happened makes it mandatory that we review your planet's classification. That is why I am here. Specifically, I have come to obtain your recommendations on this subject.'

Darzek stared. 'You want *my* recommendations?'

'You have taken an oath, Jan Darzek. You may not have been aware of the full implications of that act. The oath made you one of us – and among us, all who have been associated with a problem have an equal right to state opinions and make recommendations. Yours will be considered quite as carefully as mine. You know the transmitter's potential for space travel. It is true that your present transmitter does not have that potential, but if your scientists merely grasped the *idea* of such potential, of the transmitter that works without a receiver and the transmitter that transmits itself, it is possible that they would concentrate on the problem and solve it. May I have your opinion on that, please.'

'They'd solve it,' Darzek conceded. 'Sooner or later. I think too that you may be underestimating our scientists. The invention of the transmitter may not have been the accident you assume it was.'

'Have you a recommendation?'

'Certainly. You admit yourself there's no danger in our present transmitter. It represents a tremendous human achievement, and I see no justification whatsoever in your depriving us of it merely because at some future time it might become dangerous to you. Leave it alone. Leave us alone. And if you insist upon hindering us, we are at least entitled to a just compensation, to an equal measure of help.'

'Your recommendation has been noted and will be considered. Have you anything further to say?'

'Yes,' Darzek said. 'I think you're wrong about the darkness – about our darkness. We have saints and sinners, moral people and immoral people, men with admirable ethics and men with no ethics at all, and every shade of difference in between. It seems to me that you're attempting to measure us according to a scale of values where everything is either black or white – good or evil. I don't know myself if man is ready for amicable relations with alien peoples, but I'm positive that he isn't hopeless. If man is really as depraved as you say he is, then your people are far worse. With your tremendous technology you could banish hunger and want from Earth, strengthen the weak and contain the oppressive. Instead of building, you destroy. Instead of helping man to his natural destiny, you thwart him. A moral person who finds a fellow creature lying in the gutter doesn't try to keep him there. He helps him out. My recommendation is that you take a long careful look at your own color of darkness.'

'It has been noted and will be considered. There remains one singular problem: What shall we do with the human, Jan Darzek?'

Darzek gestured indifferently. 'That's certainly a minor problem.'

'We do not consider it so.'

'I suppose you refer to erasing my memory. Some of the things that happened I might have looked back on with pleasure in my old age, but I'm sure that I shall have other memories that will serve the purpose. It would be nice to be able to remember the way the Earth looked from the Moon. I had other things on my mind at the time, and I only glanced at it, but it would be nice to remember. Most of all I hate to part with the memories of Ysaye, and Alice, and the others. They taught me something about myself that I'll probably never learn again.'

'Is there nothing else?'

'Why ask? You couldn't leave me part of a memory. I'd go nuts trying to fasten it onto something, or figure out where I got it.'

'No decision has been reached with regard to the classification of your planet and your people, but it has been decided that Jan Darzek shall have his own free choice in the matter of his memory.

'You mean – you'll let me keep it all?'

'If that is your choice. All, or any part of it.'

'Then I'd better not say anything else. Bring out your eraser – I don't want a choice. If I were to choose I'd have to accept the responsibilty for what followed, and there may be issues at stake that I couldn't even comprehend.'

'You are an awesome individual, Jan Darzek.' She got to her feet and held the space suit in front of him. 'Do you recognize it?'

'It's a suit like those my people use on the Moon. It's – ' his eyes fell on the dangling air hose ' – why, it's the one I stole!'

'The one you stole, and used to memorable effect. Listen, Jan Darzek. There is a distant planet – more distant, perhaps, than I could make you understand in the time that I have. On that planet is a structure whose nature would be difficult to explain to you, though you would probably call it a museum. It is no mere repository of curiosities as are such museums of yours that I have seen. It, and its contents, are venerated beyond the values your language is able to express. This suit shall be displayed there, and not among the least significant of the treasures that building contains. As long as our civilization lasts – and that should be long indeed, for it is yet vigorous and expanding, and not even the gloomiest of our prognosticators professes to see an end to it – the peoples of the galaxy shall gaze upon this suit, and read of the epic of Jan Darzek, and marvel. In distant centuries perhaps even your own people will be among them. Does it please you to have attained so brilliant a measure of immortality? There are many of my people who would willingly endure much in order to achieve far less.'

'I'd say that it's a trifle exaggerated. I don't ordinarily do epic things on an empty stomach.'

'You sacrificed your own life to save the lives of the five who could only be called your enemies.'

'I didn't sacrifice my life, I didn't save their lives, and I don't consider them my enemies. What happened was a team effort. I contributed. So did Ysaye. Alice did the most. Even those who did nothing helped by not interfering where all of their training told them they should intefere.'

172

'They were watching,' the alien said slowly. 'They saw the difficulties you experienced in returning to them, when you could so easily have remained with your own people. Then you gave them your oxygen. If you had not done so Alice would have come too late. You deliberately sacrificed yourself in a cause that must have appeared hopeless at the time. It appeared hopeless to them.'

'I'm a natural born optimist.'

'You are a feebly civilized inhabitant of a remote and utterly insignificant planet, with no more than a rudimentary moral sense, and – your act has created consternation in every headquarters all the way back to Supreme.'

'You left out something,' Darzek said dryly. 'My darkness is also the wrong color.'

'Do you state that as an opinion?'

'As an indictment of whoever is in charge of colors. Shall I see them again? Alice, and Ysaye, and the others?'

'They have already departed. They left a message for me to give to you

' "When the airless wind shall sing,
    When the broken circle mends,
    When the brightest day dawns without light,
        And the brittle night comes softly without darkness,
    I shall yet remember." ' '

'It is from a poem celebrated on many worlds. Ysaye trans-translated it for you, but I fear that it does not translate well.'

'Please tell them that I understand, and return to them the same feeling.'

'Certainly.'

'Before we get on with the memory erasing, there is one thing I would like to know.'

'I am at your service, Jan Darzek.'

'What *is* the verdict?"

'The verdict?'

'About Universal Trans. And Earth. What are you going to do?'

'The verdict is not yet formulated. Even if it were, I should regretfully decline to tell you. You know something of our Code. Surely you can understand that?'

'You won't even tell me when my memory will be erased immediately afterwards?'

'Even if the Code permitted it, it would involve a needless complication and an impossible delay. The memory erasing is a prolonged and delicate operation, and we must first, with your assistance, devise substitute memories for the time of your absence. We must also have a technician prepare a wig for you. According to your photograph, the damage to your hair is somewhat conspicious.'

'Just a trifle.'

'Our technicians are highly skilled in such matters.'

'I know. I can't see the harm in your telling me, though, if it's erased right away.'

'It would be a violation of my oath – and yours. Whatever the relationship between our peoples may be in the future, Jan Darzek, none of your people shall ever know about it. Certainly not during your lifetime – or mine. Are you ready now?'

Darzek got up resignedly.

Again he could not locate the door, and he had to wait until she opened it for him.

23

Jan Darzek paid the cabdriver, tipping him exorbitantly, and stood at the curb watching him rocket away down the Chaussée de Louvain. It was a lovely day, and Brussels was a lovely city, and he would have liked to linger at least long enough to enjoy crepes suzette at a little restaurant he remembered.

But his case would not be officially terminated until he had rendered a final report – and a bill – and he shuddered to think of the work that would have piled up at his office during his absence. He turned away reluctantly, but with the confident stride of a man who has just done a difficult job well, and entered the *Gare de trans universel.*

A plump, wildly gesticulating little man intercepted him as he crossed the lobby. 'Monsieur Darzek!'

Darzek nodded gravely. 'Monsieur Vert. It is a pleasure to see you again.'

The assistant manager delivered himself of a jerky bow, and seized Darzek's hand. 'But Monsieur Darzek! Where have you been? The police we have here, the detectives from America, the engineers, all of them interfering in our operations and asking questions my head reels to think of it! "Where is Monsieur Darzek?" they ask me. "Where has he gone?" "How should I know?" I say. "I do not even see him leap into the transmitter. The gate attendant says he leaps, and poof, he is gone – " ' M. Vert snapped two plump fingers. ' "But all who use the transmitter are – poof – gone, and surely it is not my responsibility if he is not – poof – gone to the right place.' I am not certain they believed me.'

'I'll put in a good word for you,' Darzek said. 'You were most co-operative, and I didn't have an opportunity to thank you. My business was rather pressing at the time. I'll personally commend you to Mr Watkins.'

'*Très bien.* That is most generous of you. It is extremely unpleasant to be somehow thought responsible for something one knows nothing about. But Monsieur Darzek – ' The assistant manager broke off, and looked about him uneasily. ' – I do have a matter of much importance upon which I would like to confer with you. If you would be so kind.'

'Certainly,' Derzek said.

'In my office, perhaps, where we can speak privately – '

'Certainly.'

Darzek trailed after him, feeling vaguely uneasy about this development. 'There haven't been more disappearances, I hope,' he said, when they reached the office and M. Vert had firmly closed the door behind them.

M. Vert looked horrified. '*Non! Non!* Do not even suggest such a thing! If you will seat yourself, please, then we shall talk.'

Darzek sat down, and M. Vert perched on the edge of his swivel chair and began rearranging the knickknacks on his desk. He seemed embarrassed.

'I do not know precisely how to say this, Monsieur Darzek,' he said, transferring a cigarette box from the right- to the left-hand corner. 'When you were here before, you entered the Paris gate by jumping over the turnstile, and you followed a Paris passenger into the transmitter. I learned only later that you did not go to Paris. At least, I was told this so many times, by so many people, that I can only assume that it is true.'

'It's perfectly true,' Darzek said. 'I did not go to Paris.'

'*Bien,*' M. Vert said, pushing the cigarette box aside and 'Would you say that this is the fault of Universal Trans that you did not go to Paris?'

'Certainly not. I would absolve Universal Trans of any responsibility for my failure to reach Paris.'

'Excellent!' M. Vert shifted the cigarette box to the center of the desk, and beamed at Darzek. 'I am delighted to hear it. I may then discuss with you this matter that troubles me. I saw with my own eyes that you did not pass through the turnstile. You jumped completely over it. You do not deny that?'

'Why should I deny it?' Darzek said. 'It was imperative that I follow that passenger closely, and there was no time to discuss the matter with the attendant.'

'Exactly. Nevertheless, though you did not pass through the turnstile, you did not enter the Paris gate, and you did enter the Paris transmitter, and you *should* have gone to Paris. Do you not follow me?'

'I'm afraid I don't.'

'But – Monsieur Darzek! Surely you are aware that a business must be conducted in accordance with firm regulations. Though you leaped over the turnstile, you did not thereby cancel your obligation to present a ticket. You are yet owing Universal Trans for one passage to Paris!'

In the New York Terminal Darzek paused only to fill his empty cigarette case before he went to Ted Arnold's office. He lit one, marveling that a cigarette could taste so good. Considering the insipid brands that had been inflicted upon him in the past week or so, he wondered that foreigners bothered to smoke at all.

Arnold was not in, but his office door stood open, and Darzek used his telephone. 'Is Ted Arnold in the building?' he asked the operator.

'I don't know,' she said. 'Would you like me to try and locate him?'

'Please do. Tell him he's wanted in his own office immediately. Tell him the situation is critical, and if he doesn't get here at once the sun may not set today.'

'Would you mind repeating that?' the operator asked blankly.

'It's an emergency. E-m-e-r – '

'I'll tell him.'

Darzek hung up, and made himself comfortable on the sofa.

Arnold barged in ten minutes later. He stared long at Darzek, and uttered an unearthly howl, and enfolded him in a ponderous embrace.

'Stop it!' Darzek snapped. 'After passing safely through fire and water and diverse tortures, I'm not going to let myself be mashed to death in supposedly civilized surroundings.'

Arnold released him. 'Where the devil have you been?'

'That's a fine welcome. I went to Brussels, I have been in Brussels, and I have just returned from Brussels – where, incidentally, your Universal Trans terminal is operated by pirates. Where have you been?'

Have you called your office? Does Jean know?'

'She does not. With my customary loyalty to the interests of an employer, I came directly here.'

'I'll tell her. She'd probably faint of you just casually walked in on her.' He snatched the telephone, dialled a number. 'Jean – he's back! Certainly. Sitting on my sofa right now with his usual smug expression smeared all over his pretty face. I haven't asked him. He's lost weight, and he needs a haircut, but he looks all right. Better not. The Board is meeting right now, and it'll want him. Hours, maybe. Why not dinner to-night? Sure, we'll throw a party. I'll call you. 'Bye, Hon.'

'*Hon!*' Darzek exclaimed. 'You're calling Jean *Hon?*'

'You might as well know now. Jean and I are – '

'Damnation! I go out of town for a couple of weeks, and my best friend – Ted, you're the last person I'd expect to pull a dirty trick like that.'

'Old man, I had no idea you were in love with her. She's been working for you for four years, and you had plenty of time to declare yourself.'

'I'm not in love with her. It's just that she's the best office girl I've ever had, and darned useful on special assignments. In fact, she's a natural-born detective. Except for me she's the only one I've ever met. I ought to cross the wires on the nearest transmitter and stuff you into it. Justifiable homicide!'

'If you want a lifetime contact with an office girl, you have to marry her. Have you been in Brussels all this time?'

'Didn't I just say I had?'

'Ed Rucks was right. It's a big place. Just a moment.' He dialed another number. 'Shuey? It's me, beautiful. Jan Darzek has just returned from the dead. In my office. Take a note in to the Boss, will you, and tell him we'll be up at eleven. Not a minute before then. I want to hear it myself before I turn the directors loose on him.'

He hung up. 'Talk,' he said.

'About what?' Darzek asked.

'Are you serious? Rucks has been looking for you all over Europe, Universal Trans has invested a young fortune in special investigators, and we've all been worried sick. We figured out how they were doing it, and we knew you'd stopped them, but that didn't give us a clue as to where you were or what had happened to you.'

'I was in damp Belgian cellar with time hanging heavy on my hands. I can't remember when I've been so bored. I suffered intensely. I'll include that in your bill.'

'What happened to their transmitter?'

'I smashed it. I pulled it apart right down to its smallest

178

components, and with my two hands and two feet I masticated the components into snippets. You won't hear from it again. They couldn't reassemble *that* transmitter, even if they knew how.'

'I figured something like that had happened when the disappearances stopped. Incidentally, even if they could reassemble it, they couldn't bother us again. I worked out a couple of modifications.'

'Bully. Why didn't you modify before I got incarcerated?'

'I didn't know what they were doing until you tossed out that idea about some of their attempts not working.'

'Glad to hear it. I don't like to suffer in vain. Ted, I never fully respected you before I started to disassemble that transmitter. I once saw the naked entrails of a TV set, and the complexity of the thing almost made me sick. That transmitter was an absolute nightmare. How can one mind make sense of a mess like that?'

Arnold grinned. 'The mind has to be in a similar mess. So far you've avoided the number one question. Who are "they"?'

'You never asked it. And if you don't mind, I'll keep that one for the Board.'

'Suit yourself. How about a cup of coffee before we go upstairs?'

'I'll have two cups. And a piece of pie. I haven't been eating lavishly, and if there's a decent cup of coffee anywhere in Belgium, no one thought to order it for me.'

'I'll have it sent up. Want anything else?'

'Just the coffee and pie. Blueberry pie.'

'Right,' Arnold said, and phoned the order. 'You know,' he went on, settling back with his feet on his desk, 'this is the first time I've felt fully relaxed since you did the disappearing act.'

'Sorry I couldn't phone in hourly progress reports.'

'Oh, I'm not blaming you. I'm betting you dove into a pretty tense situation, for all you say about being bored. I'm surprised they let you go – or did they let you go?'

'They did. They were a long time making up their minds, and then we had some interminable negotiations, but they let me go..'

'What the devil did you have to negotiate?'

'I'll unload it to the Board. I couldn't stand it to go over it twice.'

'You can't blame me for being curious,' Arnold said. 'I've really been in a flap about this. It was the sort of problem I'd instinctively turn over to you, only you were the one who was missing. There wasn't anything I could do but send everyone out to look for you, and gnaw my nails until they found something. Which they didn't, of course.'

'And no wonder. You wouldn't tackle an engineering problem with detectives. Why go after a missing person with engineers? Your man Perrin may be a whiz in the lab, but he'll never –'

'Oh, I didn't send Perrin,' Arnold interrupted. 'Actually, I didn't send anyone. I let Rucks pick the people and do the sending.'

'Somehow I had the impression that Perrin was looking for me.'

'Perrin is on the Moon. What are you looking so blank about? Haven't you seen a newspaper? Didn't you know we were on the Moon?'

'I haven't seen a newpaper since I did my transmitter dive, and we've been on the Moon for years. But – Perrin?'

'I mean Universal Trans is on the Moon. With a transmitter. Perrin is running it. Unfortunately USSA is in control, and everyone and his brother who has a little political pull is grabbing a free Moon trip. The President went up day before yesterday – the first Chief Executive to leave this planet. It made a big splash in the papers, and the publicity is worth a fortune, but some of those asses on the Board are never satisfied. They think we should have sold the President a Moon ticket at so much per mile.'

Maybe you will be selling Moon tickets some day.'

'Sooner than that. It's all on the planning boards now. Things have been buzzing around here. We had to build special transmitters for the Moon job, and one had to be sent up by rocket, so we had to train the astronauts to operate it until we could send an engineer through, and now we're building transmitters for New Frontier City and Lunaville, and –'

'Ha! All this plus finding yourself a wife in the little time I've been gone. And you say you were just gnawing your nails and waiting for someone to find me. You may be a pretty good engineer, but as a friend you're a total fraud. Stealing my office girl –' He broke off with a scowl.

'What's the matter?' Arnold asked.

180

'Just wondering where I got the idea that Perrin was looking for me.'

A pot of coffee arrived, and the pie – a whole pie for the two of them – and they polished it off leisurely. Then they went up to the executive offices, where Miss Shue announced their arrival with all of the ceremony of a herald of old, and twice the volume and enthusiasm.

Thomas J. Watkins escorted Darzek to a waiting chair, to the accompaniment of thunderous applause. Arnold pre-empted a chair for himself, and Miss Shue remained standing by the door.

'We offer you both our congratulations and our thanks, Mr Darzek,' Watkins said. 'We know that you've been successful beyond our wildest expectations, but we have no idea what it was you did Please report in full.'

'I'd hoped that the entire Board would be present,' Darzek said.

'It is,' Watkins assured him.

'I met several directors the day I was hired. Where is Mr Grossman?'

'I should explain,' Arnold said quickly, 'that Mr Darzek has not seen a newspaper since the morning he disappeared. Grossman is no longer a director, Jan. He got confused over what was the company's money and what was his own, and he resolved the issue in favor of himself. We strongly suspect that he's your traitor, but so far he's denied it.'

'There was no traitor,' Darzek said. 'Just some directors who talked too much. Do all of you know what happened up to the time I disappeared?'

'I filled them in while we were waiting for you,' Watkins said.

'Fine. You know, then, about our identifying one of the disguised woman in the Brussels Terminal. My assistant followed her to Paris and back to Brussels, and when she apparently started for Paris a second time I managed to go through the transmitter right behind her. We came out in what proved to be a basement room. There were three men present, two of them, unfortunately, with excellent reflexes. I arrived off balance, which put me at a slight disadvantage. Some very few minutes later I was neatly tied up and laying on a heap of coal.

'I was tied up so well that it took me nearly three hours to work free. When I finally managed it I found only one man in the room with the transmitter. I dealt with the one man and smashed the transmitter thoroughly. I unwisely made a noisy job of it, others came to investigate, the odds had swollen to six to one, and I ended up back on the coal heap, much more expertly tied and under guard. That's the story of my life for the next few days, though later that first day I was transferred from the coal bin to a room that was merely filthy.

'I believe it was on the sixth day that I was moved upstairs to a bedroom, still under guard, and we began our negotiations.'

'Negotiations?' Watkins asked blankly.

'It wasn't possible for me to wire for instructions, gentlemen. I had to assume binding authority in your behalf, and you're stuck with my action whether you like it or not. Here was the situation: Their transmitter was smashed, so they couldn't engineer any more disappearances. They had me on their hands, and even if they decided to do away with me – and I don't think they ever considered it – they had no idea how much my associates knew, or how close we were to a full exposure of their activities. They had to avoid an exposure at any cost, but on the other hand, so did Universal Trans. If word about the disappearances got out, the company would have suffered an unavoidable loss of public confidence.

'That was the situation as I saw it, and eventually they agreed with me and I was able to negotiate a settlement – they to cease and desist from harassing Universal Trans, and Universal Trans to make no further attempt to identify and punish its harrassers. There remained the fact that Universal Trans had suffered no small inconvenience and considerable expense because of that harassment, and I insisted on indemnity in cash. The only really sticky point in our negotiations concerned the amount. I asked for half a million – '

'Good heavens!' Watkins exclaimed. 'Surely you didn't have the nerve!'

'You've never played poker with him,' Arnold said.

'I asked for half a million, and they said that was ridiculous, and they offered five thousand, and I said *that* was ridiculous and we tossed figures at each other for days. I wish I'd known you were going to that much expense to find me – I might have done better. Anyway here's a bank draft for the settlement, made out to the corporation. Twenty-five thousand.' He passed it to Watkins. 'Case is closed. Any questions?'

'Yes,' Watkins said. 'Who are "they"?'

'We don't know, and were making no attempt to find out.

That's the position I negotiated. Say it's someone whose interests are not precisely identical with those of Universal Trans, and keep your suspicions to yourself. I am.'

'How'd they get their transmitter from New York to Brussels?' Arnold asked.

'I never thought to ask. Air express, at a guess. They had plenty of time between the New York and the Brussels disappearances – nearly twenty hours. Does it matter?'

'Not especially. What I'd really like to know is how they got hold of the transmitter in the first place.'

'Again, I never thought to ask. But if you'll make a thorough check, I'll give you odds you'll find one missing.'

'It's possible. We had a lot of them smashed by that malfunction that bothered us for so long. Some were repairable and some weren't, and it the mixup of rebuilding them and shifting them around and getting our operations started, it's possible that one could go astray without our missing it.'

'There's one more matter to be disposed of,' Darzek said. 'I'm accustomed to dealing with confidential matters, and I make it a practice to furnish a written report only when one is specifically requested. In this case I strongly recommend against it.'

'I agree,' Watkins said. 'If a written report were submitted to me, I would destroy it as soon as I'd read it. So why bother to prepare it?'

'Thank you. That's all I have to say, gentlemen.'

Darzek leaned back and lit a cigarette for himself, marveling again how good it tasted.

Watkins was on his feet, repeating his congratulations. 'Have we a motion to accept the situation as it has been reported – and negotiated – by Mr Darzek? A second? All in favor? Passed unanimously. There remains only the matter of Mr Darzek's fee, and I would suggest, since he negotiated the settlement himself, that we merely endorse this draft over to him.'

'Twenty-five thousand sounds a little steep for a couple of weeks' work,' Darzek said. 'Even for a couple of weeks of Darzek's work, though I don't know what expenses have been incurred during my absence, or even how much money you've already advanced.'

'Come in and see me tomorrow,' Watkins said. 'We'll go over the figures. May all of our problems end on such a happy note – solved entirely to our satisfaction, at someone else's expense. Have we a motion for adjournment?'

Ed Rucks and Jean Morris were waiting in the outer office. Jean whooped, and fell into Darzek's arms. 'It's him,' she said. 'But what has he done to his hair?'

Darzek gently pushed her away. 'You might as well learn now to keep her in her place,' he said to Arnold. 'I'm going home. I want to see if the old place is still there.'

'You mean you haven't been home yet?' Jean demanded.

'I have not. My devotion to duty interferes with my material comforts.'

She backed off, and examined him critically from head to foot. 'You *have* lost weight. Of course you've been home.'

'Of course I haven't.'

'What about dinner?' Arnold asked. 'Shall we throw that party?'

'Suit yourself.'

'I'll telephone you.'

'I'll be in all afternoon,' Darzek said. 'And maybe even for the rest of the month.'

Ron Walker called for Darzek in a limousine.

'Have you gone off your rocker?' Darzek demanded, as the chauffeur closed the door. 'I've heard of padding expense accounts, but this is ridiculous.'

'I wish you and Arnold would stop harping on my expense account,' Walker said. 'You know I have to write a four-page memorandum before I can collect for a subway ride. This evening's transportation was arranged by Thomas J. Watkins.'

'What does he have to do with it?'

'He heard about the party, and made himself first vice president in charge of finances and arrangements. You've got to admit that he has a certain style. He's an awfully nice guy, and he pulls limousines and private dining rooms out of his sleeve with such a smooth touch that you forget he only does it with money. Incidentally, he's also invited himself, and after we'd agreed to let him pick up the check we didn't have the heart to turn him down.'

'Who else is coming?'

'Watkins is bringing Ed Rucks. Arnold is bringing Jean. I'm bringing you. Just three happy couples.

'Did you know about Ted and Jean?'

'I knew it before they did. Your absence threw them together. It's a good thing for both of them – I think.'

'You're probably right, but don't quote me. Where are we going?'

'Some private club I never heard of. Watkins had *that* up his sleeve, too.'

The chauffeur ceremoniously delivered them to a stately old mansion on Riverside Drive. A uniformed doorman prostrated himself and then handed them over to a monkey-suited butler, who escorted them to a small dining room on the second floor.

'The plate on the door said "Victorian Club"!' Darzek said

with awe. 'The furnishings are so modern they have to be clamped down to keep them from going into orbit, and I'll swear that odd-shaped painting was specifically designed to cover a crack in the plaster.'

Watkins greeted them smilingly, a waiter floated a tray of drinks within reach, and they found themselves gathered around a magnificent stone fireplace that housed an air conditioner. Ed Rucks pumped one of Darzek's hands and managed to knock the drink from the other. The waiter calmly supplied another drink and cleaned up the mess.

'*Victorian* Club?' Darzek said, glancing about the room.

'Named after the founders,' Watkins said, eyes twinkling. 'Six men named Victor. Originally membership was limited to Victors, but there was some difficulty in finding enough to fill the rolls, so the club was opened to Toms, Dicks, and Harrys. Ted and Jean – here they are. Shall we start?'

'Take the head of the table, Jan,' Walker said. 'And remember that a guest of honour has obligations, as well as privileges – such as leading the community singing and tipping the waiter. Jean – '

'Right beside Jan,' Jean said. 'I'm not letting him out of this room until I find out what's happened to his hair, and why he's going around telling barefaced lies.'

The others regarded Darzek with interest. 'What's wrong with his hair?' Arnold asked.

'That's what I want to know,' Jean said.

'I mean – it looks all right to me.'

'It doesn't look all right to me, and you were standing right beside him this morning when he told that lie.'

'If you must third-degree me,' Darzek said, 'you might at least have the courtesy to let me sit down first.'

They arranged themselves around the table, Arnold and Jean Morris on one side, Walker and Rucks opposite them. Arnold gallantly stood by to assist Jean with her chair – no minor operation, since the chair was backless – but she ignored him; and as Darzek seated himself at the end of the table she leaned over and snatched the wig from his head.

'There! she exclaimed triumphantly.

While the others sat paralyzed with astonishment Darzek calmly regained possession of the wig and returned it to his head. 'I'm glad this happened, Ted,' he said. 'I was much too polite to tell you what a hell-cat this female is, but since she

186

has chosen to exhibit her fiendishness in the presence of witnesses, you can't say you wern't forewarned.'

'What happened to your hair?' Jean demanded. The others continued to stare.

'Not only does she expose my most secret shame with calloused disregard for my feelings, but she has the colossal nerve to expect me – '

'What happened to your hair?'

'If you must know, I was smoking in bed, and I fell asleep. Happily my guard smelled the smoke and came to my rescue, but not before my beautiful hair was devastated. My captors did not want me to go around creating an impression that they had tested me with fire, so they took my passport photo and had this wig made. And a very good job it is, if I do say so myself.'

'It looks better when you have it on straight,' Jean said.

'Thank you,' Darzek said, adjusting it.

Jean seated herself resignedly. 'It doesn't sound like him, but I suppose it could have happened that way, and if it didn't I know that's the only explanation I'll ever get. What about the lie?'

'What lie? Darzek asked, helping himself to a roll.

'You told me this morning in the presence of witnesses, that you hadn't been home yet.'

'I'll repeat it in the presence of witnesses. At that time I hadn't been home yet.'

'Then how do you account for the fact that you disappeared wearing a light tweed sport coat, dark gabardine slacks, a green-tinted shirt, and a bow tie – not to mention those atrocious Argyle socks and brown shoes; you were confined in Brussels all the time you were gone, and you came back wearing that old sharkskin suit you should have given away years ago, a white shirt, black shoes, and a necktie you borrowed from my brother and never returned, and a pair of socks I gave you last Christmas. Just explain that. I dare you!'

'You'll never make a wife of this woman, Ted. At best she'll only be a married detective.'

'Nevertheless, it seems like a very interesting question.' Arnold said.

'*Et tu, Brute!* Very well. The tweed sport coat and gabardine slacks were subjected to trial by combat twice, on a cement floor yet, and I did not win either time. Between trials, and afterwards, I shared a small room with several tons of coal. By the time my relations with my hosts had taken a turn for the better my clothing was beyond salvage. During our negotiations a messenger had to make several trips to New York for instructions, and at my request he picked up a change of clothing from my apartment. His taste was atrocious, but I refuse to accept the responsibility for that. Any further questions?'

'Jean,' Arnold said, 'you owe him an apology.'

'I doubt it,' Jean said. 'But there's no point in spoiling a dinner party. I'll apologize now, and tell him what I think of him when I write my resignation.'

'Shall we begin?' Watkins asked, and nodded to the waiter, who wheeled a cart into the room and began to serve them.

The dinner proceeded with normal gaiety until they began to discuss desserts with the waiter. Darzek asked for the largest ice-cream sundae the establishment was capable of assembling, and Jean, after making her own selection, sweetly informed the waiter that Mr Arnold was on a diet and could not eat desserts.

'I wish I'd known that this morning,' Darzek said. 'I wouldn't have shared that blueberry pie with him.'

'Ted!' Jean wailed. 'You didn't eat a piece of pie!'

'Not a piece,' Darzek said. 'A pie. Half of one, anyway.'

'Mr Arnold will *not* have any dessert,' Jean said firmly, and the waiter moved on.

'Traitor!' Arnold muttered.

Watkins chuckled, and said it seemed as good a time as any to be offering congratulations to Arnold. 'She'll make a new man of you,' he said. 'When's the wedding?'

'We haven't decided,' Arnold said. 'I don't want to be a new man. By the way, Jan, we had a deuce of a mystery happen while you were gone. If you'd been here, I'd have put you to work on it.'

'I gather that you managed without me,' Darzek said with a grin. 'Which means it couldn't have been much of a mystery.'

'Oh, we didn't solve it. We'll never solve it. It only happened day before yesterday at the new Moon base. Perrin went in to start the day's operations, and found the transmitter sabotaged. The President and a mob of bigwigs were waiting at the Cape for a Moon excursion, and we couldn't make contact. Talk about embarrassing moments!'

'Sabotaged how?' Darzek asked.

'That's a mystery in itself. Circuits were switched around

188

fantastically, and rewired, and unwired, and cross-wired, and generally hashed up. Perrin knew the President was due, and his only idea was to get it operating again – fast. I wish now he'd taken the time to draw a diagram of what had been done to it. A few of the things he remembered made sense, in a weird sort of way. It was almost as if someone with unorthodox ideas was trying to –well – *improve* the thing.'

'That certainly would be an unorthodox motive for sabotage.'

'But who could have done it? There were only two men at the base, besides Perrin, and both of them swore they hadn't touched it. I believe them, because the person responsible had more than a rudimentary knowledge of elecronics, and they haven't. A few people would like to blame the Russians, which is absolutely ridiculous. Also, if someone wanted to sabotage a transmitter, you'd think he'd just swing a hammer and get out of there – not take the time to take it apart and rewire it. Perrin swears there was a mysterious stranger in the vicinity, which might be interesting if anyone could explain how he got there and where he went afterwards. Mysterious strangers on the Moon quickly become dead strangers, unless they have a well-established base of operations. No, this is one mystery that not even Darzek could solve.'

'Thanks a lot, old man, but I couldn't care less,' Darzek said. 'I get my full quota of mystery on Earth.'

'Am I correct in assuming that this is not for publication?' Walker asked Arnold.

'You are.'

'Damn you!'

'USSA may release something in a day or two. I told them they should change the name of that Abenezra to Crater of Mystery. First there's an explosion that leaves no traces, and then our transmitter is sabotaged by a nonexistent mysterious stranger, and now they tell me things have started to disappear up there. Anyway, there won't be any more tampering with the transmitter. We've put up a metal hut that can be locked.

'What about an explosion?' Darzek asked.

'That's ancient history. There wasn't any, only several people saw it, and – Ron, dig up some old papers so Jan can read about the explosion.

'We have a file at the office,' Jean said. 'But he wouldn't

have read about it even if he'd been here. Current events on the Moon don't interest him.'

The waiter served the desserts, and Darzek, gloating over his enormous sundae, paused with his spoon in mid-air. 'Oddly enough, the other night I did have a dream about the Moon. I was there, looking up at the Earth. It was very realistic. The Earth was a beautiful, glowing crescent. I wasn't aware that the Earth had phases, just like the Moon.'

'I don't suppose there've been more than a million photographs of those phases published,' Arnold said.

'Have there? I never paid any attention. Anyway, it struck me as a remarkable discovery.'

'At least your astronomy has improved since the last time you dreamed you were on the Moon.'

'How's that?'

'You told me you dreamed you were looking *down* at the Earth. This time you say you were looking up. That's a radical change for the better.'

'If you say so. I don't remember any other dream.'

'Too bad you didn't know about Ted's Moon mystery.' Jean said. 'While you were dreaming you were on the Moon you could have solved it for him. Did you see anything else of interest up there?'

'As a matter of fact, I did. I met some Moon people. Men and women.'

'Maybe he's normal after all,' Jean said. 'What did the women look like?'

'They were enormous. Eight feet high, maybe ten, and broad as a barn door. They were wrapped up like an Egyptian mummy, and what I could see of their flesh was a kind of blue-looking.'

'There's nothing unreasonable about that. The nights up there get pretty cold.'

'These women weren't cold. They were very warm, and more human than any human female I've ever met. They had four fingers on each hand, and their faces looked as if they'd been run over by a steam roller, and I thought they were beautiful. Don't ask me why.'

'My God!' Jean exclaimed. 'No wonder he's a bachelor. Who could complete with a vision like that?'

'Have you told your analyst about that dream?' Ron Walker asked.

'I haven't got an analyst.'

u'd better get one fast. Ted — what's the matter with

old was staring at Darzek, his face frozen in a look of
tupefaction. His mouth worked futilely; finally he man-
speak. '*Four* fingers?'

ght,' Darzek said.

'Four *webbed* fingers?'

'Right.'

'Dressed with some of kind of cloth wrapped all around and
around her, and the whole face caved in, like, and fat from
the front and skinny from the side, and eyes without any color,
and – '

'So you know her, too,' Darzek said.

'Same person?'

'Same person.'

'You two are making this up,' Jean said.

'We aren't, Hon – honest we aren't. We just must have had
the same dream, except that I only saw one of them. Did she
say anything to you?'

'I don't think she did,' Darzek said.

'She didn't speak to me, but she showed me two formulas
and a transmitter diagram, and I woke up right afterwards
and wrote them down, and this morning –'

'Naturally she'd know better than to show *me* anything
like that,' Darzek said.

'This morning I looked at them, and they made sense.' He
turned to Watkins. I've been thinking about all that red tape
we had to go through to get a transmitter on the Moon, and
all the trouble USSA has given us since we got there. I think
we should operate our own Moon projects.'

'I agree. But how do we get our transmitters to the Moon
without USSA's help?'

'All we have to do is design a transmitter that will operate
without a receiver. This one I dreamed about will do it. I'm
sure of that. We can go anywhere on the Moon we want to go.
We can go to Mars, or Saturn, or Pluto – anyhere in the
Solar System, or outside it, if there's anywhere outside of
it to go. We can double our capacity here on Earth by using
all of our transmitters to transmit, rather than half of them
to receive. Whoever your Moon woman is, Jan, I feel doggone
grateful to her. This idea –'

'He's still dreaming, Darzek told Jean. 'Kick him.'

She did – sharply – and Arnold winced and bent over to rub

his shin. 'Just the same, I'm going to build one. I know work.'

'You have trouble ahead of you, Jean,' Darzek sai
Moon woman is evidently a fellow scientist. That,
natural beauty, makes her a formidable rival. I see
hope for you.'

'What's that?'

'Put him back on desserts. Then he won't have such dreams.'

'No one took you off desserts. How did you happen to have the same dream?'

'In every man's inner life there is an area so intensely personal – '

'I'll haul both of you to an analyst,' Jean said, 'and find out where those dreams came from.'

Darzek blissfully took another spoonful of sundae. 'What makes you so sure that you'd like to know? ' he asked.